She lifted
to back o...

He was looking down at her, his probing eyes meeting her own gaze with such intensity that she caught her breath.

Green eyes. He had green eyes capable of registering a range of moods—humor, softness and, when they narrowed, a kind of tough, cold anger that could be dangerous. Could make a woman shiver. She had always been able to read those moods. But that had been then. Now she wasn't at all sure.

Managing to breathe again, she asked him curtly, "What?"

He didn't answer her. He simply kept staring.

"Casey, go away, will you? This commission is much too important to me to risk you screwing it up by your hanging around me like this."

He didn't move.

Voice shaky now, his presence unnerving her, she pleaded softly, "Please, just leave."

Dear Reader,

I have to confess I have a love affair with the islands of the Caribbean and their people. I've been fortunate to travel to that area on several occasions. Each time I was able to visit different islands. No two are alike as far as looks, history and culture. The one thing they have in common is the fabulous colors, which are a joy to experience.

I knew early on that I wanted one day to set a Harlequin Romantic Suspense book in the Caribbean, but nothing seemed to strike the right chord. That all changed some months back when I met the feisty Brenna Coleman and the man from her past, Casey McBride. These two battling characters involved me in an incredible mystery on the island of St. Sebastian. Before you read on, I must tell you that St. Sebastian is not a place you can find on any map, but it does combine the best elements of the Caribbean. That being said, I'll leave you here and let Brenna and Casey take you along with them for all the rest.

Jean Thomas

LETHAL
AFFAIR

—

Jean Thomas

HARLEQUIN®ROMANTIC SUSPENSE

Recycling programs
for this product may
not exist in your area.

ISBN-13: 978-0-373-27868-8

LETHAL AFFAIR

Copyright © 2014 by Jean Thomas

Printed in U.S.A.

Books by Jean Thomas

Harlequin Romantic Suspense

AWOL with the Operative #1694
The Lieutenant by Her Side #1742
Lethal Affair #1798

Other titles by this author available in ebook format.

JEAN THOMAS

aka Jean Barrett, lives in Wisconsin in an English-style cottage on a Lake Michigan shore bluff. The view from her office window would be a magnificent one if it weren't blocked by a big fat computer that keeps demanding her attention.

This author of twenty-six romances was a teacher before she left the classroom to write full-time. A longtime member of Romance Writers of America, Jean is a proud winner of three national awards and has appeared on several bestseller lists. When she isn't at the keyboard, she likes to take long walks that churn up new story ideas or work in the garden, which never seems to churn up anything but dirt. Of course, there are always books to be read. Romantic suspense stories are her favorite. No surprise there. Visit Jean at jeanthomas-author.com.

To my brother-in-law, Lonnie Stellpflug. Here's the book I promised you, Lonnie. I'm sorry it's not one of the Westerns you love so much, but it has as much adventure and emotion as a stirring Western. Enjoy.

Prologue

Casey couldn't imagine what Will Coleman wanted to see him about. It had been—what? Almost two years when they'd last met? Not since… Well, no point in going there. It was enough to remember their encounter had been an awkward one. Understandable, considering the circumstances.

That was why Casey had been so surprised when Will called him this morning, asking for this meeting. Surprised and curious, too. He could swear there'd been a kind of urgency in Will's tone. And something else. A note of mystery, which Will had refused to explain over the phone.

It was this that had won Casey's consent to leave the warmth of his apartment on an afternoon like this one. Mystery being in essence his business.

No one could say Casey McBride didn't love Chicago. But, hell, this was April. The weather should have been kind. Not like this, with snowflakes slashing through the air, driven by a mean wind sweeping down Rush Street.

He'd had to park a block away. A *long* block at that. Or so it seemed as, coat collar up around his ears, he finally battled his way to the door of Digger's Sports Bar.

Ah, shelter at last, Casey thought.

He stood inside the entrance, swiping the back of his hand across his eyes to rid himself of the tears the wind had provoked. It gave him a moment to adjust his vision to the dimness of the place.

Digger's was the traditional sports bar. Big screen TVs located in several strategic spots. The upper portions of its walls hung with assorted jerseys. The lower halves devoted to signed photographs of players on Chicago teams—the Bears, Bulls, Blackhawks and Casey's favorite, the Cubs.

He located Will's lanky figure standing next to a booth at the far end of the room, signaling to him with a raised hand. Will could have had just about any one of the booths, since this wasn't the Happy Hour for the newspaper crowd who frequented Digger's. Casey could only guess that Will, himself a sports writer for the *Tribune,* had chosen both the time and the rear booth as ideal for a private meeting.

Casey joined Will. The two men shook hands.

"Thanks for coming, Case. I appreciate it, especially when…well, you know."

"Water under the bridge, man." It wasn't, but why make the poor guy uncomfortable for something that hadn't been his fault?

Peeling off his coat and dumping it into a corner of the booth, Casey slid himself in beside it. Will settled himself across from him. The server rounded the end of the bar and approached their table. Both men ordered draft beers.

Will was silent until the beers were delivered and the server retreated. Casey waited, pretending to be patient.

Only when they were alone again did Will, leaning forward, speak.

"Sorry to be so secretive like this, Case, but word has a way of getting around when it's about someone so well-known in the city. And I'd rather it didn't."

There was an earnest tone in Will's voice, a solemn expression on his face. Didn't necessarily mean anything. Will had the kind of long, thin face that looked serious whatever his mood.

Casey paused long enough to sample his beer, deciding he hadn't tasted any better. Unless he counted a hot summer afternoon at Wrigley Field watching his beloved Cubs. "So, who are we talking about here?"

"Marcus Bradley. You familiar with the name?"

"I'd have to be living under a manhole cover not to be. Chicago billionaire who made his major bucks in electronics, right?"

"That's the one."

"Okay, what about him?"

Will paused, sucking in what looked like a long breath to nerve himself before answering him. "Brenna is involved with him."

Casey used his beer to collect himself, sipping at it slowly. Will had yet to touch his own mug. He was watching Casey, waiting for his reaction. He was going to be disappointed if he thought his news was going to matter to him.

"In case you've forgotten, Will, your sister and I stopped being interested in each other a long time ago." It was what he had convinced himself, anyway, although from time to time he'd had to remind himself of that.

"I'm worried about her, Case."

That was no surprise. With their parents gone, and no other close relatives that Casey knew about, the two of them had always been tight. Only Will had had a habit of being just a bit too overly protective of Brenna. It seemed like that hadn't changed.

"Why? Why should you be worried? From what I've heard, Marcus Bradley is not only rich but handsome, currently single and well liked. Aside from an age difference—he's in his late fifties, though that doesn't seem to matter these days—I'd say he's a match for a woman who knows her own mind. And Brenna," he added dryly, "always knew her own mind."

No jealousy here, McBride, he tried to convince himself. *You're no longer entitled to it.*

"Thing is, Brenna insists they're not involved romantically. That Bradley is only interested in her art."

"Well, then."

Will shook his head. "I don't trust the guy. Okay, so he's suave and charming, if you like the type, but there's something not genuine about him. Something that isn't quite right."

"Will, why did you ask me here? If it's just to complain about Marcus Bradley—"

"No, it's more than that. See, Bradley has this vacation home on St. Sebastian. You know the place?"

"Not really. An island in the Caribbean, isn't it?"

Will nodded. "He's building a luxury resort there."

"And?"

"Brenna is there with him now. She's supposed to be producing a series of paintings, island scenes for this resort."

"What's wrong with that?"

"I'm uneasy about her being there. I tried to talk her out of going, but she wouldn't listen. Said I was being ridiculous about something perfectly innocent and legitimate."

"Maybe you are."

"That was then. But since she left, I had the chance to talk to one of the investigative reporters in the newsroom of the *Trib*. I'd heard he was interested in Bradley."

"What did you learn?"

"That Bradley is a respected philanthropist."

"And that's a reason for you to be concerned?"

"No, of course not, except my reporter hinted there've been rumors of, as he put it, 'less virtuous activities.'"

"Like what?"

"He wouldn't say, other than they were nothing he was able to pin down that would warrant a story his editor would risk a lawsuit for. But…"

"You're still uneasy."

"Yeah, I keep having this feeling I can't shake. Like there's something wrong about the whole setup with Bradley. Like he has an agenda he didn't share with Brenna."

"Sounds like you have an agenda of your own. And maybe I'm it." Fearing he already knew the explanation, Casey hunched forward, demanding sharply, "Just why am I here, Will?"

"I need you, Case. I need what you are, a special ops FBI agent with all the skills required to protect the sister who means everything to me. If something *is* wrong, if she should end up at risk…"

Casey leaned back, laughing. It was a laugh without mirth. "You want me to go down there to St. Sebastian. You want me to be there for her."

"You could do it. I know you're available. I know you're on temporary suspension from the bureau while a case that you were a part of that went bad is under investigation."

"How did you learn that? It hasn't been made public."

"I have my sources. You forget I'm a reporter myself, even if my news is in the sports section."

"Yeah, I could do it. Not in any official capacity, naturally. I could visit this island for you and not let myself be concerned that I might be taking a chance on screwing up being cleared at the agency, which I expect to be the outcome of the investigation. I *could* do it, but I'm not going to."

"I'd pay all your expenses."

"That's not the problem. The problem is Brenna. Do I have to remind you, Will, that I'm no longer engaged to your sister? I haven't set eyes on her since she gave my ring back to me two years ago."

"So?"

"So, after the way we broke up, she'd no more welcome my interference than she did yours. Not that I'd let that stop me if I thought she was in trouble. Come on, man, face it. Your suspicions are groundless, the product of your imagination."

"I take it that's a refusal."

"It is. Sorry, Will, but whatever my past feelings for your sister, I have no intention of chasing down to this St. Sebastian to help a woman who doesn't want or need my help. You've got to start remembering that Brenna is intelligent and independent. She can take care of herself if she has to."

"That your final answer?"

"Afraid so."

Will got to his feet, placed several bills on the table to cover their drinks and a tip and picked up his coat. "Thanks, anyway, for listening to me, Case."

Not until he was gone, leaving him sitting there, did Casey realize Will had never touched his beer.

Casey should have been on his way himself, but he remained there in the booth, suddenly feeling lousy for disappointing a man who had once been a close friend.

He caught himself gazing unhappily at the photos on

the walls. But it wasn't any of the sports figures he saw up there. It was the radiant face of Brenna Coleman.

He couldn't help it. Against his better judgment, *much* against it, he found himself reliving memories of the long, intimate months they had shared. There was one sizzling evening in particular Casey would never forget. It was the first time they had made love.

He had driven them in his convertible that wet summer night to one of the less popular Lake Michigan beaches, parking in a deserted spot looking out at the dark waters.

"You ever come down here with a boyfriend when you were in high school to watch the submarine races?" he'd teased her with that old euphemism for making out at the beach.

Brenna pretended she hadn't, innocently asking him to explain what couldn't be possible. He'd enlightened her without words, tangling his hands in her silky hair to draw her into his arms where he'd covered her lush mouth with his own.

Her responses to his deep, lusty kisses had convinced him this wasn't the first time she had experienced those submarine races at the beach. In the end, like a couple of hormonal teenagers instead of the adults they were, they'd climbed eagerly into the back of the convertible. Thanks to the weatherman on channel nine, he'd raised the top earlier, so they were private enough while, between kisses, they tore at each other's clothes.

It wasn't the most comfortable arrangement trying to fit their naked bodies together on that seat, but it was one hell of a memorable one. He could still feel Brenna's arms and legs wrapped tightly around him, still taste her tongue on his, still hear her whimpers of pleasure as the rain pinged softly on the roof.

The possibility of some police cruiser coming along to

catch them made it all the more exciting. Maybe that was why their climaxes had been so cataclysmic.

Sitting there in the booth, Casey felt himself growing aroused just thinking about that night. Damn, he didn't want this.

He dragged his cell phone out of his back pocket. He hesitated only briefly before, his mind made up, he dialed the number of another FBI agent at the Chicago division of the bureau over on Roosevelt Road. To his satisfaction, Ken Boynton, a trusted buddy, was at his desk and picked up immediately.

"What's up?" Boynton asked after Casey had identified himself.

"Hey, Kenny, I need a favor. I'd like you to check and tell me if there's anything on the bureau's radar about Marcus Bradley."

"*The* Marcus Bradley?"

"That's the one."

"Jeez, Casey, you don't ask much. You know the records are classified, and with you on suspension…"

"Who's going to know if you don't tell them?"

There was an audible sigh from the other end followed by a reluctant "All right, hold on while I look."

Casey heard the tapping of keys as Ken called up the files on his computer. He waited patiently until the agent reported back.

"Okay, here it is."

What Casey listened to wasn't much, but it was enough. *Just* enough to convince him, after he thanked Ken and hung up, that he needed a holiday in the sun.

Chapter 1

Brenna gazed out across the bay, frowning at the scene. It wasn't the narrow, palm-studded spur of land giving her trouble. That she had already managed without difficulty.

As she always did, she'd chosen her subject with care, convinced that, simple though it was, it would make a highly effective painting. The colors were the problem.

Without question, the waters of the Caribbean were the most gorgeous she had ever experienced, ranging from a rich aquamarine to a deep, inky blue. But to capture these incredible colors on canvas and make them believable... well, this was what eluded her.

Come on, you can conquer them, she reminded herself.

With that stubborn self-promise firmly in mind, Brenna swung her attention away from the view, prepared to mix the pigments she needed on her palette. Along with her brushes and tubes of oil paint, the palette rested on the wide tray attached to her easel.

She was reaching for it when, out of the corner of her eye, she discovered something moving off to her left, ambling in her direction along the volcanic black sand beach. A tall, barefoot figure wearing a pair of snug white pants rolled to mid-calf and a matching white shirt carelessly open down to his waist.

There was something distinctly familiar about that long-legged, easy gait. It couldn't be *him*. Not here on St. Sebastian.

But there was no denying his identity when he neared her, sporting that big, goofy grin on his bold mouth. A mouth whose sensual talents she was incapable of forgetting. Casey McBride.

Brenna never wore sunglasses when she was out on location. She felt they interfered with the truth of her painting. That was why it was necessary for her to squint her eyes against the brilliance of the tropic sun as she watched him approach her.

He did wear sunglasses, whipping them off when he reached her. Without any greeting, he leaned over the easel to inspect her painting in progress. That left Brenna free to examine him.

He hadn't changed in the two years since they'd parted. Casey was still the rugged figure he'd always been with that angular, good-looking face. And, much to her disgust, he still had the power to set her pulses racing with his mere appearance.

Careful. You can't let him know that. He'll take advantage of you if you do.

Nodding, he placed a stamp of approval on the painting with a brief "Nice."

"Thank you. Now would you like to tell me what the hell you're doing here?"

He turned to face her. "That isn't a very friendly welcome."

"I didn't intend it to be. Do I get an answer?"

His only reply was to keep on looking at her, still wearing that stupid grin. All right, it wasn't stupid. It was sexy. So, somehow, were the beads of perspiration on his powerful, bare chest. At least the portion his open shirt revealed. The sun, after all, was hot.

"Never mind explaining. I can guess. Will sent you, didn't he?"

"Could be."

"You know he did. What I can't figure out is how you found me in this particular spot."

"Now, see, I just happen to be renting one of the cottages back there." He jerked his thumb in the direction he had come from where she could see a palm-thatched roof peeking out from the trees. Below the roof was a deck projecting over the beach.

"Uh-huh."

"Yeah, and I was out on the deck taking in the view— great, isn't it?—when I spotted this woman working at her easel. 'Could that be Brenna Coleman?' I asked myself."

"And what did you answer yourself?"

"Didn't. I had to kick off my shoes—you know how I love to go barefoot—and go out on the beach for a better look-see."

"Naturally."

"Well, then I knew for sure. Who else, with that copper-colored hair blowing in the wind, could it be but Brenna herself? Lucky coincidence, huh?"

"Very," she said dryly.

She knew it was no accident, his discovering her like this. Casey had always specialized in locating the targets the FBI assigned him. She could have pursued it, but she didn't. It didn't matter, because she had a more important challenge for him.

"Let's cut the games, McBride. Exactly what did my brother have to say to convince you to come after me?"

"Not much. Hey, it's still cold back in Chicago, and being in the mood for a vacation in a warm place—"

"I've never known you to take a vacation."

"Kind of forced on me. I'm on suspension from the bureau."

Knowing how dedicated he was to his work, she realized how hard this had to be for him. "I'm sorry, Casey. What happened?"

"Long story. Why don't we save it for another time? Anyway, the island here sounded just about right. 'That's great,' Will said. 'While you're there and if you have the chance, you can check in on Brenna.'"

"He said that, did he?"

"More or less."

"No, he didn't. I'll tell you what he said. He said, 'Gee, Casey, would you mind watching over my sister for me? I don't like the company she's keeping.'"

"He didn't put it exactly like that. But, okay, close enough. He's concerned about you, Brenna, and maybe he has reason to be."

"What reason?"

"This is for your ears only. Something I wouldn't tell you if you didn't need to be aware of it. Happens that your friend, Marcus Bradley, is a member of a cabal of elitists, a group suspicious enough that the FBI is keeping an eye on them."

Brenna blew out the breath she'd been holding with a sound of exasperation. "You're as bad as Will. Like I told him, and I'm telling you, there are always rumors about the very rich. And in this case, FBI or not, they're crazy rumors. Marcus is not only a friend, he's a generous benefactor. Along with his other charitable projects, he's building a resort here on St. Sebastian in order to bring much-needed revenue and jobs to the island's poor."

"Heard that. Good for him. Meanwhile, you're staying with him in his villa. Cozy."

She was close, *very* close to snatching up a brush, dipping it in fresh paint and swiping it across his nose. "You've been investigating me, Agent McBride, and I don't like it. You don't deserve to know it, but I'm not staying in the villa. I'm staying in the guesthouse."

"That so?"

"Yes. Furthermore, whatever my connection with Marcus, it's not your business or Will's. Nor do I need you or anyone else playing watchdog."

"Got it. But, uh, would you mind telling me something?"

"Like what?"

Casey jerked that strong, square chin of his in the direction of the road a few hundred feet off the beach. A late-model Jaguar sedan was parked there in the shade of a banyan tree. Its driver, leaning against the car as he smoked a cigarette, was eyeing them.

"What do you call him, Brenna, if not a watchdog? Guy seems real interested in us. He belong to you?"

"That's Julio, and all he's doing is passing the time waiting for me. He works for Marcus, who asked him to drive me around the island so I could paint the scenes he wants when his resort is finished. He's not a watchdog."

Brenna's attention had been fixed on Julio and the car. When she turned back to face Casey, she found him standing close to her. So close she could feel the heat of his hard body.

She lifted her chin, meaning to ask him to back off.

Mistake. He was looking down at her, his probing eyes meeting her own gaze with such intensity that she caught her breath.

Green eyes. He had green eyes capable of registering a range of moods—humor, softness and, when they narrowed, a kind of tough, cold anger that could be dangerous. Could make a woman shiver. She had always been able to read those moods. But that had been then. Now she wasn't at all sure.

And something else. Casey's right eyelid drooped a little. A sexy, bedroom kind of thing that never failed to fascinate women.

Managing to breathe again, she asked him curtly, "What?"

He didn't answer her. He simply kept staring.

"Casey, go away, will you? This commission is much too important to me to risk you screwing it up by your hanging around me like this."

He didn't move.

Voice shaky now, his presence unnerving her, she pleaded softly, "Please, just leave."

To her relief, he backed away from her silently. Only when he was a safe distance away did he speak.

"If you should get into any trouble, Brenna, and need me, I'll be here for you."

How was she supposed to reply to that? She didn't know, not with that sober tone in his voice, the equally sober look now on his face. He waited for a few seconds, but when she had no response for him, he turned and started to walk away.

Brenna found herself seized by a sudden, unexpected guilt. The same guilt she had suffered two years ago. Until now, she'd been able to convince herself she'd overcome that guilt, successfully put it behind her. Apparently not.

She couldn't prevent herself from calling after him. "Casey, wait."

He turned back, his dark eyebrows raised questioningly.

Even though she had expressed it at the time, she felt the need to tell him again. "I—I'm sorry I hurt you when I broke our engagement," she told him quietly. "But I hurt, too, Casey. *I hurt, too.*"

"I know," he said, his voice deep, husky.

And that was all. His hand lifting in parting, he turned again and moved back up the beach the way he had come. He left her with the forlorn, unwanted memories of what they had once shared. The love he had lavished on her both physically and emotionally, and what it had cost her to sacrifice them.

She went on gazing after his striking figure, damning him for reawakening all those potent feelings. Angry with herself, too, for her weakness, for still finding herself attracted to him.

Enough of this.

Facing her easel again, she considered the painting on it. It seemed to look back at her, demanding her renewed attention. Brenna complied, picking up a brush and her palette, prepared to attack the canvas. This time with a fierceness determined to shut out the image of Casey McBride.

The sprawling villa, Moorish in style, was perched on an elevated point of land overlooking the sea on one side. Stretched below on the other side were the winking lights of Georgetown, St. Sebastian's capital and only city.

Brenna thought how different the setting here was by day. The stuccoed white walls of the villa glared with pride in the tropic sun. But now, at night, those same walls, with their arches and plastered domes, were subdued into something that resembled a soft, shadowy gray.

She was looking at the lamplit boats bobbing in the harbor that fronted Georgetown when Marcus spoke to her.

"How was your day?" he asked her in that gentle voice that had what she felt was a hypnotic quality to it. "Pleasant, I hope."

They were having a late dinner on the open terrace. The perfect meal consisted, among other dishes, of pepper pot soup, an island favorite, and freshly caught, baked grouper.

"It was," she said, meeting his gaze across the candles that glowed in their hurricane globes on the table.

His hair gleamed in that same light. Pure silver hair, without a touch of any other color in it, framed his patrician face. Brenna supposed most people would describe that face as distinguished. It certainly reflected the breeding of an impressive ancestry. And even in his late fifties as he was, with some noticeable lines, Marcus Bradley could be called handsome.

His blue eyes, however, had the clarity of a much younger man's. Observant eyes that, at the moment, were watching her with a sharpness that made her slightly uncomfortable. Made her turn the direction of the conversation to a subject that would distract him from what she was beginning to suspect was an interest in her that was more personal than just her art.

"So how was *your* day?" she inquired brightly. "You were going to spend it at the resort's building site, weren't you?"

"I was and did. It's coming along, although like most large building projects, it has its problems."

"Oh? What are they?"

"Nothing that you'd find particularly interesting, I'm afraid."

She knew how invested he was in his resort, both financially and emotionally, and she wanted to keep him discussing it now. "I'd love to see the place, Marcus."

"I'll have to take you there sometime, but right now it's in a pretty rough state for any touring. Let's get back to your own day. How is the painting coming?"

Her effort had failed. "I think you'll like the scene I'm working on when it's finished. It's still in a rough state, too. Traditional, of course, but that's what you wanted, isn't it?"

"Yes. A seascape, I believe?"

"Basically. On location from one of the beaches."

"I see."

The blue eyes continued to search her as she briefly described the scene for him. This was growing awkward. She had the distinct feeling he knew she was withholding something from him, and that he also knew what that something was.

Marcus nodded slowly when she was finished. Then, stabbing a forkful of fish, he said smoothly, casually, "I hear you had a visitor on the beach."

Casey. He'd learned about Casey. There could only be one source of information for that. Julio had reported it to him. Brenna had insisted the driver was not a watchdog when Casey implied he was just that. But now she wasn't so certain that Julio's employer hadn't planted him to specifically spy on her.

"Just a tourist wandering by and stopping to look at what I was painting," she said with what she hoped was a believable, innocent explanation. "I'm used to it. It's a common occurrence when artists are painting on location."

Brenna regretted the necessity of her lie, but she was afraid that Marcus wouldn't appreciate learning the FBI agent she'd once been engaged to had turned up on the island. To her relief, he seemed to accept her explanation.

Placing his fork on his plate, he leaned toward her. "You mustn't mind your driver looking out for you," he said mildly. "I'm afraid there's no shortage of crime on islands like St. Sebastian where there's so much poverty."

"I understand." She found another, safer topic. "If you keep on feeding me like this, Marcus, I'm not going to fit into any of my clothes when I get back to Chicago."

"Gilda *is* a marvelous cook," he conceded.

Gilda, she knew, was his housekeeper here, as well as Julio's wife.

"Are you ready for coffee yet?"

"If you don't mind," Brenna told her host after dinner, "I'm going to call it an early night."

"Not a bad idea. I'm ready to turn in myself. We've both had a long day."

"I'll leave you here then," she said, rising from the table.

"Why don't I walk you back to the guesthouse before you leave?"

"That isn't necessary, Marcus."

"I insist," he said, rounding the table to join her.

The guesthouse was behind the villa and the paved walkway to it was well lit. There was no reason for him to escort her. Brenna felt like she was being guarded, maybe a bit too closely, and she didn't like the idea. But she didn't feel she could afford to object, either to his company on the walk or his good-night kiss on her cheek when he left her at her door.

He's paying you a lot of money for those paintings. What are you going to do? Risk offending him?

There was more to it than that, she reminded herself after letting herself into her quarters. How could she for-

get all he'd done for her back in Chicago? Not only buy-
ing two of her pictures when they met at the art gallery
that held her first showing but broadcasting her talent to
his wealthy friends, making possible the success she was
now enjoying.

A lot to be grateful for.

Except Marcus Bradley wasn't the first individual to
admire her work. Casey was responsible for that.

Much as she might have wanted to, Brenna was unable
to prevent herself from remembering their first meeting
as she went around turning on the lights in the elegantly
furnished suite she was occupying.

She'd been working in an art supply store at the time.
Casey had strolled into the place to buy a set of paints
and brushes for his nephew's birthday. That first sight of
him—hard body, tousled, dark brown hair—had been like
experiencing heat lightning.

The store had permitted her to display a few of her
paintings. She was wrapping Casey's purchase when he
called out, "Hey, who did this?"

She looked up to find him, thumbs hooked into the
pockets of his jeans, gazing at her painting of the Chicago
skyline with storm clouds gathering behind it.

"I did," she answered.

"And these others?"

"I'm guilty of those, too."

"They're good. *Damn* good."

His compliment had lit a warm glow inside her. As
compelling as the man himself. And that's how it had
begun for them. With that stormy painting.

Speaking of which—

She crossed the sitting room to check on today's painting where it rested on the easel in the corner, making sure
it was drying properly.

She was getting ready for bed when her cell phone chimed, startling her. Who on earth—

It needed only the few seconds she took to pluck the phone out of her bag to guess who it was.

She answered the call with an irritated "Casey, how did you get this number?"

"From Will, of course, before I left home. I needed to be sure I could contact you down here. He said you had a GSM cell. Me, too."

Brenna knew that, overseas like this, they would not have been able to connect otherwise.

"You'll need to take down my own number."

"Why?"

"To reach me if you need me. Why else?"

"Casey, I'm not going to need you."

"Just do it, will you?"

It was easier not to argue with him. "Fine," she sighed, finding paper and pencil on the desk where her bag lay. "What is it?"

He relayed the number to her.

"Happy now?" she asked him after jotting the number down.

"Reasonably so. How are you doing? Okay?"

"Why wouldn't I be?"

"Just wanted to check."

"Don't." What was it with these two guys, Marcus and now Casey, determined to watch over her? "Look, I'm going to hang up now. I was just headed for bed when you called."

They exchanged good-nights. Minutes later, after turning off all the lights in the suite, Brenna crawled into bed. She expected to be asleep within seconds of laying her head on the pillow. It didn't work that way.

Casey kept her awake. She couldn't seem to rid herself of the image of him that rose in the dark and stayed there.

It was as if that strong, forceful body was actually in the room with her, standing over her, wearing the same wounded look on his face he had worn the day she'd given his ring back to him.

But she didn't want to go there again. Hadn't she already suffered enough torment for weeks after? She had, yes, and in the end managed to survive it, too.

She didn't deserve to fight that battle all over, spend a sleepless night being haunted by Casey McBride. And she didn't. She finally willed herself into a deep, uninterrupted sleep.

Uninterrupted, that is, until what must have been hours later when she came awake with a restless inability to understand why. It took her a few minutes to realize she could no longer hear the peaceful hum of the air conditioner.

Brenna had learned that, in the deep hours of the night, the tropical heat of the day, even a steamy heat, was known to cool down to a degree that was downright chilly. Had to be the reason why the thermostat had shut down the air conditioner. It was no longer needed.

The temperature of the bedroom was comfortable enough without it, but the air in here felt stuffy now. She had to open a window.

She didn't bother turning on a lamp. It wasn't necessary. The security lights outside that bathed the property provided enough illumination through the blinds to guide her from the bed to the nearest window. Lifting the sash, she knelt on the carpet to breathe in the fresh air.

A breeze off the land not only cooled her face, it carried with it the wonderful scents of the spices that were grown on the island. Then, suddenly, she caught a whiff of something less pleasant. The odor of a cigarette. It had to be close by for her to smell it like this.

Peering through the slats of the blind she hadn't bothered to raise, Brenna was able to immediately detect the source of the smoke. Julio was out there, a burning cigarette in hand as he paced along the path that circled the guesthouse.

This was no casual, midnight walk. His gait was too purposeful, too deliberate for that. Marcus must have ordered him to patrol her quarters. There was something else. He'd paused to crush his cigarette on the ground. Even in the shadows, the glow from the security light mounted overhead was sufficient enough for her to read his face.

There was no other word to describe his expression. *Sinister.*

She didn't like it. Didn't like that look on his face. Didn't like Julio being out there. Didn't like his keeping watch on her, because that's what it was.

Could Casey be right? Was she making herself vulnerable to some unknown, potential danger just by being here at the villa?

Casey couldn't sleep. He was concerned about Brenna, convinced that Marcus Bradley was an unpredictable presence in her life. This was why he was here on the deck, listening to the waves crashing on the beach, instead of in his bed.

He could tell the tide was coming in. There was no moon, but he could see a luminescence like foxfire on the crests of the waves, marking their position.

He had to be honest with himself. There was something more than just Bradley troubling him.

It was the memories of Brenna and him and why their

affair had gone wrong. He had no business revisiting those memories, but he couldn't help himself. Couldn't stop himself from placing the blame for their breakup where it belonged. With himself.

And there it is, McBride. The self-accusation you deserve.

Because hadn't he known from the beginning that persuading her to marry him was a mistake? Brenna had made no secret of her fear for his safety. She'd been raised on it by a mother who'd lost her husband, a Chicago fireman who'd died in a warehouse blaze.

"It devastated her, Casey," Brenna had confided to him. "It killed her in the end. Mom just seemed to fade away on Will and me."

Casey had sympathized with their loss, but he hadn't seriously listened to Brenna's argument that his work as an FBI agent was every bit as dangerous, perhaps even more so than that of a fireman. She had made repeated efforts during the course of their engagement to talk him into leaving the field and taking a safe desk job at the bureau.

But he knew that wasn't for him. He craved the adventure out there.

It might have turned out all right if, on assignment in the Mideast to rescue an officer from the American embassy captured by terrorists, he hadn't been caught and held himself. The FBI was unable to tell Brenna during those long, nightmare weeks whether he was alive or dead.

In the end, a release for both the officer and Casey had been negotiated, but it was too late for Brenna and him.

"I can't take it anymore, Casey. I love you, but I can't live with the fear of losing a husband. I just *can't*. It's easier to live with the heartache of letting you go."

That's when Brenna had returned his ring to him. When his bitterness had followed. In time he had overcome that bitterness, but he'd never been able to forget her or what they had shared.

And now here they were, thrown together again.

Oh, hell, was this going to turn out to be another bad mistake?

He looked up at the stars overhead, brilliant in the night sky, and realized he had no answer for himself.

Chapter 2

The first thing Brenna did when she emerged from the guesthouse the next morning, besides noting that it was going to be another clear, beautiful day, was to deliberately seek out Julio. Providing, that is, he wasn't asleep in his bed after patrolling her quarters all night.

She found him near the garage, where he was washing the Jaguar in the driveway. He looked much too alert to have spent the entire night without sleep. She decided he'd either deserted his post at some point or been replaced by another member of the staff at the villa. For all she knew, Marcus had a whole army of them working in shifts to guard her around the clock.

Or maybe, thanks to Casey's paranoia on the subject of Marcus, she was simply letting her imagination run wild.

As it must have last night, she thought, when she had sworn the expression on Julio's face was a grim, sinister one. His was nothing remotely like that this morning.

He was all harmless smiles, greeting her with a cheerful, "Good morning, miss. I will have the car ready for you after breakfast."

She returned the greeting, adding a careless "Thank you, Julio, but I won't need you to drive me anywhere."

"You are not doing the painting today?"

"Not today, no. I'm planning on walking down to town, where I'll probably spend most of the day scouting subjects for possible paintings at some other time. There are a lot of interesting colonial buildings in the city, as well as some fascinating stuff along the harbor, don't you think?"

He looked alarmed at her intention. "There are certain quarters in Georgetown that are not safe, miss."

"Well, I won't be going anywhere near those."

"But you will let me go with you."

And have her feel all day like she was a prisoner, like she did last night? Not a chance.

"Oh, I don't think that will be necessary. I'll be fine on my own," she insisted. "It isn't far to town, and with its being downhill all the way, it should be a pleasant stroll."

"But if you should be tired when you are ready to come back…"

"Then I'll just grab a taxi," she assured him brightly, hoping he understood that, behind the brightness, was a stubborn determination that would permit no further opposition.

Brenna could feel him gazing after her unhappily when she left him and headed toward the villa.

Too bad. Because, like it or not, my friend, I mean to be free of you, at least for today and maybe all the other days I'm here on the island. And you can just report that to your employer and see where it gets you.

Breakfast was waiting for her on the terrace. Marcus was not.

Brenna must have looked puzzled by his absence, because the round-faced, plump housekeeper who was clearing his place at the table informed her, "If you are looking for Mr. Bradley, miss, I am sorry to tell you he has already gone to the place of the building of the resort. He is to meet the architect there at an early hour, you understand."

"Oh, it doesn't matter, Gilda. I didn't need to see him for anything."

Actually, Brenna was relieved that Marcus wasn't here. He would have wanted to know what her plans were for the day, and she didn't want to have to lie to him again. He would learn eventually, anyway, from Julio that she'd insisted on going off on her own.

Well, what of it? She was not going to have any of them trying to control her, and that included Casey.

"What can I get you for the breakfast, miss?"

"I'll just have coffee and one of the muffins from the basket there. They look delicious, Gilda. And maybe a glass of juice, too. Whatever you have."

The housekeeper brought her a small pitcher of fresh papaya juice and while Brenna drank it and ate her muffin she consulted the guidebook for St. Sebastian she'd bought for herself the morning of her arrival on the island.

What she ought to be doing today, Brenna thought with a guilty sigh, was going back to the beach to finish yesterday's work. But that would have meant Julio transporting both her and all her gear, as well as the possibility of running into Casey again.

And what she wanted, and meant to have, were several hours to herself. Not that she was going to ignore her obligation to Marcus. Which was why, when she set off on foot for Georgetown below, she went equipped with a tote bag containing her camera, sketchbook and the guidebook.

Brenna hadn't lied to Julio when she'd told him she

meant to scout out subjects for future paintings. What she'd omitted, however, was her plan to save those interesting colonial buildings for another occasion. This time the camera and the sketchbook were going to record another destination.

There was no shortage of taxis in the busy streets of the city, most of them used American cars that had seen better days. But any one of them was sufficient for her purpose. She had no trouble hailing a cab.

"The airport, please," she directed the local driver, who flashed her an enormous grin with teeth so white they were blinding. His speed at the wheel was less pleasing, making her immensely grateful the airport was only a few miles from town.

Brenna was vastly relieved when he managed to drop her safely at the front of the terminal before racing off again to find a new fare. Entering the building, she made her way to the desk of St. Sebastian's only car rental agency.

The young woman behind the counter greeted her with a wide smile and a kindly "Help you, miss?"

"Yes, please. I'd like to rent a car. Whatever you have that would be easy for me to manage."

The cheerful smile of the attendant vanished, replaced by a regretful shake of her head. "I am much sorry, miss, but there is no car for me to check out, only ones for me to check in. Which," she added, "is not yet happening this morning."

"Are you telling me there's nothing at all available? Not even for the day?"

"Sadly, our fleet of rentals is not a large one, and the last of them was claimed an hour or so ago. But, miss, if you would like to leave me your name and a phone number..."

Brenna decided against that measure. It could mean

waiting for who knew how long, wasting her time hoping for a rental car to be returned.

Cabs were plentiful at the airport. It looked like her only disappointing choice was to hail one of them to take her back into town. She'd spend the day doing what she'd told Julio she would do, actually scouting painting subjects in the city. That would teach her to be deceptive.

The sunlight when she exited the terminal had her squinting against its intensity. Juggling her purse and tote with her head lowered, she searched for her sunglasses, found them and slid them into place.

The first sight that met her gaze when she looked up was Casey McBride. He leaned against the side of a silver Toyota, muscular arms locked across his chest and wearing a sly smile that said he was pleased with himself.

"All right, how did you find me this time?"

"Nothing complicated. Just cruising around Georgetown, you know, seeing the sights, when I spotted you grabbing the cab."

"Another lucky coincidence, huh?"

"Looks like it."

"I'd say it was more like you were waiting for me to turn up, probably watching the villa until I did."

"Me? Never. How are things at the villa, anyway?"

"Fine."

She had no intention of mentioning last night and Julio. If Casey got one whiff of that, he would be on her to move out of the guesthouse and relocate elsewhere. No way was she going to jeopardize her career by alienating Marcus with an action like that.

"So, you weren't playing secret agent, hmm? You just went and tailed my cab in that silver chariot there for— what? The fun of it? Where'd you get it, anyway? Oh, no," she said, "it was you, wasn't it, who got the last rental car?"

"Don't tell me I went and snatched it out from under you? Sorry, but I need transportation."

"So do I."

"I thought that was being provided for you. So where is your shadow today?" Casey looked around, as if he expected Julio to be lurking nearby.

"I suppose you could say I gave him the slip. A lot of good it did me, because now it looks like I went and traded one shadow for another one."

"Yeah, but I'm a much friendlier one."

He removed his sunglasses, as if to convince her with a full view of his face how harmless he was. It didn't work. "I'm not so sure of that."

"Well, let's say a social one anyway. Didn't look to me like the driver Bradley assigned you qualified for that."

"That's the point. I didn't want friendly, social or any other kind of accompaniment. This was to be a solitary outing."

"Feeling crowded, are we? Like maybe too many people sticking too close?"

"I just felt like being on my own today."

"You could get that by going back to town."

She hesitated too long. That perceptive mind of his, so valued by the FBI, guessed she was hiding something. "Or could it be that you have some other particular destination in mind?"

Her silence confirmed it for him.

"Tell you what," he drawled in his faint Kentucky accent, "I've got the car and the time. So why don't you let me drive you there?"

"I don't think so."

"No?" He lifted those broad shoulders of his in a little shrug. "Of course, there is an alternative. You could always hire a taxi for the day. A cab driver should be impersonal enough for you. Providing, that is, you don't mind the expense or the reckless speed these guys down here travel on questionable roads."

"I've experienced enough of that already, thank you."

"There you go then. You either abandon your intention or choose me, a safe driver."

"You've covered it all, haven't you?"

"Come on, Brenna. What's holding you back? I promise to behave myself."

"I seem to remember some occasions when you didn't."

"But not today. Guaranteed." He opened the passenger door of the Toyota, holding it for her temptingly. Here she was about to make a mistake with a stubborn, take-charge agent determined to safeguard her.

Oh, hell, she thought, harmless or not, either way she wasn't going to be able to lose him.

"You win."

Settling herself into the passenger seat, she placed her tote and purse on the floor at her feet. Casey was about to close the door after her when he realized something.

"No painting gear?"

"Not this time."

"Why is that?"

She launched into a brief art lesson. "Painting on location is great. It can lend a kind of immediacy to a canvas you don't get in a studio. It can also be a nuisance having to transport all your materials to the site, or ending up with the kind of weather that decides to shift its mood."

"Does that mean you're playing truant today, Rembrandt?"

"Not really." She reached a hand down to pat the side of her tote. "I've got my camera and sketchbook to record the subject I'm considering for another painting. What I capture might be enough to justify a studio picture. Your eyes are beginning to glaze over. You're excused from class."

Laughing, he slammed the door, rounded the car and climbed in behind the wheel. After buckling his belt and putting his sunglasses back on, he turned to her. "Okay, what is this mysterious destination we're headed for?"

"A place called Braided Falls up in the highlands. It's supposed to be spectacular. That's what the guidebook says, anyway. Hey, what are we waiting for?"

She could be damned exasperating, Casey thought as he swung the Toyota around and headed them back toward Georgetown, which she'd indicated was the route they needed to go.

On the other hand, she could also be bewitching with that flaming copper hair, amber-colored eyes known to spark with anger when she was provoked to it and a lush, seductive mouth. Not to mention those long, elegant legs, which were on full view in a pair of pale green shorts paired with a matching green-and-white-striped tee.

There was something else he could tell with his sneaky, sidelong glance. With the free spirit of a true artist, she wasn't wearing a bra under the tee. Damn, how was he supposed to deal with that and not lose control of the wheel?

He'd promised Brenna to behave himself, but with her assets so close like this in the confinement of the car, Casey wasn't so sure now he *could* restrain himself.

Try, he ordered himself.

They were approaching the city when, to his relief, he was distracted by a glimpse of her guidebook open on her lap.

"What are you doing?"

"Unfolding the map provided inside."

"What for?"

"We'll need it to get to the falls."

"Uh, both the car and our phones are equipped with GPS."

"Not reliable functions here on St. Sebastian, says the guide," she informed him. "A paper map is a safer bet. You'll have to go straight through Georgetown to reach the shore road on the other side. That'll take us to the highlands road."

For the next fifteen minutes, Casey concentrated on weaving through the dense traffic of the city. After passing a cricket field, which Brenna reported was the favorite sport here on the island—another gem from the guidebook, Casey assumed—they found themselves on the open shore highway with the broad, blue Caribbean on their right and on their left an unbroken expanse of vegetation.

"What are you doing?" he challenged Brenna when he glanced over and saw her lowering the passenger window. "We've got air-conditioning operating in here."

"I know, but I'd rather breathe the warm, outside air."

"Why?"

"Because," she explained, her head practically hanging out the window, "it carries such wonderful scents. Can you smell them? The cinnamon, the nutmeg and that sweet fragrance…that's frangipani. I saw it growing at the villa. They're enough to make you drunk on them."

"If you say so," Casey said. Personally, he'd much rather be inhaling Brenna's own faint, flowery scent, which he'd been enjoying with a sensual freedom before she'd opened the window.

Maybe she *was* drunk. That might explain why, after traveling another mile down the road, she cried out, "Pull over!"

God Almighty, was he about to hit a goat? The nuisances seemed to be wandering everywhere on the island, often in the road. Casey dutifully parked at the side of the highway, where he was reminded that scents weren't enough for Brenna.

"What now?"

"The flamboyant tree over there! Isn't it magnificent?"

"Yeah," he agreed. The tree was in full bloom, like a crimson torch. Why hadn't he remembered that scents alone wouldn't satisfy her? Brenna lived for color. It was a heady wine for her.

Casey recalled how she never wore drab colors if she could help it. And even on those rare, formal occasions, like her gallery showings, when she wore a form-fitting black dress that emphasized her hips and breasts, she'd always managed to accent it with a bright neck scarf or a carefully selected piece of jewelry.

You remember too much about her, McBride. Not healthy. Not when you're no longer a couple.

He needed to stop being aware of her beside him. Needed to stop thinking about her and Bradley. He had no right to any jealousy. Concern, yes. Because, like her brother, he didn't trust Marcus Bradley and Brenna's living arrangement with him. Just that. Nothing else, he ordered himself.

They moved on up the highway, Brenna switching from flowers to birds. Scarlet ibises, a blue tanager, jeweled hummingbirds. They were as plentiful as the flowers.

Or they were until she instructed him to leave the highway for the road that would take them up into the highlands.

"Where are they?" she wondered. "All the flowers and birds?"

She was right. There was suddenly none of them in evidence. The contrast between the shore highway behind them and the road here was startling, with its dark, shadowed green growth close on either side of them. Like an impenetrable jungle, Casey thought.

Brenna was silent now as they traveled along the gloomy tunnel. Even the engine seemed quieter to him.

"It's…weird, isn't it?" she finally remarked. "Not the same St. Sebastian at all."

"Another one, anyhow. Ah, here we go. Sunshine up ahead again."

The Toyota emerged from the dim passage that was the road into the open. The change should have been encouraging, cheerful even. Somehow, it wasn't.

The thick forest was still off to their left, but on the right the land had been cleared away to accommodate expansive fields. They must have once grown crops, but now they were nothing but weeds.

"What's left of an old sugar plantation, I bet," Brenna said. "I read in the guidebook that in the slave days the island once exported a lot of sugar."

Casey had slowed the car to a crawl. "Understandable," he responded. "But with the land no longer cultivated, what's with the fence?"

It was not an old fence. It was a modern, high cyclone fence that seemed to enclose the entire property. He stopped the Toyota in front of a pair of padlocked gates.

Behind them, in the distance up a narrow driveway, was a galleried mansion from another century. Shuttered, it looked abandoned and decaying.

"They called a place like that the great house in the plantation days," she said.

"Yeah, but why would the security of a fence and locked gates be necessary now? It's odd."

"It's eerie, is what it is. Come on, Casey," she urged with a shudder, "let's go on."

He didn't argue with her. He sent the silver chariot, as she'd referred to it back at the airport, along the road again.

The route began to climb, winding into the first of the highlands. The vegetation thinned again here.

Rounding a bend, Casey sighted what seemed to be a small, dilapidated general store at the side of the road. He pulled into the gravel parking lot in front of it.

"Why are we stopping here?" Brenna wanted to know.

"I'm thirsty. Let's see if we can get a couple of bottles of water. And while we're at it, maybe some answers."

Chapter 3

The area was modest in size, but every foot of it was crammed from floor to ceiling with merchandise. Had there been time for it, Brenna would have treated herself to a tour of those shelves. Mixed in with a jumble of modern products were such old-fashioned wares as rolls of fly paper and dust-coated, metal electric fans.

A curtain of beads hung in a doorway at the rear. Suddenly it rattled, parting for a young black man who appeared from a back room wearing one of the island's famous smiles and a head of dyed orange hair.

"Welcome to de store," he greeted them. "What can I git for you?"

Brenna knew that St. Sebastian had been British owned before it was granted the independence it had requested. This explained the English that was spoken by the native population, although with a flavor of its own possessing a melodic cadence she loved to hear. This young man's speech was a strong example of that.

"We'd like two bottles of water," Casey said. "Cold, please, if you have them."

"What you tink? We don't have cold here?" Chuckling, he turned away, removed a pair of bottled waters from a cooler and placed them on the counter he stood behind.

Casey paid for them and handed one of the bottles to Brenna.

"De steel band, dey play tonight in Georgetown. Dey something when dey come togedder. Tickets don't cost you much."

"Maybe another time," Casey said. "But there is something I'd like to ask."

"Sure."

"We passed this old plantation back down the road. The one with the high fence around it. What can you tell us about it?"

The exuberant smile on the clerk's face vanished. He was no longer looking at them. His gaze had shifted to something behind them.

Mystified, Brenna turned. An equally puzzled Casey also twisted around. No one else had entered the store. She figured the clerk must be staring through the front window at what was outside.

And this, she convinced herself, was another car that hadn't been there when she and Casey arrived. It was parked directly across the way at the side of the road, an old sedan as dark a green as the deeply shadowed stretch of jungle she'd been grateful to leave behind them.

The window on the driver's side of the car had been lowered, revealing the figure at the wheel. He was looking in their direction, a man with a Nordic face, a buzz cut, and cold, blue eyes.

Brenna and Casey faced the clerk again, waiting for the answer to Casey's question. His dark gaze turned reluctantly back to them.

"Mon, we don't talk about dat place."

"Why is that?" Casey persisted.

"You givin' me too much worry," he mumbled.

They were clearly being dismissed.

The green sedan was gone when they left the store.

"What was that all about?" Brenna wondered when they'd settled themselves in their own car. "The guy was spooked. You could see it in his face."

Casey shook his head. "Dunno. Maybe our mystery plantation is haunted, and the guy in the green heap is its ghost."

"With old legends in the West Indies so common, that's not so funny."

"But nothing to do with us." Casey started the Toyota and backed out onto the road. "Come on, let's go find your waterfall."

His intention wasn't so simply achieved. A mile or so farther up the road Brenna caught a movement in the angled outside mirror on her side of the car. Leaning to the right for a better view, she was able to identify the green sedan tailing them.

She'd had no reason before this to check the road behind them, but it did seem that the vehicle had suddenly appeared out of nowhere. Tempting as it was, she resisted the urge to call it a phantom. Casey would have loved teasing her about more ghosts.

"Casey—"

"Yeah, I see him. Spotted him in my rearview," he said, indicating the driver's mirror above his head.

"Um, you don't think he's deliberately following us? I mean, his car back at the store was headed in the direction we're going. Now he's somehow ended up behind us."

"Could be he waited off on some side lane for us to pass and then pulled out."

"But why? Why should he want to follow us?"

Casey had no explanation for her. His only response after a few seconds was a simple request. "Break out that map of yours again, will you?"

"You want me to see if that side lane behind us does exist?"

"Nope. I want you to see if there's another road ahead of us branching off this one."

That didn't make sense to her. "For what reason?"

"I want to test something."

Brenna waited for a further explanation, but again he gave her none. Grumbling to herself, she consulted the map as he'd asked.

"There is another road up ahead on the right, but it doesn't make any more sense than your wanting to know it's there."

"Why is that?"

"Because after winding all over the place, it ends up looping back to join this one. And this one is a much shorter, more direct route to the falls."

"The other road…lots of twists and turns, huh?"

"Yes."

Casey nodded, looking satisfied. Why, she couldn't imagine, and this time she didn't bother asking him.

"I suppose," she theorized, "since its being there at all doesn't make sense when it doesn't go anywhere but back to this road, it must have been constructed earlier. And then this one was built later, cutting off the old one to make a shorter route."

"Sounds right. Our green sedan is still behind us," he added, casting a fast glance into his rearview mirror. "Keep checking on it for me, will you? I'm going to be too busy before long to do it myself."

He does love keeping me guessing, doesn't he? Brenna

thought wryly. But she obeyed his newest request, turning in her seat as much as the restraint of the belt would permit. Her view through the back window was considerably more accurate than what her outside mirror provided.

She waited a minute to report, "He's sticking with us."

"Coming up just ahead. Hang on."

She did and learned why when, without slowing, Casey sharply and abruptly swung the Toyota into the side road he must have been watching for and found.

She was watching, as well. "The green demon turned, too," she announced.

"Good."

She understood now just what Casey was testing. He wanted to learn whether the green sedan only seemed to be following them or if this was a deliberate pursuit. Well, he'd evidently determined which was correct, but Brenna wasn't certain it had been worth the risk.

She was even less certain of that when the Toyota bounced over a deep pothole, jolting her harshly. The road had obviously not been kept in repair. There'd been no reason to when the newer road was built. Worse than being in a rough condition with its broken pavement, it was narrow and without any guardrails. And now that they were fully in the forested highlands, with long drops over the side... Unnerving.

"Casey, this isn't smart. The road is bad, and there's nothing along it. If that guy tailing us is dangerous and should catch up with us out here in the middle of nowhere..."

"He won't. I'll lose him before that happens."

"You're awfully sure of yourself."

He turned his head just long enough to favor her with one of his smug grins. "Hey, I'm an experienced FBI agent, remember? I know how to chase the bad guys and

I know how to outrun them. Besides, that heap back there is in no shape to keep up with us. You'll see."

Maddening. He was maddening.

Moreover, Casey failed to ease his foot on the accelerator, and with the tortuous road growing more treacherous with every mile, she thought he might have realized that was imperative. He didn't.

Brenna felt dizzy with all the rapid twists and turns. And when she found herself looking over the side into a deep gorge, and had a vision of the Toyota plunging into it, her giddiness morphed into absolute terror.

Casey's only reaction to their perilous situation was a placid "Nice scenery up here, huh? I'd say they're more mountains than highlands."

"And I say I'm going to lose my breakfast if you don't slow down."

Much to her relief, he braked the car to, if not a crawl, at least a cautious speed. "Look," he said.

"At what?"

"At what you were supposed to be on the lookout for. Your green demon is no longer behind us. He must have decided we weren't worth it and headed back. Told you he'd give up."

"Aren't you the clever one? So, why are we stopping then?" she wondered when he pulled the Toyota over to the side and put the shift gear into Park. "The direct road can't be much farther."

He turned to face her. "Because I have some questions for you."

"Such as?"

"Kind of funny, isn't it, that some guy should turn up out of nowhere and decide to follow us?"

"Why should you imagine I would have an answer for that any more than you do?"

"I don't know, Brenna. We had a pretty good view of him back at the store. It's got me wondering whether you might have realized who he is."

"What kind of question is that? Of course I don't know who he is. Why on earth would I?"

"Maybe you saw him hanging around at the villa and recognized him from there. Could be Bradley is using thugs like him to keep tabs on you."

"To an extent like this? That's nuts, even if he did have a reason to have me watched, and I can't imagine what that could possibly be. Why is it that you insist on connecting anything at all negative with Marcus?"

"Just trying to cover the possibilities."

"Well, don't. Can we please forget this and go on?"

"All right," he said, shifting back into Drive, "let's find your falls."

She was ready to put the whole episode behind her. Wanted to do just that. Except Casey left her reluctantly remembering Julio last night outside the guesthouse.

A graveled parking area had been provided for visitors to the falls.

"Looks like we've got the place to ourselves," Casey observed, pulling into the small, empty lot.

Brenna left her tote and purse in the car, taking only her camera with her. By the time Casey locked the Toyota and joined her, she had located a sign posted at the mouth of a trail, the arrow on it indicating the direction of the attraction.

"It can't be far," she said. "I can hear the sound of the water from here."

The trail was wide enough to permit them to walk side by side. Although the ever-protective Casey offered no comment on this feature, Brenna knew it satisfied him to be able to keep her close. There was no point in objecting. He wouldn't have listened.

A few hundred yards brought them through the forest to their destination. They suddenly found themselves in the open, standing on the lip of a ravine.

Casey spoke his approval in her ear. "It doesn't disappoint, does it?"

She shook her head, marveling at the sight. She understood why it was called Braided Falls. There was no single stream of water tumbling over the ledge high above them on their right, but three distinctly separate ones. Several feet along their descent, the projecting rocks of the cliff face squeezed them together into one cascade. A little lower, and they separated again, then still lower joined once more, like strands of hair twined into a fat braid.

A pool at the bottom rimmed with moss and banks of ferns finally received the waters. From here they rushed through the ravine they had carved, their course taking them beneath a sturdy, hanging bridge that faced the falls.

"I'm going out on the bridge," Brenna announced. "I should get some great shots from there."

"I guess it wouldn't be there if it wasn't safe," Casey agreed.

By the time he'd followed her to the center of the bridge, she was busy with her Nikon compact, adjusting it for color, sharpness and clarity. She was ready to record a series of photographs when she heard it.

"Listen!"

"What?" Casey questioned. "All I can hear is the roar of the falls."

"Not that. It's the sound of drums coming from somewhere off the other side of the bridge."

"You're imagining it."

She shook her head in denial. "I don't think so. There's

a path there. I'm going to follow it and see what I can learn about those drums. I don't think they can be the usual steel ones. Could be really interesting."

Before he could stop her, she was off the bridge and hurrying along the path.

"Brenna, come back here!" he yelled after her. "Damn it, now who's being reckless?"

She ignored him, knowing he would catch up with her. He did, muttering, "You're going to get into trouble with this appetite of yours for local color."

"You should talk. You weren't worried about trouble when you took us over that rotten road."

"So we're even."

They left it there, the drums growing louder as they proceeded on through the forest. Sunlight ahead of them poured down into what promised to be a large clearing. When the path widened, Brenna could see a collection of small houses. More like shacks really, their peeling wooden walls painted in the rainbow hues favored by the natives everywhere on the island. Vibrant colors that had faded but which she still admired.

"It's a village."

"A poor one, from the looks of it," Casey said.

Brenna could make out garden plots devoted to vegetables, banana plants at the sides of the houses and scrawny chickens scratching in the dust, but nowhere was there a sign of human life that would explain the drums. It was odd.

The path divided here, the branch on the right curving around a blind corner. Casey nodded in that direction. "It's coming from around there."

They followed the sound, turning with the path that brought them to the edge of another clearing, the origin of the drums and probably the strangest sight Brenna had ever seen.

Kneeling on the ground in a wide circle was a collection of women, none of them old and none of them probably younger than their upper teens. There were only three men present. Two of them were seated back to back in the center of the clearing, slapping out an alternating rhythm on a pair of hip drums.

Added to the beat was a shaking rattle in the hand of the third, older man wearing a fantastic headdress, his dark face streaked with white paint. In his other hand was a pot. Progressing slowly, regally around the circle from woman to woman, his forefinger dipping into the pot, he smeared a careful symbol on the forehead of each, his lips moving in what Brenna convinced herself was an incantation.

"If I didn't know any better," Casey mumbled, "I'd say what we're seeing here is an episode from *Survivor*."

"It isn't funny, Casey. I think we've wandered into a private, and probably very sacred, ceremony of some kind, and maybe we'd better—"

She got no further. There was a sudden, somber silence. The two men had abruptly stopped smacking their drums and were staring at the pair of intruders. The entire gathering had discovered them, including their leader, who was plainly unhappy with their presence.

Glaring at them across the clearing, he stretched out his hand that gripped the rattle and shook it at them menacingly. Shouting out some dire threat Brenna didn't understand, he started toward them.

Casey didn't wait. His hand closing on her wrist, he started to thrust Brenna protectively behind him. Another shout from a different source stopped him in midaction. The witch doctor, or whatever he was, never reached them. That second shout effectively halted him, too, in the middle of the clearing.

Brenna was as startled as the rest of them when an

attractive young woman, with skin the color of smooth milk chocolate, charged into the clearing from the direction of the village.

"I'm guessing that's our shouter," Casey said.

Whoever she was, she was fearless, Brenna thought. Without the least hesitation and no evidence of intimidation, she approached the glowering witch doctor.

She had to stop thinking of him as that. Other than the apparent leader of this group, she didn't know what he was exactly.

As she and Casey watched, their savior began to lecture the fellow. Or so it seemed from the tone of her voice, because from their position they couldn't make out her words. But whatever they were, her target was actually listening to them.

"I knew it," Casey insisted. "*I just knew it.* It's a reality TV series. Has to be."

She wished he'd be serious. This was a *serious* situation. On the other hand, she had no right to complain about his attitude when he'd tried to prevent her from coming here. Although it seemed the bold young woman must have won them their exoneration since the leader, with the sulky look of a child, turned his back on them and retreated to the other side of the circle.

Brenna watched the woman as she approached Casey and her, thinking, *she's different from the others. It's something in her attitude.*

It wasn't just her friendly smile either. It was her language when she reached them, an apology she expressed without any hint of the native dialect. "Sorry about that, folks."

"It looks like we owe you a vote of thanks," Casey told her. "You know, the cavalry riding to the rescue at the last minute."

She received his gratitude with a laugh. "Oh, you weren't in any danger. He was just upset because of that." She nodded at the camera in Brenna's hand.

"I wouldn't have photographed any of this," Brenna hastened to assure her. "Certainly not without permission."

"I appreciate that. My people don't mind having their pictures taken by the tourists, but they do like to be asked first. I'm guessing you came to see the falls and heard the drums."

"We did, yes."

Their deliverer glanced back over her shoulder. "Um, if you don't mind, why don't we leave the ceremony here to continue, and I'll walk you back and try to explain."

Casey waited until they were out of sight of the clearing, where the drums had resumed beating, and on the path to the falls before asking, "What was that we were seeing? Voodoo?"

"Not voodoo, no, though it is similar but with different rituals. Both of them originated from Africa, but this one is called obeah."

"And the guy in charge?"

"Well, whatever you do, don't call him a witch doctor. He hates that. He considers himself an obeah priest, and when he's conducting a ceremony his name is Lubomba. And when he's not," she confided, following another melodic laugh, "he's plain Frankie Wilson. Works on a melon farm outside a village below ours. Like most of our men do whenever the work is available."

Brenna stopped on the path, Casey and the young woman stopping with her. "Speaking of names, I'm thinking introductions are in order here. I'm Brenna Coleman, and this is Casey McBride."

She shook their offered hands. "And I'm Zena King."

"You, uh, live in the village then, Zena?"

"I'm from the village, but just visiting family there right now. Why do you— Oh, I understand. It's my English being so different from my people's. There's a reason for that."

They strolled on toward the falls, the sound of the drums fading behind them while Zena offered a second explanation.

"My village is a poor one. Most of the villages are on the island. The only schooling here is not regular or very good. I was lucky. Because I was considered exceptionally bright, my parents had the opportunity to send me at a young age to a Catholic boarding school in Georgetown."

"And that's where you learned to speak without an accent," Brenna assumed.

"The nuns were excellent teachers. Also very strict. I'll always be grateful to them for preparing me for a higher education."

"In Georgetown?" Casey asked.

Zena shook her head. "In Florida. I was able to earn a scholarship at a medical school in Miami. Like I said, I'm home for a couple of weeks to visit family."

"Ah, you're studying to be a doctor maybe," Casey said.

"Nothing that grand. I'm training to be a nurse-practitioner. When I qualify, I'll come back here to offer my people the kind of medical help they badly need. Right now, with the nearest doctor in Georgetown, they think it's the obeah priest who can help them."

They were nearing the falls. Brenna could hear the waters pouring over the ledge. "Am I right in supposing that's what the ceremony in the clearing was about?" she asked. "Some kind of medical crisis?"

"In a way," Zena said, leaving Brenna to wonder what this mystery was about.

They had reached the falls. The three of them stopped in the middle of the bridge where they gazed for a silent moment at the flowing waters. Zena, who seemed to have reached a decision, spoke to them again.

"It's complicated. I don't want you thinking my people are worshipping some primitive African god. Most of them, including Frankie Wilson when he's in the mood, are actually devout Christians. But they're also superstitious, and sometimes when the situation is desperate enough and their prayers aren't answered, they'll turn to the old religion, hoping for a solution."

"Desperate how?" Brenna questioned.

Zena hesitated, as if searching for the right words to enlighten them. "Did you notice the sad faces in the circle?"

"I did. I also noticed that, except for the two drummers and the priest, all of them were women."

"There's a reason for that. You have to understand that children aren't just important to the islanders, they're everything. The arrival of new babies is always celebrated. But—and I know this is hard to believe, because I can hardly believe it myself—there hasn't been a single baby conceived in my village over the past eight months."

"You're telling us," Casey said in wonder, "that this is what the ceremony back there was all about? This obeah priest doing his thing to lift what the women are convinced is a curse?"

Chapter 4

"That's exactly what you were seeing," Zena told them.
She went on to elaborate, "Of course, there are children
in the village, some of them infants, but no pregnancies
since last August."

"I'm supposing it wasn't for want of trying," Casey
said.

"You can trust me when I say the villagers have never
had any problem in that department."

"But wasn't there any effort to consult a doctor?"
Brenna asked.

"A doctor *was* persuaded to come up to the village.
The women most eager to get pregnant, the youngest ones
who have yet to have babies, were more than willing to
be examined."

"And?"

Zena shook her head. "Nothing. The doctor—and he's
a capable one—could find no reason for their infertility."

"What about the men?" Brenna wanted to know.

Zena rolled her eyes. "You don't know the St. Sebastian males if you think any of them would even consider himself incapable of fathering a child. Much too proud to submit to any test. I suppose it is unlikely at that that every husband, or for that matter, lover, would be sterile."

No more unlikely than the infertility of the women, Brenna thought, but she refrained from voicing it.

Zena changed the subject. "Do you have a car nearby?"

"Over in the parking lot," Casey said.

"Why don't I walk you there before we say goodbye?"

Casey waited until they reached the Toyota before he verbalized a consideration that must have occurred to him on the trail from the bridge. "This infertility thing…is it possible there was some kind of epidemic in the village that could be responsible?"

"Nothing like that. In fact, the village has been healthy since it got itself a safe supply of drinking water last year. It wasn't the case before then. I don't know. It all seems a mystery with nothing to explain it."

"Where does the new supply come from?" Casey asked.

"A deep well was drilled."

"And the village was able to afford that?"

"Not the village, no. I wasn't here then, but they tell me a wealthy benefactor who preferred to remain anonymous provided it."

Before saying their goodbyes to Zena, they thanked her for befriending them and wished her well in her training.

They were on the road when Brenna expressed her sorrow. "What a tragedy. An entire village with its women suddenly barren. That's got to be one for the medical records."

Casey agreed and was silent after that. Whatever his thoughts were, he didn't share them with her.

It wasn't until they were descending the highlands that

she realized she'd never gotten either her photographs or sketches of Braided Falls. It was too late to turn back. She'd have to wait for another day.

They had reached the cyclone fence that enclosed the old sugar plantation when Casey slowed the Toyota.

Now he slows down, she thought, when what she wanted him to do was speed on by. The place was too creepy for comfort.

He not only slowed, he stopped the car altogether in front of the closed gates to the drive.

"You see what I see, Rembrandt?"

She couldn't help noticing it. Parked outside the main door of the mansion was the dark green sedan that had followed them earlier.

When Brenna had no response for him, Casey turned to look at her. Was it his imagination, or had she turned pale under that golden tan that so became her?

"No thought on the subject?" he asked her.

"Please, can we just forget it and go on?"

She doesn't want to discuss the car, he realized, complying with her request. Probably doesn't want to even think about it. Its presence, both earlier and now, seemed to scare her.

But Casey couldn't forget what they'd referred to as the green demon as he headed them toward the shore highway. His mind, trained by the best instruction Quantico had to offer its agents, examined the puzzle.

The vehicle wouldn't have followed them, as it had tried to do, without a reason. The obvious explanation was the driver had wanted to know just where they were going. But why? Casey's FBI training had no answer for that. Couldn't be expected to provide answers without the information he lacked.

No sense in denying it. He had the questions, just not the solutions. Questions like why the clerk at the general store had been frightened by his discovery of the green sedan out front. And why it was now parked in front of the great house behind the locked gates. What connection did its driver have with that sinister plantation?

Those thoughts alone were enough to keep Casey's brain busy. Because it seemed to be a day for puzzles. He couldn't forget the most significant of them. Zena King's village. It just didn't make sense that a whole village could go barren.

It had to be a coincidence that he and Brenna had been confronted by two major mysteries, one following directly after the other. Casey resisted the urge to try to relate the plantation, the driver of the green demon and the village in any way. Much too unlikely to even consider such a possibility. Or was it?

Managing to put the whole thing out of his mind, at least for now, he resumed paying attention to Brenna. She looked like she was recovered from her alarm over their second sighting of the green demon. They were on the shore highway now, and she was contentedly occupied with finding new flowers and birds outside her window.

He was occupied with her. Hell, he would have been better off still worrying about puzzles than getting all bothered now by the woman beside him. Whatever their different moods of the day, shifting with the frequent events that had triggered them, Casey had never lost his awareness of the sexual tension that existed between Brenna and him. Nor did he think he'd be wrong in swearing she had been just as conscious of it, as well.

This heat he was experiencing whenever his gaze drifted in her direction had him frustrated with need. And what could he do about it? Nothing. She had made it clear on more than one occasion that she was off-limits to him now.

But he could look, even though it did raise his temperature with no possibility of release. And so he did, stealing frequent glances.

Damn, but she was one alluring woman with that abundant, copper hair any healthy man would love to run his fingers through. Probably while longing next to get his hands on those breasts. Breasts that, without a bra, enabled him to fully appreciate their lushness. Even that smattering of freckles across her nose—

"Watch!" she cried out. "You're drifting across the center line!"

Sweet Jesus, what was he doing? Trying to get them into an accident?

Casey immediately corrected their position on the road. After that, he made a determined effort to keep his eyes off Brenna and on his driving.

They had reached Georgetown when he managed to think of his stomach and not his libido. "I just remembered we missed lunch. It's not too late. There's this little seafood place on the harbor. My treat."

"Thanks, but I'll just grab something up at the villa. I want to make use of what's left of the day. I've been neglecting my work. I don't need to be on location to finish the seascape in the corner of the guesthouse I'm using as a studio. The light is good there."

Back to business, huh? Disappointed or not, he couldn't argue with her. She'd only agreed to come with him this morning because she needed the transportation he offered and not his company.

"So, I'll deliver you to the villa."

She shook her head emphatically. "No, please drop me at the bottom of the hill. It's an easy walk up from there."

He understood. She didn't want to chance being seen with him by any of the staff and having one of them report it to Marcus Bradley. Bradley wouldn't like it. It was a realization that soured him.

Casey concentrated on dealing with the traffic as they crossed to the other side of the city, not speaking again until he stopped to let her off where she indicated.

"What about tomorrow? The silver chariot here and I will be available to chauffeur you wherever you might want to go."

"I appreciate that, but I plan to stick close to town here on foot. The cab driver who drove me out to the airport this morning mentioned it was market day in the center of the city tomorrow. The stalls should offer some rich subjects."

"And you wouldn't like an escort, either by car or on foot?"

"Afraid not. I'll be careful. I hope you understand."

"Oh, sure, I get it. You want to be alone."

We'll see about that tomorrow, he promised himself.

He watched her undo her seat belt, gather up her things and start to exit the car. But she hesitated with her hand on the door handle.

"Forget something?" he asked.

She didn't answer him for a moment. Then, as if impulsively making up her mind, she twisted around to face him again. "I need to ask you something. It's been bothering me ever since you landed on the island."

"Fire away."

Another pause from her. What was it this time? Summoning the courage for whatever it was she wanted to know? She must have found it, because she suddenly blurted out her question.

"Casey, did you ever manage to forgive me for breaking off our engagement? Completely forgive me?"

He could see in her face how important this was to her. And, unlike Brenna, he didn't need to hesitate. He answered her, not with words, but with a swift, decisive action that allowed her no chance to resist.

It was an action that involved his arms reaching out and drawing her so tightly up against him she was unable to escape. An action that involved his mouth descending to angle across hers in a forceful kiss meant to leave her in no doubt about whether or not he'd ever forgiven her.

It was also a kiss he'd been longing to give her from the moment he had discovered her the other day on the beach. A kiss that he made certain permitted him to savor the faintly flowery scent of her he had been missing all these months. A kiss that he refused to make anything but lengthy and thorough.

Whether she intended it or not, her mouth opened to him. It was all the invitation Casey needed to slide his tongue inside where he experienced the familiar, heady taste of her. He captured her own tongue in a hot wetness that threatened to spiral both his emotions and his need in a lower area out of control before he managed the wisdom to release her.

His voice was as raspy as a file when he asked her, "Does that answer your question?"

She was breathing hard, unable to form a reply. Her purse and tote had slid back onto the floor. Collecting them again, she fumbled for the handle and opened the door. She couldn't get out of the car and away from him fast enough. He watched her hurry up the hill toward the villa.

Nice performance, McBride. She'll probably never let you get anywhere near her again.

After that episode, Casey wondered how he could still be hungry when he drove off in search of the little seafood joint on the harbor front. But, heck, if he couldn't satisfy one appetite, he might as well satisfy another.

He found the place all right, but there was nowhere to park. The fishing boats had come in with their catches for the day, and the area was crowded with customers wanting fresh fish.

He had no choice but to park two blocks away and walk back to the restaurant.

The waterfront was a busy place. There were vessels everywhere at the docks loading and unloading. Mostly unloading. He knew that on islands like St. Sebastian much of what was consumed had to come in from elsewhere.

He paused to watch steel drums, the kind that contained chemicals and other liquids, being transferred from a freighter into a secure, fenced enclosure. The burly white guy directing the operation had a long ponytail and tattoos covering his bare arms. He also had an unpleasant disposition. Casey didn't much care for the way he growled at the native workers under his command. But it wasn't his business to interfere.

With anger simmering, Casey moved on. He was nearing the restaurant, working his way through the crowd, when he felt something hard pressed tight against his back.

This wasn't the first time in his FBI career he'd experienced this kind of thing. Not a frequent occurrence but enough to identify the barrel of a gun.

Great. Just great. As if he hadn't already had enough excitement over the past few hours, he was about to be mugged.

He had no weapon of his own. His Glock had been confiscated, along with his FBI identification folder, back in Chicago when he was placed on suspension. And although his training had taught him several tactics for defeating an opponent, even with a gun in his back, he didn't dare use one of them. There were too many people here, kids as well, and he wasn't going to risk one of them being shot.

All this went through Casey's mind in no more than the span of several seconds before he muttered a resentful but resigned "All right, let's not hurt anyone. My wallet is in my back pocket. Just take it and clear off."

He could feel a breath stir near his ear as a rough voice informed him sharply, "Sorry, but this ain't any robbery."

No native dialect, but Casey did detect a slight foreign accent. Eastern European, he thought. He'd heard them before in his work. He figured the gun must be a small one and that the guy holding it had to be pressed against him so closely that no one seemed to be noticing.

"If it isn't a robbery, then what do you want?"

"Just to warn you, that's all."

What in the— "Warn me about what?"

The voice that hissed back at him had the venom of a deadly snake in it. "Stay away from her, McBride. If you know what's good for you, stay far away from her."

And that was it. Casey could feel the barrel of the gun retreating from his back. He should have waited for a moment more than he did to be sure it was safe before he whirled around, but he was afraid of losing his enemy. As it was, there was no sign of anyone like that. Whoever he was, he'd managed to melt off into the crowd and disappear, leaving Casey with a fuming inability to deal with him.

It wasn't until then that it occurred to Casey. He had known his name. The bastard had *known* his name. With that came another realization. Marcus Bradley. Yeah, he would swear to it. That was the explanation here. Bradley had connections, probably had spies everywhere on the island. And one of them had told him that Casey Mc-Bride had been seen in the company of Brenna Coleman. And Bradley didn't like it.

That was the *her* Casey had been warned to stay away from. Like hell he would.

The first thing Brenna did when she reached the guest-house was to hurry into the well-lighted bathroom and peer into the mirror. She expected to see her lips redder and more plump, but there was no change in her face.

Only the eyes that stared back at her were different. There was a wildness in them. And why shouldn't there be when she was still shaken from Casey's mind-numbing kiss? There had been nothing sweet or tender about it. It had been a fierce demonstration of masculine posses-siveness.

She should have been furious with him when he let her go. Why hadn't she been? Why wasn't she furious with him now?

Maybe because she didn't have anyone to blame but herself. After all, hadn't she willingly contributed to that savage kiss?

In want of some relief for her cheeks that felt as if they were flushed with a fever, she ran the tap and splashed cold water on her face. It helped. At least physically. Emo-tionally, she was a mess.

They had been parted for two years, convinced them-selves they had gotten over each other long ago. Had that been a lie she'd inflicted on herself? And had he, as well? Was she, in truth, still in love with Casey McBride?

Dear God, she couldn't let herself get involved on that level all over again with him. Couldn't relive the hell of being sick with worry about his safety whenever he was on some dangerous assignment.

What was she going to do about him? Brenna asked herself as she wandered back into the sitting room. She stood there for a moment gazing at the unfinished seascape on the easel.

She knew what she needed to do. Work. It always helped keep her mind clear when she had a brush in one hand and a palette in the other.

And it did help to steady her nerves when she got busy, determined to complete the painting. For now, anyway.

Brenna would have preferred not sharing dinner with Marcus that evening. But asking for a tray in the guest-house would have raised questions, probably brought him to her door to express a concern for her absence. It was easier to join him at the table on the terrace.

Marcus looked tired. It was an opportunity to defer any questions about her and instead ask him what was troubling him.

"Rough day?" she wondered, dipping her spoon into the savory turtle soup Gilda had served them.

"It was a bit," he admitted.

"Oh? Trouble at the site?"

"I'm afraid so. We have a problem with missing building materials. It's not uncommon for theft to occur whenever construction is underway on the island, but this time it's also tools. The poverty, you know, makes things that can be sold or traded attractive. I'm sorry to have to do it, but I'm afraid we'll have to post nighttime guards at the site."

"That's too bad."

Gilda brought in a platter of steaming pork roast, island vegetables and two plates and placed them in front of Marcus, knowing he liked to serve the entrée himself to his guests. Removing the soup bowls, she retreated to the kitchen.

He was silent while he helped Brenna to a generous portion of the pork and passed her plate to her. It was only after he served himself that he spoke again.

"What did you do today?"

"I spent a portion of it in town hunting for other subjects to paint." It wasn't totally a lie. She *had* gone down to the city to catch a taxi to the airport.

"And the other part of it?"

"In the guesthouse. I finished the seascape there. When it's dry, I'll show it to you." She was glad this was the truth. She hated lying to Marcus.

"I'll look forward to that."

"I think you'll like it. It turned out well."

He was quiet again, his cool blue eyes searching her face in the gleam of the candlelight. His possible suspicion made her uneasy.

"I understand," he said softly, "that you also spent some time with your friend from the beach."

Not just possible suspicion, she thought, but a certainty. She should have known better than to try to hide anything from him. Marcus Bradley had the kind of power and connections to uncover whatever secrets he wanted.

"He gave me a lift back to the villa."

"Did he? I heard it was a bit more than that. Do you think it's wise, Brenna, being with him? He is, after all, under investigation."

So Marcus knew that, too. And if he knew that much, then he also had to know her "friend from the beach" was her ex-fiancé. "And just how did you manage to find out Casey McBride turned up here?" she challenged him.

Marcus was disturbingly casual about it as he cut into

his pork. "Most of the island's resort keepers are very good about letting me know who's staying with them."

"Marcus, I don't appreciate all this surveillance. I think it's my business where I go and who I see."

"You musn't mind if I'm concerned about you, Brenna," he said, his voice low and soothing. "After all, you're my guest. I feel responsible for you while you're here on the island. Why don't we forget all about it? You haven't touched your pork. It's one of Gilda's specialties."

Brenna resisted the urge to scrape her chair back from the table and march back to the guesthouse. She couldn't afford to alienate Marcus. He had paid her a generous advance on the paintings he expected her to produce, money she had loaned to a friend back in Chicago who had a baby on the way and whose husband had lost his job. A sum that Brenna didn't have to repay Marcus. She had no choice but to fulfill her commission and that meant keeping her anger in check.

Chapter 5

Brenna refused to spend another restless night being unnerved by guards who might be pacing around the guesthouse. If either Julio or any of Marcus's other minions were out there wearing themselves out, she didn't care. She went to bed and slept without once checking from a single window.

To her relief, however, Marcus once again failed to join her for breakfast. Gilda informed Brenna that her employer had departed for the construction site just as he did yesterday.

"Would you tell Julio for me," Brenna asked the housekeeper as she ate another simple breakfast, "that I won't be needing either him or the car this morning? I plan to spend most of my time down in Georgetown visiting the market day there."

And if they wanted to check that out, let them. Because that's exactly where she would be. On foot and alone.

* * *

The city center teemed with people. Brenna wormed her way through the crowds, moving from stall to stall, delighted with the explosions of color on every side.

The natives, who used every opportunity to be festive in mood, were in holiday dress. Loud colors that might be considered vulgar in other lands but here in the West Indies were nothing but pleasing to the eye.

Even so, Brenna decided, the clothing couldn't compete with the stalls themselves. Each one offered its own special merchandise. A table piled high with fruits—the bright yellow of ripe bananas, the inviting green of limes and plantain, the warm brown of coconuts. Another table featured nothing but fresh vegetables that ranged from shiny red tomatoes to orange-fleshed yams. There were live, squawking chickens, too, in slatted wooden cages.

Not everything was food. Some of the tables displayed handcrafted articles meant to appeal to the tourists. Baskets of every size and shape and whimsical wooden carvings of island birds and animals painted in happy colors. Brenna found her hand itching to have a brush in it instead of a camera.

And over it all was the noise, the cacophony of voices raised in exchanges of bargaining, merchants loudly crying their wares, and somewhere unseen to Brenna the sound of a calypso steel band.

She was focusing her Nikon on a stall overflowing with flowers bursting with a profusion of colors, when a familiar, deep voice close behind her asked cheerfully, "Mind some company?"

Casey.

Brenna turned to face him, not sure whether she was annoyed or glad to see him.

"And just how did you spot me this time?"

"Easy. Even in all these mobs that hair of yours stands out like a beacon."

"Uh-huh. Just another coincidence. You couldn't have possibly remembered that I told you I meant to visit market day this morning or have been deliberately searching for me. Now could you?"

He made a tsking noise. "Just when did you get so suspicious, Rembrandt?"

"Since you showed up on that beach and denied you were here to play protector."

"You haven't answered my question."

"Which question would that be? Oh, yes, the one where you wondered if I would mind some company. I suppose it wouldn't matter if I objected. You'd tag along with me, anyway."

"Probably."

"I have one rule, though. No more outbursts like yesterday's."

His hand went to his chest in a solemn act of crossing his heart. "Swear."

She didn't trust him, but she'd already decided that his characteristic humor was not unwelcome. He'd always been fun to be with in that respect. And as long as he kept it light…

"So," he said, falling into step beside her as they wandered among the stalls, "did you get to finish that painting after I dropped you off yesterday?"

"I did, thank you. How about you? What did you get up to with the rest of your day?"

"Just playing tourist and checking out the sights."

Withholding information came with the FBI territory, and Casey had always managed to be excellent in that department. But Brenna had learned during their engagement when to believe his performances and when not to. The signs were there this time. A voice that was just a shade too casual. His gaze drifting off in another direction. He was definitely keeping something from her.

Before she could press him about it, he sidetracked her with an enthusiastic "Hey, look! Limbo dancers!"

They had arrived at the edge of a small square where the dancers, accompanied by the calypso steel band, were entertaining the crowd gathered around them.

Casey shook his head in wonder. "Man, how do they manage to get their bodies that low and still clear the pole?"

So, he had no intention of sharing with her exactly what had happened yesterday afternoon after they had parted. He apparently had his reason. Brenna left it at that.

After watching the dancers for another few moments, they moved on, comfortably silent now with each other as they checked out more stalls. Brenna's attention was drawn to one of them in particular. Arranged across its surfaces was a collection of handcrafted straw handbags and totes in distinctive designs.

"Did you make these?" she asked the elderly woman tending the stand.

"Yeh, I made them wit dese." Grinning broadly, she held up a pair of gnarled hands. "You like the bags, huh?"

"They're wonderful! I've got to have this one!" Brenna pounced on a handbag whose artful weaving spoke to her.

"Hey, gal, git me some paper and I wrap dis bag for de lady."

"That's not necessary, really. I'll take it just as it—"

Brenna broke off in midsentence as a young woman, who'd been busy down behind the booth, rose up in view. Zena King! She supposed Casey must be as surprised as she was.

"Hello," Zena greeted them. "Well, this is pleasant running into you again. How are you liking our market day?"

"It's great," Casey said. "Heck, even better now that we find *you* here. What were you doing crouched down there? Practicing CPR?"

Zena laughed. "No, I don't get to play nurse today. I was checking the stock."

"You're working at the stall?" Brenna asked.

"Well, helping out, anyway." She turned to the elderly woman beside her. "This is my Aunt Cleo. Auntie, these are some new friends I made yesterday, Brenna Coleman and Casey McBride."

"You friend of Zena, den I give you special price on dat bag."

"You will not," Brenna insisted. "It's a bargain price as it is for a handbag of this quality."

Aunt Cleo looked pleased by the compliment.

"Auntie does an amazing job with her products, doesn't she?"

They talked for another few minutes about the materials Aunt Cleo used to weave her creations, and then Brenna changed the subject. "Zena, there's something I didn't get around to asking you yesterday. You never told us the name of your village, and I couldn't find it on my guidebook map."

"Freedom. It's called Freedom. I know that's an unusual name for a community, but there was a reason for calling it that. Back in the 1800s when the slaves were freed, a group of my ancestors were given that piece of land in the highlands to settle. And no longer being slaves…"

Brenna understood. "They called their village Freedom. Perfect."

"I have another question for you about the name of a place," Casey said. "You mind?"

"Ask," Zena invited him.

"On our way up to the falls and back again we passed this humongous, abandoned-looking house behind a fence. You know what it's called?"

"That isn't a road we use. We have another, closer road on the other side of the village that goes to Georgetown. And having lived my school years down here instead of up in Freedom, the house you're talking about isn't..." She looked to Cleo to help her out. "Auntie, you must be familiar with the place."

The old woman scowled and shook her head. She either doesn't know the answer to Casey's question, Brenna thought, or she's reluctant to provide it.

"Oh, wait," Zena spoke up, "I think I do know the house you're talking about. It's called...yes, White Rose Plantation. That's got to be it. White Rose Plantation."

A beautiful name, Brenna decided, for what had struck her yesterday, and did again now, as having a sinister character about it. No wonder Aunt Cleo had refused to discuss it.

After paying for the handbag and tucking it into her tote, she and Casey were ready to move on again when Zena detained them.

"Are you in a hurry, or could you spare me a little time? There's something I'd like to talk to you about. In private," she added quickly.

Brenna and Casey exchanged puzzled glances.

"Sure," he agreed for both of them. "But with all these people around..."

"There's a sidewalk café I know about away from the traffic here. We could go there and have coffee and be private enough at this hour. Auntie, would you mind if I left you on your own for a bit?"

"Who you tink tend this stall you're away? Go, go."

Zena led the way to the sidewalk café located on a back street. As she had promised, there was no market day in progress here. The area was quiet.

They chose a table shaded by an overhanging awning, and far enough removed from the few other occupied tables to prevent their conversation from being overheard.

After they were settled in their chairs and had their coffees delivered to them, Casey leaned toward Zena with a grave "So what is it you want to discuss? You sounded pretty serious back there."

Zena drank from her mug, as if needing a moment to introduce an awkward subject. "Before I tell you," she finally said, directing her words to Casey, "I have a confession to make. When I met you yesterday, I had this strong impression that you're…well, frankly, a man of authority."

"He likes to think he is," Brenna answered dryly for him. "But, in all honesty, it is true. He's with the FBI."

Zena looked very impressed.

"Whoa, hold on," Casey said. "If it's an FBI agent you need, I can't help you. I have no official sanction to operate here on St. Sebastian. In any case, I'm currently on suspension from the bureau."

"Zena," Brenna asked her earnestly, "are you in some kind of trouble?"

"No, no, nothing like that. But I suppose it's possible I could be, though probably not."

Casey, as incisive as always, permitted no more delays. "You'd better tell us just what this is all about."

The three of them, Brenna noticed, were no longer interested in their mugs of coffee as Zena launched into an explanation.

"It's because of what we talked about at the falls. About

the women of Freedom not being able to reproduce and there seeming to be no reason for it. You asked about the new water supply, Casey, and I got to thinking about that after you left. It doesn't make sense, I know, but maybe…"

"Go on," Casey urged.

"What if something got introduced into this new well, *deliberately* introduced, and it made the women infertile? I know that sounds crazy. But I couldn't let it go. I kept thinking about how the problem started not long after the well was drilled. And that's why I ended up calling a friend back in Miami, who works in this reputable lab there, and told him all about it."

"What did he say?" Brenna asked.

"He felt it was unlikely, but he promised to ask some of the chemists there in the lab what they thought about it. He's going to get back to me tomorrow morning. It's possible I would be invited to send a sealed water sample, which I'd have to be careful not to contaminate, to the lab for analysis."

"If something was put into the water," Brenna reasoned, "it would have to be colorless, odorless and without any suspicious taste. Otherwise, it would have been detected by those who consumed it. Particularly you with your training."

"Exactly, and I didn't detect anything like that in my visits. All the same, I'm not taking any chances now. Hopefully, I was never in the village long enough to be affected, but I've been using bottled water since yesterday."

"I think that's a wise precaution," Brenna said.

"And I think," Casey said, putting down his mug after finally tasting his coffee, "I'd like to know why there's a possibility of you being in some kind of trouble."

Brenna followed Casey's example, drinking her own coffee now while she listened to Zena's response.

"It's just that if someone did put something into the water, and that person learned I discovered it was there and tried to convince the villagers not to use the well any longer, which I would do, he wouldn't be happy about it."

"No, he wouldn't," Casey agreed. "Not if he went to some lengths to tamper with it."

"But like I said," Zena hastened to add, "it's probably all my imagination. Why would anyone want to make a whole village of women incapable of conceiving, even if he was capable of doing such a wicked thing?"

Casey was silent, concentrating again on his coffee. Brenna understood that grim look on his face. It never failed to appear whenever he'd been assigned to one of his vital FBI operations.

"Look," he said at last, leaning forward again toward Zena, "I can't be an FBI agent for you, but I can be a friend if you should need me. I don't want you to hesitate to contact me if at any point you feel you might be in danger."

"Thank you. I appreciate that."

"I'll give you my cell number. Meanwhile, I'm going to ask you to be careful. Don't talk to anyone about this, and stick close to people you trust."

"I will."

Brenna, watching Casey extract a business card from his wallet with his private number on it, above which he wrote where he was staying at the Fair Winds cottages before he handed it to Zena, had a request of her own. "I think we'd both like to know what you hear from your friend in the morning. Why don't you call Casey, and he can pass it on to me?"

Casey immediately vetoed that plan. "No good. It's one thing for Zena to phone me in a situation of need. I'm all for that. But for this other..." He shook his head.

"Phone calls can be monitored by the people who have the means to do it. We don't want to risk someone hearing what we don't want them to know. It's better if we meet in person. What's the chance of you coming down here again tomorrow?"

"Doubtful," Zena said. "The only transportation I have available to me is this old rattletrap of a truck that belongs to Aunt Cleo's son. He's willing to drive his mother to Georgetown for market days, and I'm welcome to ride along whenever I'm visiting Freedom, but I heard him say he's going to need the truck tomorrow at the melon farm where he works."

Brenna had a solution. "I have an idea. Why don't the three of us meet instead on the bridge at the falls? I need to go up there again, anyway. I never did get my photos of the place. Casey?"

She knew what he must be thinking by the look he sent her. He couldn't believe she'd actually be willing to let him chauffeur her again to Braided Falls.

"Sounds like a plan," he agreed.

Zena also agreed to the arrangement. After Casey suggested a time for the meeting that suited all of them, she consulted her watch. "I should get back to Auntie. She may need me again at the stall."

Casey insisted on paying for the coffees. Zena thanked them again and hurried off.

"I should be on my way, too," Brenna said, collecting her purse and tote.

"Where to now?" Casey asked after handling the bill and a tip for their server who, apparently having noticed the signs of their departure, had immediately appeared at their table.

"Back to the guesthouse," she said, on her feet now. "I've seen enough down here for today. I want to get my camera's memory card up on the computer and print out a few of the best subjects. I still have the afternoon. I should be able to start on another painting."

"You brought a computer and a printer with you from Chicago?"

"Hardly. Marcus provides his guests with them."

"Generous of him. I'll walk with you. Don't look so alarmed, Rembrandt. I'm only going as far as the bottom of the hill where I dropped you off yesterday. The Toyota is parked near there."

How could she object when he'd already spent most of the morning with her? And behaved himself the whole time. Of course, it would matter if someone Marcus knew, maybe even one of his staff, saw them together and ended up reporting it to him. But that could have happened anytime during the morning.

"Let's go then," she said.

It was only when they'd started off side by side that Brenna wondered if she'd made a mistake when Casey, his voice at a seductive level, asked her softly, "So, you think I'm a figure of authority, huh?"

He *would* go and remember that. "Don't look so smug. It wasn't a compliment. It was a statement of fact."

"If you say so."

Things only got worse after that. When they returned to the area of the stalls, and it was necessary for them to draw close together in order to work their way through the crowds, his hip bumped at least twice against hers. Then his hand, dangling down at his side, began to brush against her own hand.

Were they accidental, merely innocent contacts, or intentional? Either way, the result was the same. They left her with yearnings she had no business feeling. That and striving for a self-control she was unable to achieve until they finally reached the bottom of the hill.

"We separate here," she reminded him.

"Right. Where do you want to meet tomorrow?"

"How about the square where the limbo dancers were performing? I noticed some interesting buildings there that should make a good painting. I ought to have time to work on it after we get back from the falls. It will mean transporting my gear to the square, but I can call a taxi for that."

She realized Julio would want to drive her himself if he saw her leaving the guesthouse with her painting materials. She would have to avoid him. Marcus, too, if he hadn't already left for the construction site by then. She would manage it somehow.

Brenna was relieved when she and Casey settled on a time for him to pick her up, and they could part. She guessed he was probably watching her when she headed up the hill, but at least she was putting a safe distance between them. What she was unable to put behind her were the conflicted feelings she had for Casey McBride that chased wildly through her mind. They stayed with her all the way to the villa.

She found Gilda in the villa's state-of-the-art kitchen. She asked the housekeeper to fix her a sandwich she could take with her to the guesthouse. That and a banana were all the lunch she wanted.

Only when Brenna was back in her quarters, and concentrating on her work, was she able to forget about Casey. At least for now.

Removing the memory card from her Nikon, she loaded it on the computer. She sat eating her sandwich and the banana while studying the photographs on the screen.

There would be no market day tomorrow. The square would be empty. What she planned to do, however, was lift a selection of today's stalls from her photos and introduce them into the scene. Combined with the background of the square, they should make a vibrant, eye-catching painting.

Choosing several of the best photographs, she printed them out to carry them with her tomorrow. She needed to protect them, and that required an envelope. There should be envelopes in the desk in front of her.

She started with the top drawer and moved on down to the other drawers below it, pulling them out one by one. There was no sign of envelopes. Only when she reached the bottom drawer, which refused to open until she applied a bit of force, did she find what she wanted. A stack of manila envelopes waited at the back of the drawer.

Brenna helped herself to one of them, slid the photos inside and placed the envelope beside the computer. She shoved the drawer shut. Or tried to. It went only part of the way and then, as before, stuck. Something was holding it fast, this time stubbornly.

Removing the drawer altogether from the desk, she slid her hand deep inside the opening and felt around. At the far back, her fingers contacted what felt like scrunched up paper on the dusty bottom of the desk.

Ah, the culprit.

A corner of the thing must have gotten caught in one of the drawer slides. It took a little tugging to free it. Only when she got it into the light and smoothed it out on the desk top did it reveal itself as an envelope. Not a manila one this time but a stationery variety. A good, ivory-colored stationery.

It must have been placed on top of the stack of manila envelopes and then, over time, had worked its way over the back edge of the drawer and out of sight below, where eventually it had caused the problem with the drawer.

There was no writing on the face of the envelope, but it was just thick enough to promise something inside. Brenna gazed down at it for an indecisive moment. Should she?

Chapter 6

The envelope was not sealed. That made Brenna feel a little less guilty about investigating its content. At least that's what she tried to convince herself as she slid a single, folded sheet of paper out of the envelope.

She spread it open on the desk. Like the envelope that had contained it, it had been punished by the constant opening and closing of the drawer. She used the heel of her hand to flatten the worst of the wrinkles.

It was a letter. Or at least the beginning of one dated in June of last year. Private correspondence, of course, and she struggled again with guilt over her intention to read it.

It was handwritten and not signed, but the flowing, almost delicate style of the penmanship told her a woman had been its author. That and a faint scent of the gardenia fragrance that lingered on the ivory paper.

Brenna read it with wonder seasoned by a growing sense of uneasiness.

Dear Glory,
I shouldn't be writing this to you, but I could no lon-
ger stop myself from needing to confide in someone
who'll understand and sympathize.
I know I can trust you not to reveal what I'm about
to tell you to anyone. Curtis would be extremely
angry with me if he so much as guessed, especially
after all his warnings to me.
I wish to God I'd never come down to this island.
I can't believe what's happening here, much less
that Curtis is involved in it. It's wrong, so terribly
wrong. Frankly, I'm beginning to be frightened by—

The letter abruptly broke off there, as if its author had
been suddenly interrupted. Brenna could picture her hast-
ily folding it, sliding it into the envelope and thrusting it
into the bottom drawer.

Whoever she was, she couldn't have been discovered
writing her secret, unfinished letter. Not if it had remained
all this time at the back of the drawer and then at some
point under the drawer.

Brenna sat back on the desk chair, question after question racing through her mind. Who was the woman who
had penned the letter? Like her, a guest at the villa? What
had she been about to disclose, why had she never completed the letter, and what had become of her? And who
were Glory and Curtis?

Questions without answers. There was the final question, too. What should she do with the letter? Put it back
in the envelope and return it to the drawer?

That was Brenna's first inclination. But in the end, after
refolding it and squeezing it again into its envelope, she
placed the letter instead in her purse with the intention

of showing it to Casey tomorrow. Maybe he could make some sense out of its mystery.

But that would be a big mistake. She knew what he'd do if he saw the thing. He'd insist that she move out of the guesthouse. Not just away from the villa either, but back home. And he wouldn't rest until he got them both back on a plane to Chicago.

She couldn't leave. She had to fulfill her obligation to Marcus to produce the paintings. If she failed to do that, she would have to repay the advance he'd given her, and she no longer had the money. And, along with that, she would be sacrificing her reputation as a reliable artist.

Reading the letter had been a mistake on more than one level. She had violated a correspondence she'd never been meant to see. For another reason, its contents left her feeling unclean. As if, had the author completed her letter and Brenna had been able to see all of it, she would have been participating in something profane.

Whatever the explanation for her reaction, criminal or innocent, she suddenly felt the need for a bath. Pushing back from the desk, she went into the bathroom and ran a tub. Once undressed and immersed in the hot water, she vigorously soaped herself all over.

Brenna felt better afterwards, her body more relaxed as she went on soaking there in the tub. Her mind, however, refused to be at peace. It insisted on reviewing the seemingly disjointed events she'd experienced over the past few days.

Casey turning up on St. Sebastian to protect her from what she was convinced didn't exist. The sighting of the mysterious White Rose Plantation. The fear in the eyes of the young man at the general store. The green sedan and its driver chasing after them for no apparent reason. Meeting Zena King and hearing about her village and its tragic problem. Aunt Cleo's reluctance to admit any knowledge of White Rose Plantation.

None of them, counting the letter she'd just discovered, seemed to Brenna in any way connected with one another. They were like pieces that wouldn't fit because they were all from different jigsaw puzzles. Or were they?

Marcus phoned her later that afternoon with an apology.

"I'm sorry to say I won't be with you for dinner this evening. I'm eating in Georgetown with business friends who flew in from Chicago. I'd invite you to join us, but I'm afraid you'd be nothing but bored. They want to discuss the casino that will adjoin the resort. They're financing that portion of it."

"Please don't apologize, Marcus. Gilda will see to it that I'm well fed right here. I'll probably turn in early. I'm going to be starting another painting tomorrow in town."

Brenna was relieved when they ended the call. She wouldn't have to face Marcus over dinner this evening, or tell him more lies when he questioned her about how she spent her day.

She did retire early, but it took her a long while before she fell asleep. Casey's image planted itself in her head and refused to go away. She kept remembering his heated, passionate kiss from yesterday.

There were other more disturbing memories. Hottest among them were those mornings when they were engaged. She would wake up with a drowsy awareness of Casey spooned against her in the bed. He would be half asleep, that stone-hard erection of his seemingly with a mind of its own as it pressed against her, pleading for entry.

You can't let yourself fall in love with him all over

again. Can't suffer the fear of losing him when he goes off on another risky FBI assignment. You just can't, she chided herself.

Giving his ring back to him and letting him go had been the hardest thing she'd ever done. It had taken her months to get over it. No, she wasn't going to relive that anguish.

Brenna was set up with her easel when Casey arrived to pick her up. He found her with a charcoal stick in hand. She had already sketched the buildings on the side of the square she'd chosen. They were appealing two- and three-story structures with shuttered French windows, iron balconies and red-tiled roofs. She was busy now blocking out several stalls in the foreground. The paint, he knew, would come later.

"Nice," he said, leaning over her shoulder to view the canvas.

"Do you know that's the only word you ever use to describe my work? *Nice.*"

"What's put you in a grouchy mood this morning?"

"Sorry. It's just that you're late. I was beginning to wonder if you'd forgotten about me."

"Not a chance. I'm late because I didn't notice until I was almost here that the silver chariot was running on fumes. I had to find a gas station for a fill-up, and believe me they're not on every street corner like back home."

"You're forgiven. But I don't know if Zena will forgive you. She's going to be waiting on that bridge and wondering where we are."

"Relax. I'll make up for any lost time when we're on the road."

"Oh, no, you won't. I'll thank you not to treat me to any more of your NASCAR races like the other day."

He grinned at her. "Yes, ma'am. What are you going to do with the easel and your other gear?"

"Load it all in the trunk of the Toyota. I can't risk leaving it here until we get back."

Casey refrained from pointing out that, if she hadn't erected the easel in the first place, they wouldn't need to be wasting further time. But that was Brenna. When she was fired up about a subject, she couldn't wait to make a start on it. But, hey, wasn't that one of the reasons why he'd fallen in love with her?

That was another time, McBride. And you've put that behind you. Remember?

Yeah, he remembered. Didn't mean he couldn't still be turned on by that sweet body of hers. Which was something he definitely needed to control, and somehow managed to do as he helped her stow her things in the trunk.

Casey waited until they were clear of the city traffic and out on the coast highway before asking her, "So, anything interesting happen up at the villa after I last saw you yesterday?"

"No, why should something have happened? It was all very ordinary. Why do you ask?"

"Just wondering if Bradley learned I spent time with you at the market and asked you about it?"

"I didn't see him. He had dinner in town with friends, and I went to bed early."

She's withholding something, he thought. *My question worried her, and she answered it with too much haste.*

He decided not to press it. She wouldn't like that. Anyway, if she was keeping something from him, it couldn't be very important, or she would tell him about it. Or would she? he wondered.

Besides, Casey had his own secret he was hiding. He had no intention, though, of sharing with her the episode of the gun that had been shoved into his back, and the nasty warning following it to keep away from Brenna Coleman. She'd be alarmed if she heard that, insist that he heed the warning for his own safety.

But there was something he did need for her to learn, and he used this opportunity to do it.

"You haven't asked me what *I* did after I left you."

"Okay. What *did* you do?"

"Learn some interesting information."

"You were investigating?"

"Not exactly."

"Casey, stop being evasive. You always did have an FBI habit of doing that. You wanted me to know, so tell me."

"Right. It's just that I had a chance to talk to a couple of local guys. Don't ask me why they trusted me. They just did. Maybe because I was sympathetic, ready and willing to listen to them when they opened up to me."

"About what?"

"In this case, it wasn't a what but a who. Marcus Bradley."

Casey had realized Brenna wouldn't appreciate his introducing this particular subject. He was right. A swift glance in her direction was all he needed to tell him she was suddenly rigid, a sure sign of defensiveness.

"And?" she asked coolly.

"The man has big influence on the island, too much influence. No, now don't start getting your back up. Just listen to me. It seems his money has bought him the kind of power that has him in control of the officials that count. The men and women who were elected to serve the people here but instead serve Bradley. Brenna, he owns St. Sebastian."

"That's absurd," she scoffed. "He's an American. All he can own is the land he purchased. And haven't I already told you he's using it with the intention of benefitting the island?"

"Yeah, I remember. A luxury resort that will employ the natives. But what do you want to bet they won't be hired in any managerial positions? They'll be doing the menial jobs, the kind of work most of the people are already doing on these islands. Serving the tourists. In this case, the rich ones."

"You don't know that. And even if what you're saying is true, the taxes alone on the kind of place he's building would help to relieve the poverty here."

"Would they?"

"Look, I'm not going to argue with you about what's probably nothing but a lot of gossip."

She had him there. Casey's information had come from a bar he'd visited, where the two native men who'd befriended him had told him more than they ordinarily would because their tongues had been considerably loosened by the local rum. Not the most reliable source maybe, but he'd felt then, as he did now, that it bore a certain truth. Marcus Bradley was not all he appeared to be.

Brenna chose that moment to distract him, and herself, by indicating a small church with a squat bell tower on the shore side of the highway. "Now there's a painting possibility," she said. "It looks very old. Built out of volcanic rock, I think."

"You want me to stop so you can snap some pictures of it?"

"Maybe on the way back. I don't want to make us any later than we are."

She was quiet after that, the amber, long-lashed eyes he'd always admired searching for other interesting subjects.

Casey waited until they turned on the road to Braided

Falls to renew their conversation, raising another question he knew would only make her unhappy again. But he couldn't resist asking it, needing to hear her response.

"Did it ever occur to you, Brenna, that the benefactor who provided that deep well for Freedom was Marcus Bradley?"

At first Casey thought she wasn't going to answer him. Then, after a lengthy pause, she admitted, "It occurred to me. On the other hand…"

"What?"

"There's nothing to say Marcus did pay to have the well drilled. There are a lot of people with big money willing to spread it around."

"Granted."

"And even if Marcus did give the village a new water supply, it doesn't mean he had something put into it. That could have been someone else entirely. Besides," she pointed out, "we don't even know yet that it was altered in any way. It's only a possibility until Zena learns otherwise."

"True," Casey agreed.

He left it there. Privately, however, his worst suspicions about Bradley seemed to increase with each day he spent on St. Sebastian. Along with his fears for Brenna's safety. But he had a long way to go before he could convince her those fears had any real merit.

There was something, though, that did seem to trouble her without any convincing. White Rose Plantation. He noticed when they passed it several minutes later that she averted her gaze from that side of the road.

She really has a bad feeling about that place, doesn't she? he thought.

It was a reason for him not to slow the car when they reached the gate, but he wanted to check on something.

It took only a few seconds for him to learn there was no sign of the green sedan parked in front of the mansion.

Casey drove on, hurrying them now toward their rendezvous with Zena King. They left White Rose behind them, but his curiosity about it stayed with him. He wondered who owned the plantation.

There was no sign of Zena on the bridge.

"She must have given up on us," Brenna said.

Casey shook his head. "We're not that late. She's probably just been delayed, like we were. Give her time."

They waited in silence. The only sound was the splash of the waterfall. Brenna fixed her gaze on the path to Freedom, hoping to see Zena swing into view at any second. When she failed to appear as the minutes dragged by, she expressed her concern to Casey.

"Something's wrong. We ought to go to the village and try to find her."

"Bad idea. Zena wouldn't have agreed we meet here on the bridge if she hadn't wanted our conversation to be private."

"You're right. If we show up in the village, it's apt to bring questions she'd prefer weren't asked. Not if she's trying for now to keep a lid on this thing. But what do you suppose is keeping her?"

"Could be she hasn't heard yet from her friend in Miami and is waiting on that. Look, we came up here not just to see Zena but so you could get the pictures you missed the other day. Why don't you get a start on that?"

She understood. His suggestion was meant to keep her from worrying needlessly, and it was a good one. Plucking her camera out of the tote, she got busy recording a series of photographs of the falls from both sides of the stream, as well as from the center of the bridge. She included the deep, dark pool under the cascades.

The whole time she worked, a relaxed, patient Casey leaned his arms on the rail of the bridge, devoting his mesmerized attention to the flow beneath him.

When Brenna felt she'd snapped enough photos of the falls and the pool, and Zena had yet to materialize, she reversed her direction and considered the waters after they passed under the bridge. There was no dramatic activity on this side, but it could on its own make an interesting scene, with the current searching its way downstream between the high banks.

She was looking for the best angle when she saw the band of crimson trailing out from behind a black boulder, its massive head surfacing at the side of the stream like an ancient beast.

Blood? No, it couldn't be. Whatever she was seeing was too brightly scarlet to be blood, had too much form to be anything but something with a definite substance. Not liquid at all. What then? Maybe a red scarf or a red sash floating just beneath the surface.

The water in that spot was quiet, but not altogether still. A gentle current there stirred something just on the other side of the crimson band.

Brenna stared at it for a very long time, struggling to identify it. Denying its reality in the end. Until she could no longer pretend it wasn't what she suspected it was.

An arm! A human arm stretched out from behind the boulder! Her reaction was not just alarm. It was horror. Pure horror.

Flashing around, she clamped her free hand over Casey's forearm. He was immediately alert, turning to her. "What is it? What's wrong?"

Brenna looked back. "Down there," she said, her voice hoarse. "Next to the boulder."

She allowed him a moment to concentrate on what she'd indicated before demanding, "It is, isn't it? A body!"

"The arm of one, anyway. As for the rest—" He considered her with narrowed eyes. "Are you going to be okay if I leave you for a few minutes? Just long enough for a close look at exactly what's behind the boulder. Or what isn't."

She nodded, murmuring, "Be careful."

Her gaze followed him as he left the bridge, scrambling down the steep embankment carpeted with tangled vines. The growth changed to knee-high ferns when he reached the bottom. They framed the stream on both sides as far as the eye could see.

Brenna watched him wade through the ferns, reach the boulder and squat down behind it. She covered her mouth with her hands as she went on watching him.

He rose at last, his lifted gaze briefly meeting hers before he started back. Even from here, Brenna could see how troubled those green eyes of his were, how grave in expression. Swinging himself up onto the bridge, he came silently toward her.

Why didn't he speak? Why didn't he tell her? But she already knew. From the moment she'd sighted that arm, the truth had attached itself to her with a slowly mounting certainty.

Removing her hands from across her mouth, she whispered, "It's Zena, isn't it? Is she—"

He nodded.

"No question of it?"

"No question. I'm sorry, Brenna."

It seemed only right, natural that Casey should draw her against him. Hold her tightly to his chest, rock her in his arms. It wasn't seduction. It was comfort, and she relished it.

She had known Zena only a few days, spent less than three hours with her altogether. It didn't matter. Brenna's tears were just as real, her grief just as intense as if they had been friends for years.

Casey pressed a tissue into her hand when she signaled her readiness to be released. She mopped her cheeks dry and handed it back to him.

"Casey, we can't leave her down there like that. We have to carry her up here."

"No, Brenna. She can't be moved. The scene can't be disturbed."

"Yes, I suppose the police will need to verify it was an accident. She probably fell in, struck her head on one of the rocks and was carried—"

"It wasn't an accident, Brenna."

Stricken, she stared at him. "What are you saying? What are you telling me?"

"Zena was murdered, Brenna."

"I don't believe it," she whispered. "I *can't* believe it. Because if I let myself believe it—"

"I'm afraid it's true."

"How?"

"The signs point to her being strangled."

"The red scarf?"

Casey shook his head. "It's not a scarf. It's a sash, and it's still tied around her waist."

"Then does that mean—"

"Yeah, probably a pair of strong hands. Male hands. At least that's what the ligature marks on her throat indicate."

Brenna shuddered over the image of those hands tight around Zena's neck, choking the life out of her.

"How can we just leave her lying down there like that,

Casey, as if—as if she'd been thrown away like a piece of worthless trash? She deserves better than that."

"I agree with you, but she can't be moved."

Yes, this was a crime scene, and that meant it was not to be altered. "I understand, but if the murder itself took place elsewhere, and her body floated as far as the boulder, it's possible it could float out again downstream."

"Not likely. It's locked in behind that boulder."

"I feel helpless. Like we should be doing something."

"We are." He slid his cell out of his back pocket. "We're calling the police." She watched him check his screen and then shake his head. "I don't have a signal. What about you?"

She extracted her own phone from her purse, but when she searched for a signal, her result was equally disappointing. "What I get is too weak to be useful."

"We're too far from a tower, plus the growth is too thick up here."

"We need to go to the village," she decided. "There must be a working phone there."

"No!" Casey's reaction was so sharp it startled her.

"But they should be told—"

"Look," he said, his voice softening, "I know it seems cruel not to inform them of Zena's death, but we have to leave that to the police. If we don't, there will be villagers swarming all over this spot, trampling any and all useful evidence that still remains. And you can't suppose her family won't insist on her being carried back to the village."

"So what's our choice?"

"We leave. We drive back to Georgetown and find the nearest police station."

"Just like that?"

"Yes."

She waited until they were back in the car and on their way down from the highlands to ask the question that had been gnawing at her from the moment Casey had reluctantly told her how Zena had met her death.

"Who'd want to murder her? And *why?*"

Casey's reply was slow in coming. "Are you sure you don't already know the answer to that one yourself?"

She thought about it for a moment. "I suppose you're referring to Zena's determination to have a sample of Freedom's water supply tested."

"That would be a logical explanation, wouldn't it?"

"Well, I'd judge it to be a primary one, anyway. But I suppose far from conclusive."

"Spoken like a true detective," he said.

"But, Casey, if that was the motive for her murder, then her intention must have somehow gotten out."

"More than that. It reached the ears of the wrong person."

She nodded. "Someone who wanted to stop her from sending that sample to a laboratory. And was willing to kill to prevent it."

"Which means keeping the content of the water supply a secret is of major importance to him. Or should it be *them?*"

Brenna waited, expecting him to use what could be regarded as a perfect opportunity to implicate Marcus Bradley. Or at least suggest him as a person of interest. To her surprise, however, all he had to say was, "But at this point none of it is more than speculation."

Casey might not be wondering about Marcus, at least not out loud, but he left *her* wondering. She made a massive effort, though, to shut that possibility out of her mind. Because to even consider it meant she must acknowledge her association with a man capable of—

No, she had no solid reason to call Marcus anything but a benefactor.

Brenna's resolve failed when it came to the gruesome scene below the waterfalls. It kept replaying in her mind, kept her sorrowfully realizing that a young, vibrant woman would never become the nurse-practitioner who would return to St. Sebastian to help the people of her village. A terrible loss to the community.

She had worked herself into a state of numb grief when she realized they had reached the coast highway and that Casey was speaking to her.

"Do you still want to photograph the little church?"

She shook her head. "Not now."

They didn't talk again until they neared Georgetown, and he pulled over to the side of the highway.

"I know you're anything but in the mood for it," he said, "but I'm going to return both you and your painting gear to the square."

"You can't do that," she objected. "I need to come with you. The police will want to talk to both of us."

"They don't know you were there at the falls with me, and I'd prefer to keep it that way."

"Because?"

"What's the point in involving you when you couldn't tell them anything I can't tell them?"

"Casey, if this is about protecting me—"

"Not like you imagine. Brenna, think about it. How's Bradley going to react if he should learn you were with me in the highlands at the scene of a murder?" The look on her face must have told him all he needed to know. "Uh-huh. Trouble. Not that I wouldn't personally celebrate if he kicked you out, but there's the commission to consider."

He was right. Marcus wouldn't like it if she was connected with any publicized atrocity that could reflect negatively on him, especially at this sensitive stage of the luxury resort's construction. He could end up firing her and finding another artist.

Brenna hated the thought of another fabrication, of having to pretend she'd spent the entire day painting in the square just because of Marcus and the risk of losing the commission. How could she do that to Zena? Logical or not, Brenna did feel she was abandoning Zena by not accompanying Casey to the police station.

Whatever the moral issues of it, she found herself back in the square. Casey helped her to unload her things and set up her easel. There was a little shop nearby that sold wonderful sandwiches. Brenna was in no mood for food, but Casey insisted they both needed to eat something.

"I'll come back for you," he promised, "but be patient. This could take some time. They could very likely want me to accompany them to the crime scene."

It was only after he was gone that she realized he hadn't told her which police station he was going to, providing there was more than one, and where it was located.

Chapter 7

It was the toughest painting Brenna ever undertook. Not because it was any more challenging than scores of others she'd executed. It wasn't.

But those canvases had been painted with her full concentration in a positive state of mind. Both were lacking on this occasion. Still, she managed to soldier on, sipping from a bottle of water between strokes of her brush or nibbling on a sandwich.

The minutes crept by as she worked, her thoughts with Casey. She tried not to wonder what was happening, but she could only achieve that by grieving for Zena. And that was no better.

Considering her mood, it was ironic the painting was turning out to be one of her best. But as Brenna well knew, you could never predict the outcome of a canvas.

Her anxiety mounted as the afternoon lengthened. Casey had told her to be patient, but she was finding that increasingly difficult. She thought about phoning him, but as involved as he must be, he wouldn't have time to talk. Or possibly he wouldn't be allowed to take her call.

The day was sweltering. There was no moving air in the closed square. It helped that a straw hat protected her from the blazing sun, but even so, her head began to throb.

Where are you, Casey?

Having left her watch back at the guesthouse, she had lost track of the time. She just knew it was taking forever. Bells rang somewhere in a church tower, but she failed to count the hours. It didn't matter. All she cared about now was getting back to the air-conditioned guesthouse, swallowing a couple of aspirin and stretching out on the bed.

Sorry to desert you, Casey, but I can't take any more of this heat.

Brenna began to pack up. The painting, vivid with color, was finished except for a few details, and those she could handle later in her studio corner in the guesthouse.

She would need to call Casey before she signaled a taxi. No choice about it this time. He would be deeply concerned if he came back here to find her gone without an explanation. However, when she tried to reach him, his phone went straight to voice mail. She left a message, telling him where she was going and why.

The young cab driver who stopped for her helped her to hustle her gear into his taxi, assured her he knew exactly where the Bradley villa was and took off at the usual island speed. Which could have had disastrous consequences when, a few minutes later, the cab stopped with such sharp abruptness that Brenna was thrown forward against the belt on the backseat.

She had closed her eyes, intending to rest until their arrival at the villa, but now they were wide open, and she was bewildered. If there had been a collision, she hadn't felt it, although they were halted just a few inches behind the vehicle ahead of them.

Her driver, twisted around in his seat, was eyeing her in concern. "You okay, lady?"

"Um, yes, I'm fine. But what happened?"

"Guy ahead o' us had a fender bender. Now he an' the fella he hit talk it out."

"Oh. Well, can't we go around them or back up and go another way?"

"No. Police don' like that I leave. I must stay right here in case I need to take sides or else I git in big trouble."

This was ridiculous, Brenna thought. The drivers here couldn't go fast enough, and now suddenly they had all the time in the world.

She glanced out her side window. They were parked where a cross street met this one. At the end of it she could see the incredible blue of the Caribbean, telling her the waterfront was just a block over.

Brenna suddenly felt the need to be there, out in the open where, with any luck, there would be a refreshing, cooling breeze off the sea.

Mind made up, she spoke to her driver. "I'm going to get out and walk from here, but as soon as you're free I'd like you to take my things on to the villa. I may not be there yet when you arrive, but the housekeeper will show you where to put them. One thing, though. The painting here isn't dry. I want you to be very careful handling it."

"Sure ting."

"Okay."

She paid him the fare, added an extra generous tip and exited the vehicle.

Brenna already felt better just being out of the taxi and headed toward the waterfront. The street was a short one, the buildings on either side dropping away before she'd walked more than a hundred yards.

She was in the clear now, the wide Caribbean stretched out in front of her, the air off its expanse so bracing she could feel her headache beginning to dissolve. There was a stone seawall that invited her to perch on it, which she did.

Brenna was able to relax there for maybe five or so minutes before she remembered what the cabbie had told her about getting in serious trouble with the police if he left the scene of the fender bender, even though he himself hadn't been involved in the trivial accident. Were the cops on St. Sebastian that harsh?

It struck her then. Casey. Casey was with the police now. Was it possible they considered him a suspect in Zena's death? Were they holding him?

What in the world had she been thinking to take off for the villa, abandoning him without any compunction? She had to go back, find the police station where Casey had gone and, if necessary, speak up in his defense.

All right, so maybe Marcus would be deeply unhappy with her when he heard. But at this point she no longer cared. Rescuing Casey was all that mattered.

Brenna was prepared to do just that when she got to her feet, ready to hail the next taxi that came in sight. Before she could do that, her cell chimed.

Snatching the phone from her purse, she consulted the display, wilting in relief when she saw the call was from Casey.

"Where are you?" he demanded without greeting when she made the connection.

"Down at the waterfront by the seawall."

"I can't be more than a couple of blocks away from you. Don't move. Stay right where you are. I'm coming for you."

She didn't have to wait more than a few minutes before the silver chariot streaked into sight. There was no parking on the seawall side of the street. Casey squeezed into a spot on the other side. Emerging from the Toyota, his stalwart figure came striding toward her.

He had never looked better to her than he did now. There was no point in denying it, was there? It was getting harder to resist him.

"What are you doing here on foot? Your message said you were grabbing a taxi to take you back to the villa."

Brenna explained the situation. His wide mouth split into a grin when she ended by telling him his call came just when she was ready to head back to the center of town, fearing the police were holding him.

"You were going to rescue me, were you?"

"Don't get all puffed up about it, McBride. I was worried about you, that's all."

"After the afternoon I've had, I deserve to be pleased that someone was worried about me."

She was right then to think he might be in trouble. "Casey, what happened?"

He looked around. "Not here. Let's find somewhere we can sit down and have a cool drink."

What they wanted was located several blocks away on the waterfront. The tiny café was currently empty of customers, allowing them to occupy a table on the porch looking out on the sea. They were served two tall, frosted iced teas and then left to themselves.

After satisfying himself with a long drink of the tea, Casey swiped the back of his hand across his mouth and was ready to talk.

"They kept me waiting out front. Even though I told the officer at the reception desk I had a serious crime to report, they kept me waiting forever. I could hear them inside, two detectives hammering away at some poor, terrified kid, trying to get him to confess he'd stolen tools from a construction site."

The construction site of the luxury resort? Brenna wondered. She remembered Marcus telling her they were having trouble there with thefts. She didn't tell Casey that. He already had enough negatives against Marcus without adding that to the list.

"You know what happened when I finally did get their attention? They acted like they didn't want to know I had a murder to report. That it was a nuisance just to hear about it. These aren't nice people, Brenna."

He didn't remind her what he'd told her earlier on their way to the meeting with Zena. How Marcus Bradley's money controlled those in charge on the island. She appreciated his restraint. She was not ready to believe the worst about Marcus.

Casey paused to swallow more of his drink. Brenna waited for him to go on while sipping her own tea.

"I told them everything I could," he continued, "but they weren't satisfied. Well, I had anticipated that. If you're a cop and doing your job, then being thorough is one of the first rules."

"Did they go up to Braided Falls?"

"They went, yeah, but reluctantly so I think."

"And you went with them?"

"I did and waited while they examined the scene. I can't say it was a very scientific examination, but considering this is a small island with limited resources, it would be wrong to expect what we're used to back home."

"Casey, they did retrieve Zena's body, didn't they?"

He nodded soberly. "She's with their medical examiner right now."

"And her family? I hope her family was informed."

"One of the detectives went on to the village to tell them and to ask questions. I wanted to go with him, but I was prevented from doing that. I was made to wait with the other detective on the bridge. Brenna, I swear I could hear the howls of shock and grief all the way from Freedom."

She could imagine how awful that was. "Casey, did you tell them about Zena's suspicion where the village water supply is concerned?"

"That was practically the first thing out of my mouth after I reported her murder. It's a motive, after all."

"And?"

He made a sound of disgust. "Nothing. They said it would be considered in their investigation, but I could tell they all but dismissed it. They had another suspect in mind."

"Who?"

"Me. They kept taking me over and over the same territory when we got back here to Georgetown. How did I come to know Zena King? Why was I meeting her on the bridge? Had we fought?"

Brenna almost knocked over her glass in her haste to reach out and cover his hand on the table with her own. "Oh, Casey, I'm such a coward! I let you talk me into not going there with you, but that was wrong. I should have been there right beside you."

His fingers curled warmly around hers, sending shivers down her spine. "It wouldn't have made a difference, Brenna, except maybe to implicate you, and we agreed there was no point in risking that."

"All the same…"

"No, it's okay. They could have held me, even without any evidence, and maybe they would have done just that if I hadn't told them at the beginning I was an FBI agent on vacation."

"And they could easily verify that, couldn't they?"

"They could and did. I don't know how much that impressed them, but apparently it was enough to let me walk out of there."

"Will you have to go back?"

"Not unless I'm summoned, but I'll probably stop in anyway to keep us informed on their progress. Not that I'm expecting them to find Zena's killer. Something tells me his identity is going to remain a closely guarded secret."

Brenna waited for him to elaborate on that, but all he did was lift his glass, drain it and ask her if she wanted another one. She shook her head.

"I should be getting back to the villa. With any luck, the cab driver will have delivered my gear by now. I'd like to check to be sure it's all there."

Casey got to his feet. "I'll take you. Hey, don't look so panicked. I know better than to drive you straight to your door. I'll drop you as before at the bottom of the hill."

As long and tiring as the day had been, she had no argument against that. They didn't talk along the way. Actually, it would have been the opportunity for Brenna to ask him why he believed the killer's identity would be kept a closely guarded secret. Did he think Zena's murder could be a conspiracy? Something even ordered by a higher-up?

Without any solid information, however, these were nothing but theories. In any case, before she could ask him anything at all or even decide she wanted to, he stopped to let her out.

"You know what I'd like to do, don't you?" he said, his voice low and raspy as he turned to her. "I'd like to turn around and drive you straight back to my place, lock both of us inside, wrap myself securely around you and refuse to let you go."

Those wild, jungle-green eyes of his pinned her in his gaze. It was only with an effort that she was able to drop her own gaze from his, and that turned out to be a mistake. Instead of staring at those mesmerizing green eyes, she found herself fascinated by the seductive pulse beating visibly in the hollow of his throat.

Was there no facet of this man that wasn't dangerously sexy?

Her mouth was so dry that when she spoke it was with a croak. "Casey, I have to go."

A lie, of course, because for the first time since he'd arrived on St. Sebastian, she had no desire whatsoever to leave him. But unless she escaped…

To her relief, he didn't try to stop her. All he said was a very firm "Be safe."

"I will," she promised him, sliding out of the car.

Brenna's head was no longer throbbing as she climbed the hill. But other areas of her body definitely were.

Brenna had the day's painting up on her easel and was putting the finishing touches to it when the phone rang.

Phone?

But that wasn't the sound of her cell. What in the—

It took several more rings and a moment of bewilderment before she realized *this* phone was mounted on the wall just inside the front door of the guesthouse. She was a little breathless by the time she reached it.

Snatching the receiver from its cradle, she answered the call with a hesitant "Yes?"

"Brenna, have I caught you at a bad time?"

Marcus. It was Marcus. "No, I was just— Marcus, where are you?"

"In the villa." He sounded surprised by her question. "Brenna, I'm calling from the main house."

She put her free hand to her forehead, feeling like an idiot. Of course. He was calling her on the house phone. He'd explained on her first day here how, if she needed or wanted anything, she could communicate directly with the villa without having to use an outside line. It was something she'd completely forgotten about.

"I was a little distracted I'm afraid," she apologized. "I get that way when I'm busy at the easel."

"And I interrupted. Well, I won't keep you. I just wanted to make certain you'll be free to join us for dinner."

"Us?"

"Yes, I'm entertaining a guest this evening."

"Marcus, if this is at all formal, I don't have anything suitable to wear."

"It's perfectly casual, Brenna. He's eager to meet you, by the way. I've been telling him about your work. If it's convenient, why don't you bring your latest painting with you? Six-thirty in the library. We'll have drinks there before we head for dinner on the terrace."

He ended the call before she had a chance to learn any more. The mystery guest would have to remain just that until six-thirty.

Brenna no more believed in hate at first sight than she did in love at first sight. In her opinion, both demanded a period of getting-to-know-you before either emotion could be determined. Which was why, in this moment, she was irritated with herself.

She had no reason to immediately dislike this man before they had even spoken to each other. But she did. Why? The gauntness of his face? His paper-white skin? A pair of silver eyes that looked at her too intently?

It wasn't fair to judge someone by their appearance. So why was she doing it?

She had no answer for herself or any time to hunt for one since Marcus was introducing them.

"This is my good friend, Curtis Hoffmann, Brenna."

"My pleasure, Miss Coleman," he said, offering a dry, bony hand for her to shake.

Curtis. Curtis. Where had she either heard or read that name? And recently, too.

"I see you brought the painting," Marcus said, indicating the table just inside the library door, where she had laid the picture. "May we see it?"

"Of course." Brenna fetched the painting and brought it over to the grouping of chairs, where the two men had been seated when she first entered the room. "You're welcome to handle it as long as you hold it by the edges. It's not dry in places."

Marcus and his guest examined the work, generously admiring it.

"Beautiful, Miss Coleman," Hoffmann said. "I wonder. Do you ever do murals?"

"I've never tried, but I suppose it's possible I could manage one."

Hoffmann turned to Marcus. "I was thinking how splendid an island mural would look in the casino."

Marcus agreed, explaining to Brenna, "Curtis is one of the major investors in the casino portion of the resort. But here, I'm ignoring my duties as a host. Curtis, I believe you prefer a dry martini. Brenna?"

"Uh, wine for me. Red, if you have it."

The bar at one end of the room was apparently well stocked. Marcus fixed their drinks and, seated facing one another in the grouping of chairs, they sipped them.

The library, Brenna noted, was as luxuriously appointed as the rest of the villa, but she didn't feel comfortable being in it. It was possible, though, that Curtis Hoffmann was as responsible for that as the room itself.

She had absolutely no right to feel this way. The man was perfectly cordial to her. But there was something cold and calculating about him. If she believed in vampires, she might suspect he was one.

The men talked about the progress of the resort, directing polite comments to her from time to time. To Brenna's relief, the subject of doing a mural did not come up again. She had already decided she would have no enthusiasm for such a project.

Hoffmann, however, did return his attention to her painting, where it was now propped against a lamp on a nearby table. "I don't think I've ever seen that square. In Georgetown, is it?"

"Yes."

"And those flower stalls…are they there all the time?"

"No, those were elsewhere yesterday at market day in the city. I photographed them and then painted them in for effect today from the prints back here in my studio corner."

"A marvelous display. My wife would have enjoyed seeing those stalls."

The mention of an absent wife triggered a sudden memory for Brenna. She knew now where she had so recently encountered the name *Curtis.* It had been twice written in the unfinished, disturbing letter she'd found in the desk. It seemed only logical the author of that letter was this man's wife.

"Your wife isn't here on St. Sebastian with you?" she asked him casually.

"She preferred to remain back in Chicago on this trip."

Those chilling, silver eyes were trained on her again,

as if questioning her interest in his wife. She had nothing to volunteer. A moment later one of the staff arrived to tell them dinner was ready to be served on the terrace.

Gilda had outdone herself with a delectable beef burgundy, a medley of fresh vegetables and, for dessert, a pie made from limes grown on the island. Because this was a more complicated meal than usual, the housekeeper had a young Hispanic woman helping her to serve and clear away the courses.

Knowing that both Gilda and Julio were also Hispanic, Brenna wondered if the young woman was related to them, perhaps even their daughter. Not that it mattered, but it did raise a new awareness in Brenna. She had noticed from her first arrival here that the staff at the villa, although from different backgrounds, were all fair-skinned.

There had been no reason to question or think about this. Until now, when it occurred to her that with the native population of the island being largely of African descent, it was odd that not one of them was employed at the villa. Was that purely by chance, or—

"Brenna, you seem to be preoccupied with something. Everything okay?"

She was conscious then of Marcus speaking to her. "Sorry. Were you asking me something?"

"Curtis is wondering what your next painting subject will be?"

"Oh. Well, I haven't decided, but I was thinking of a harbor scene. Boats can be very interesting."

She had actually intended Braided Falls to be her next subject, but that had been before her discovery of Zena's body. Now, it was out of the question.

Come to think of it, there had been no mention of the murder all evening. Was it possible that Marcus hadn't heard of it yet? Or that, not knowing the victim, the story wasn't of interest to him?

It *was* possible, however, that he could have learned she'd been with Casey for part of the day. In which case he was likely to ask her about this, and she would politely decline to answer him.

Brenna was ready for that challenge, but it never occurred. The evening ended with her going back to the guesthouse, a quick shower and her bed. The sleep she'd been counting on after her exhausting day was long in coming, though.

Her mind refused to shut down the troubling images of Zena King lying there in the water, the waves of heat shimmering in the square and Casey ravishing her with his potent green eyes.

Just at what point she did finally drift off she couldn't say. But she must have slept long and solidly, because it was many hours later when she awakened. Since she had tightly closed the blinds at the windows in order not to be disturbed by the security lamps outside, it was not possible to read the clock or her watch. She could only suppose, therefore, that she sensed that much time had passed.

Strange. Just as strange as trying to explain to herself what had so suddenly awakened her out of a deep sleep when it was still night outside. The answer came a moment later.

There was the sound of a soft, cautious movement nearby. Totally alert now, Brenna lifted her head from the pillow, listening, her heart beginning to hammer with fear.

Breathing. She could hear breathing that was not her own. She was no longer alone in the room. Someone was here in the darkness with her.

Chapter 8

He was blind in the darkness. The only way he knew she was awake and must be aware of his presence was the faint, careful rustle of her movement on the bed. The sound was all he needed to lead him in that direction.

"Don't make a sound," he whispered urgently.

He could feel his knees press against the side of the bed, telling him he was within reach of his objective. If she failed to obey his warning, didn't recognize his voice, he was ready to clap his hand over her mouth to silence her.

Hell, she wouldn't like that. She was capable of retaliating by getting some fleshy part of his hand between her teeth and biting down on it hard enough to draw blood.

He was relieved to be spared that possibility. There was no cry, only a hissed "Casey! What are you doing here? How did you get in?"

He decided to answer Brenna's second question first. It would be much simpler to get that out of the way before handling the lengthy explanation her first question demanded.

"Picked your lock."

"Why did I ask? Routine for an FBI agent, right?"

"Depends on the lock."

It sounded now like she'd scooted up against the headboard when she responded, "Don't be such a smug smart-ass. Marcus has one of the staff doing sentry duty out there every night. I'm surprised you managed to get by him."

"You mean the guy leaning against the wall of the villa? He must have been in the service if he can be asleep like that and still on his feet."

"Don't tell me. I know. If you hadn't found him like that, you would still have managed to avoid him and get inside. But there's the risk now of us being overheard."

"Which is why we need to keep our voices down and stay close while we talk."

To achieve that, Casey perched himself on the edge of the bed without waiting for her invitation. What he would have preferred doing was crawling in there with her and holding her body so tightly against his she would be begging him for more than just an embrace. But circumstances ruled that out.

It was time to get serious.

"Brenna," he began, leaning toward her, "you asked me what I was doing here. Believe me, my reason is an essential one."

"I'm listening."

"My night has been far from idle. To begin with, I had an email from your brother. Will talked again with his buddy in the newsroom of the *Tribune*. The investigative reporter, remember? The guy is persistent. He managed to dig out more info on Marcus Bradley."

"Like?"

"Like Bradley and his cabal aren't just billionaire elitists. They're secret racists, Brenna. White supremacists dangerous to anyone who tries to interfere with them."

"Is this information reliable?" She didn't seem overly surprised by his revelation.

"Not solid enough for him to go to press with it yet, but he's headed there. And Will wants you headed in another direction. Home."

As Casey expected, Brenna ignored that part. It wasn't new. "What else? You implied there's more."

"Yeah." Casey sucked in air. He would need that air for this next one. "After chewing over your brother's email, I managed to get in a couple of hours of sleep. That was before there was this banging on my door."

"You had a visitor at your beach cottage? At that time of night?"

"He said he had to wait until after midnight when everyone was asleep to sneak away. Otherwise, they would have wanted to know where he was going and why, and he had sworn to keep his errand a secret one."

Casey could feel her stirring impatiently on the bed. "Who? Who are we talking about?"

"A young local kid. He couldn't have been more than fifteen or sixteen and scared as hell. Would you believe he rode this old bike of his all the way down from Freedom in the dark?"

"I don't blame him for being scared, all on his own all that way and at that hour."

Casey shook his head. "I don't think that's why he was afraid. I think he was terrified of being caught."

It had to be Brenna this time who needed the air. He could hear her inhaling before she spoke. "Freedom. You said he came from Freedom, Zena's village."

"Zena sent him, Brenna. The kid's name is Teddy King. Her brother."

"Dear Lord."

"Yeah, that's what I thought. That, and that Zena must have somehow discovered she was in danger, which is why she had Teddy promise that if anything happened to her he was to come to me. Remember, I told her the other day where I was staying, so she would have been able to pass that on to her brother."

"But why? What reason would she have for sending the boy to you?"

"Because she gave him a package to deliver to me. I wanted him to wait while I unwrapped it, but he was too nervous to hang around. Refused my offer, too, to put his bike on the back of the Toyota and let me drive him home. He said he was better off alone, that he rode the back roads all the time and knew them as well at night as in the day. Personally, I think he didn't want to risk being seen with me. That said, he shoved the package into my hands and took off into the dark."

"I hope he's all right."

"I've already convinced myself to believe that he is." He wouldn't let either himself or Brenna think otherwise.

"Casey, about the package…"

"You can guess what it contained, can't you?"

"I think so. The water sample from the well in Freedom. I'm right, aren't I?"

"You are, yeah. I don't know if there was an original sample Zena kept with her, but I'm supposing she feared she might be prevented from sending it, so it's only logical to theorize she created a duplicate sample as insurance."

"And instructed her brother to get it to you if anything happened to her."

"Exactly. It arrived in a pocket-size, tightly sealed as-

pirin bottle, along with a letter from her pleading with
me to see that the bottle was delivered to the Miami lab
that agreed to test it. She included a name and address,
accompanying it with a warning for me to make certain
the bottle was kept sealed until it reached its destination.
If it was in any way contaminated, a chemical analysis
would be worthless."

"Zena was counting on you, Casey."

"Yeah, she was, and I don't intend to fail her."

Brenna was silent. Thoughtfully so, he decided. She
must have made up her mind about something, because
there was a sudden movement from her end of the bed.

"What are you doing?"

"Getting out of bed. There's something I want to show
you. Wait here. I'll get it."

He could hear her bare feet padding across the floor,
followed seconds later by the squeak of what sounded like
a drawer being pulled out in the sitting room. She was
back a moment or so later.

"Let's go into the bathroom," she said. "There are no
windows in there. With the door shut, it will be safe to
turn on a light."

The bedroom and the sitting room were not wells of
complete blackness. Light from outside found its way
through slits in the blinds, a very feeble light but it was
just enough to enable Casey to follow Brenna into the ad-
joining bathroom.

He made certain the door was firmly closed behind
him. She was apparently familiar with the location of the
switches, because directly after the click of the door, light
bloomed in the bathroom.

Casey caught his breath at the sight of what he hadn't
been able to see until now. What he hadn't even imag-
ined until now. It had been more than two years since

he'd seen Brenna naked. She wasn't naked now, but as far as his male hormones were concerned she damn well might have been.

Her long, sleekly smooth legs, bare from her feet up, ended in what appeared to be a pair of brief panties. Hard to tell for certain because a T-shirt covered her from her neck to just below her crotch. It should have provided a form of fairly modest sleepwear, right? Not so. The tee was a thin one. So extremely thin he could plainly see the pink nipples of her full breasts.

Heat pooled instantly in Casey's groin.

"Up here, McBride," she ordered him.

"Uh, I was looking at what's in your hand."

"Sure you were."

Casey didn't pursue it. Neither did Brenna. She handed him the blank envelope she had fetched from the sitting room. Before lifting the flap and examining what he could feel was inside, he paused for a moment to get his raw state of lust under control.

That accomplished—adequately so, he hoped—he turned the envelope over in his hand, raised the flap and withdrew the single folded sheet of paper from inside. He spread it open and angled it to the light.

A handwritten letter. He quickly scanned its content. Or what there was of it, anyway. He made certain when he looked up this time that it was only Brenna's gaze he encountered.

"Where did you find this?" he questioned her, unable to help sounding like what he was. An FBI agent.

"In the bottom drawer of the sitting-room desk. Or, to be accurate about it, under the drawer. I investigated because something was making the drawer stick."

Had the letter been tucked down there to hide it,

Casey wondered, or had it somehow landed there un-intentionally?

"It's unsigned, and it's unfinished," he stated flatly.

"But interesting."

"It's more than that. You know what the author is prob-ably referring to, don't you? What's got her so shocked and worried?"

"I think so," Brenna admitted, lowering herself onto the closed lid of the toilet, as if suddenly needing a sup-port under her. "I think she must have learned that Mar-cus and her husband were involved in something wicked connected with Freedom's water supply."

"Brenna, when did you find this letter?"

She didn't answer him at first. When she did, it was with a clear reluctance. "The afternoon of market day when I came back here to print out the photos on my memory card."

"And you're just now showing it to me?"

Her tone changed from reluctant to obstinate. "You know why I withheld it. You would have been after me again to leave the villa and get off the island."

"Damn right I would have."

"There you are."

"But you're showing it to me now. Why?"

"Because I learned who the mysterious Curtis is. I met him at dinner last night. He's Curtis Hoffmann, a close friend of Marcus's staying here at the villa. There was something almost obscene about him."

"And that's it? That's your single reason for letting me see the letter, which I'm supposing from all indications was written by his wife?"

"Isn't that enough?"

"No, it isn't. I think there's something more, Brenna. I think, after adding up all the pieces, you've come to the same conclusion I have. That Marcus Bradley is probably responsible for Zena King's death. Oh, he wouldn't have murdered her with his own hands, but he engineered it somehow. He had to eliminate her to protect his secret. That is what you believe now, isn't it?"

Casey was challenging her. Brenna knew she could no longer oppose his arguments about Marcus.

"All right," she admitted, "it is what I believe now. I suppose on some level I sensed all along there was something wrong about Marcus. But the truth is, I deceived myself about who Marcus Bradley really is, because I so wanted the success he offered me. I'll always be ashamed of that."

"It's human nature to be ambitious, Brenna. To ignore your conscience because of it is also understandable. To go on ignoring that conscience, though…well, that's another matter. But you never let yourself get that far."

She tipped her head to one side, considering him. "I've never known you to be a philosopher."

He leaned against the door behind him. "Being on suspension gives a guy a lot of free time. I've spent a good amount of it reading."

"I'm impressed." She was silent for a few seconds, and then she asked him suddenly, "Casey, why are you here?"

His eyes widened in surprise. "I thought I've been making myself pretty clear on that."

"Oh, I didn't mean it like that. I mean, why did you show up at this ungodly hour of the night? All that you've been telling me could have waited until daylight. In fact, you could have called me and explained everything over the phone."

"No, I couldn't."

"Why not?"

"Because you and I are getting off this island. *Now.*"

"You're serious."

"You bet I am. In fact, opposition or not, I should have hauled you out of here long ago. But now we can't afford to wait." He checked his watch. "There'll be signs of daylight in another hour. We have to get out now while it's still dark, or we risk being stopped. You understand? You're not safe here. As for me, I need to deliver that water sample in Miami before Bradley finds out that I have it."

"All right," she agreed mildly.

Those sexy green eyes of his gazed at her in disbelief. "Just like that?"

"Just like that."

"It's a holy miracle."

"Should I start packing?"

"No," he instructed her sharply, "we don't have time for that. Just take your passport, wallet and whatever essentials you can stuff into a couple of totes and your purse. I'm sorry, but you'll have to leave your painting gear behind."

"Meaning we have to travel light and fast."

"That's about it. I'm counting on no one discovering your absence from here until we're in the air."

"Can we find a flight this early in the day?"

"Maybe nothing to Miami, but there's bound to be a plane to somewhere. Getting away from St. Sebastian is what matters. We can make connections from elsewhere to Florida."

Casey handed the letter back to her. "Take this with you. We might need it." He paused before opening the bathroom door. "Think you can manage in the dark out there to dress and gather what you need?"

Brenna got to her feet and switched off the bathroom

light, plunging them into blackness. "I can feel my way well enough."

"I'll keep a lookout at one of the bedroom windows. There's enough light with the security lamps outside to tell me if anyone is on the move. Ready?"

"Ready."

Casey opened the bathroom door, and they slipped out into the dark bedroom. The next minutes were hurried ones for her, as hurried anyway as it was possible to get with only the faintest glimmer of light. Familiarity with the guesthouse, as well as the location of her possessions, helped immensely.

Brenna chose a casual, comfortable outfit to wear in the form of a pair of dark slacks and a simple, plain top. Neither garment boasted any of the vivid colors she favored. She reasoned it was best to avoid them on this occasion in order not to draw any attention to herself. Her copper hair was bad enough, but if it became necessary, she could stuff her hair under the baseball cap she slipped into one of her totes.

After that, it was not so easy to select what should go in the other tote and what should be left behind. A change of undergarments was essential and her Nikon, small enough to deserve space.

It had already been determined that her painting supplies would have to be abandoned. The seascape and the painting of the square, as well as her sketches, would remain. They belonged to Marcus now. A part of his generous advance had paid for them. As for all the rest she owed him, and would not now be delivering…well, there was time to figure that out after she'd returned to Chicago. One thing was for sure. She couldn't ask for the money back she'd loaned to her friends at home. The couple needed it too desperately.

What was she doing wasting time worrying about this stuff?

The underlying truth was she was nervous. Fearing discovery before she and Casey could get away. There was one certainty. She might not know what Marcus Bradley's reaction would be when he learned she had cleared out, but whatever it was, it would be far from good.

"Brenna," Casey called softly from his vigil at the window, "what's taking you?"

She had filled the two totes with as much as they would hold. "I'm set to go."

"Then let's roll."

He led the way to the front door where he halted her. "Wait here. I'm going to do a fast check outside to be sure it's clear."

"Was Julio still leaning against the wall asleep when you left the window?"

"No, he's gone."

Brenna was alarmed. "And you weren't going to say anything to me? Casey, you can't go out there! He could be waiting in the shadows with a gun!"

Before she could stop him, he was already out the door. Talk about nerves! He left her imagining the worst. That he would either be shot or would end up easily breaking poor Julio's neck, as she was sure his FBI training had taught him the skill.

Danger or not, Brenna was set to go after him when Casey was suddenly back, slipping inside the guesthouse.

"No sign of any guard outside. Whoever was on the last shift either decided to call it quits for what's left of the night or needed to take a leak. You have the key with you for the front door?"

"Right here." She produced it from her purse. "I suppose I should leave it behind."

"No. Take it with you and lock the door behind us. You don't want to risk any of them testing the door and finding it unlocked before they have a good reason to start suspecting something's wrong."

"I guess," she said sheepishly, "that's why I'm paid for being an artist, and you're paid to be a special agent."

Once they were outside, she did as he asked and locked the door.

"Okay," he said, taking one of the totes from her to carry, "we've caught the break we need. Let's not waste it."

Casey swiftly preceded her down the hill to the safe spot where he had left the Toyota. Only when they were out of range of the security lamps or any shouted challenge from the villa did Brenna think about relaxing.

The first, faint light of daybreak was tinting the horizon when Casey wound through the gray, nearly empty streets of Georgetown toward the road leading to the airport.

He had learned to read Brenna in all her moods. Even now, after their long separation, those moods were familiar to him. They registered in the shifting expressions on her face. A quick glance at her beside him told Casey all he needed to know.

"Okay, Rembrandt, what's got you so deep in thought?"

She frequently denied what she called his bogus mind reading. Not this time. "I was thinking…if the water sample proves to contain what Zena expected, some kind of chemicals blocking pregnancy, will the proof of that be enough to take Marcus down? Including whoever else might be in on it with him?"

Casey considered her question for a moment before answering. "Probably not by itself, no. But with what the FBI is building, along with what Will's journalist friend is compiling from people willing to talk, Bradley should definitely face charges. The trouble is, his money has bought all kinds of support for him here on St. Sebastian. The kind of support that may allow him to get away with Zena's murder."

If Brenna was disappointed in his judgment, she kept it to herself, although he knew she would bitterly object to any vindication of Zena's killer.

The light in the sky was strengthening as, having now reached the open road, they raced toward the airport.

Casey coached Brenna with a couple of rules before they arrived at the terminal. "I want you to remember two things. Until we're off this island, neither one of us touches our cell phones. Whatever the emergency seems to be, we keep our phones off."

"I understand. Any calls can be traced to us and where we are."

"Exactly."

"What else?"

"No credit card use. Keep the cards in your wallet until we're home. Activity on them can also be traced. Strictly cash transactions."

"Uh, that might be a problem. I don't have that much cash on me."

"But I do. I've been hitting the ATM machines around Georgetown. I've built up all the cash we'll need."

"You've been anticipating this situation?"

"I believe in preparing for negative possibilities, even when they're unlikely to occur. You know that."

"Yes, you were always thorough."

Speaking of which…

It was time again for Casey to check the rearview mirror, which he had been regularly doing since the start of their departure in the Toyota. The traffic at this early hour was almost nonexistent on this particular road, making it easy for him to be confident they weren't being followed.

It was better to be certain, however, even though it was too soon for any chase. Brenna wasn't apt to be missed until breakfast, and then the hunt would begin. But by then, if all went well, they would be flying high over the Caribbean, far out of reach.

The sun was up by the time they reached the terminal. There was already activity out on the field in the form of a cargo jet maneuvering into a takeoff position.

"We'll turn the car in before we hit the ticket counter," Casey said, parking the Toyota in the designated rental lot. "Might make a difference if we have to run for a plane."

Not that he expected them to be that lucky, he thought as they gathered their things and headed into the terminal, but there was always the chance.

This was not Chicago's O'Hare Airport. There was only one ticket counter and no frustrating line ahead of them when, completing their business at the rental car desk to return the silver Toyota, they appeared in front of the solitary ticket agent ready to serve them.

Or, as Casey grimly determined a few minutes later, ready to screw them.

"What do you mean," he demanded, "there are no available seats on any of the flights either today or tomorrow? I'm not specifying it absolutely has to be a U.S.A.-bound flight, man. Anywhere in the West Indies would be fine, as long as we can make some connection there back to the U.S."

The young man, well-groomed, handsome, looked like a mixture of races familiar in the West Indies—some Asian, some African, some Caucasian. But no detectable local dialect.

"I am sorry, sir, but this is a small airport with a limited air service, and we're simply booked full."

"Both days?"

"I'm afraid so."

He's lying, Casey told himself. He could hear it in the agent's voice, see it in the way he avoided direct eye contact with Casey.

"Uh-huh. And what about the day after tomorrow? Any chance of reserving two seats for then?"

"Only if there are any cancellations. I could put you on the waiting list."

"Yeah, I bet you could." Casey had the urge to reach across the counter and grab the guy by the throat. He would do it, too, if he thought shaking the truth out of the agent would work.

Brenna at his side was obviously aware of his anger. She placed a hand on his arm, murmuring a low warning out of the side of her mouth. "Someone at ten o'clock near the gate. Looks like he could be security. Hadn't we better go?"

Chapter 9

Casey waited until they got outside the front entrance to mutter a gruff "We've got a problem."

"The agent was lying, wasn't he? He could have sold us seats on one of the flights out this morning."

"Oh, yeah."

"I think I understand just why he didn't, but you'd better let me hear your explanation so we'll both know we're on the same page."

"We could make you an FBI agent yet, Coleman."

"And replace the paint brush in my hand with a pistol? No, thank you. Getting back to our dilemma…it's Marcus, isn't it? He's put out a net to prevent our escape from St. Sebastian."

Casey nodded. "I counted on his not discovering this soon that you were gone, but I obviously underestimated him. Real trouble is the bastard's got so much money he can pay just about anyone who matters on the island to do what he asks. That apparently includes the ticket agent back there. What do you want to bet he's already phoning the villa to report we're here?"

"So what are we going to do?"

Casey was impressed by Brenna's calm restraint. "Wave down the next taxi that comes by."

"And go where? To your rental cottage on the beach?"

"That's the first place Bradley's goons will look for us, although I have an idea he's not in any great rush to find us. Why should he be? He has every reason to be confident we're boxed in and can't get away. That he can reel us in any time he's ready."

"And can he?"

"Not if I can help it. Men like him often have bloated egos that fail to consider their opponents have weapons, too. All of which is to say I lined up a few emergency surprises of my own to throw at him in the event we got grounded here. For those we need to go back to Georgetown."

"What are these emergency measures?"

"I'll tell you when we get there."

"Always the mystery with you, McBride."

"It's just that telling you now could be a waste of time. Circumstances can change, making adjustments necessary. Better if I explain when we know exactly what the situation is."

A moment later a taxi swung into sight. Casey held up his hand for it. The driver pulled up to the front entrance to collect them. After Casey and Brenna settled themselves on the backseat of the cab, he leaned forward to speak to the grizzled driver.

"You know where Crooked Lane is, don't you?"

The old man, looking over his shoulder, gazed at Casey

wide-eyed. "Mon, dat deep into black folks' neighbor-hood. Why you want ta go dere?"

"To pay you a nice fare, with an even nicer tip, if you can get us there with no questions asked."

The driver nodded, tearing off in the direction of Georgetown.

Brenna didn't bother to question him on this one. Her only observation was, "After what you told me yesterday, I suppose there's every reason why we wouldn't ask the police to help us."

"Only one. They're more likely to help Marcus Brad-ley than us."

"Meaning we're on our own and on the run."

"That just about describes it." He found her hand on the seat, warm and smooth, and squeezed it gently. "That worry you?"

"I'd be lying if I said I wasn't…well, maybe *concerned* is a better word."

"Anything specific?"

"Yes. Casey, do you suppose Marcus knows you have that water sample?"

"With the money he has in so many pockets on this island working for him, there's a good chance he does know by now."

"He'll want it back," she said. "And he'll make every effort to get it."

"Of course."

He hated that Brenna had to be involved in this thing. And that at this stage, all he had was a fierce self-promise to do whatever was in his power to make sure she stayed safe.

To that end, he remained alert. And that, thank God, enabled him a few miles farther on down the road to put his self-promise to work.

Speeding toward them was a familiar-looking green sedan. No way of knowing whether it was the same car that followed them that morning they were headed to Braided Falls, but Casey wasn't waiting to make sure.

"Brenna," he ordered her sharply, "slide down in the seat out of sight! *Fast!*"

She could have asked him why. Could have objected. But his tone must have relayed the urgency of the moment, letting her know how necessary it was for her to obey his command. Her action was immediate and swift.

Casey also lowered himself, but only far enough to minimize being sighted and recognized by the occupants of the other car. He kept his face to the level of his nose above the bottom of the window on his side, making his eyes clear of any obstruction.

The approaching sedan flashed by the taxi. What Casey could see was pretty much a blur. All he could make out were two men in the front seat. As for the car itself…that required a quick second look through the rear window of the taxi.

His gaze this time zeroed in on the dent in the trunk lid of the rapidly receding sedan. That deep dent was known to him. He remembered observing it the morning when the dark green vehicle had parked across the road from the general store. There was no mistaking the identity of the sedan.

"You can come up now," Casey murmured.

Brenna pulled herself back into a normal position on the seat. "Just why were we playing hide-and-seek? Our driver must think we lost our minds."

"We were taking cover from the car that passed us going the other way."

"Why?"

"It happened to be the green demon. You remember the green demon, don't you, Rembrandt?"

"All too well. So it was headed toward the airport. Can that mean what I think it means?"

"That it was on its way to try to intercept us. I'd guess that's a fair assumption."

"So we're already being hunted. It seems like you were wrong, Casey. That Marcus is in a hurry to have us caught."

"He wants that water sample."

"I'm supposing," Brenna said, "that whoever is in the car didn't spot you, or they would have turned around and chased our taxi. How about you? Did you get any look at them?"

"Only a quick glimpse, just enough to know there were two men in the front seat and that the driver was blond."

"The driver of the demon that morning on our way to the falls was blond. A mean-looking one," she added unhappily. "I hope you have that backup plan all ready to go when we get to Georgetown."

Their cab driver put them down at the mouth of Crooked Lane. This was as far as he was able to go. Crooked Lane was not only crooked, it was also extremely narrow, not wide enough to accommodate anything on wheels larger than bicycles, motor scooters and one of the occasional motorcycles that were rare on St. Sebastian. Most of the traffic was on foot.

The first thing Casey did when they were alone was to try to ease Brenna's concern. "It's not likely those two goons will be able to track us here."

"But if they should?"

"This is what we'll be doing. After we cover the first block, we're going to separate."

Her face wore an immediate expression of alarm. "You're going to leave me on my own?"

"I don't like it either, but it's the safest plan. They'll assume rightly that I'm the one who's got the water sample, and they'll both come after me."

"And if they don't? If one of them comes after me?"

"I've got that figured, too. After I leave you, you'll walk another block on just as quickly as you can. When you come to the corner, there'll be a little restaurant called Tonya's. Go into the place. Don't pause in the dining room. Head straight through the swing door at the back into the kitchen."

"What if I'm stopped in the dining room by one of the waitstaff?"

"No one will challenge you."

"And you know that how?"

"I just do. Now listen, will you? We don't have time to waste. You'll find Tonya in the kitchen. She's always there seated at this big table working on the next meal. She'll help you."

Casey realized Brenna was deeply confused by now and was longing for an explanation, but they needed to be underway. She had the weight of her two totes balanced in either hand. He bore his single, zippered athletic bag in his left hand, leaving his right hand free to cup her elbow protectively as he guided her up the sidewalk.

Crooked Lane was crowded with pedestrians, all of them black. White faces were rare in this neighborhood, which explained the curious glances from passersby. Casey could see those glances worried Brenna.

"What are you doing?" he asked her. "Remembering what our cab driver said after I gave him the address?"

"I thought he might be implying this area wouldn't be safe for us."

"Naw," he scoffed, "he was just surprised, is all. Brenna, I don't know about other islands in the Caribbean, but places like this in Georgetown aren't like the ghettos in our big cities. You're welcome here, as long as you're not any member of Marcus Bradley's crowd. Then you're the enemy and not a friend. And believe me, they know the difference."

Brenna cast a sidelong look at him. "How did you learn all this?"

"What did you think I was doing all that time you were busy elsewhere? Loafing on the beach?"

"No, I can't picture you ever doing that. So you occupied yourself exploring neighborhoods like this one. And apparently making friends. Like the mysterious Tonya."

He grinned at her. "Well, I had to eat somewhere. If you remember, I was never a cook. One of the maids where I was staying recommended Tonya's. Told me the place wasn't much, but the food was the best on the island. She was right. I asked to compliment Tonya, and they sent me into the kitchen. She doesn't often leave the kitchen. You'll see why when you meet her."

"But how is this woman going to know to help me?"

"I described your red hair. She was eager to see it. Okay, maybe I did suggest it was possible, although improbable, a time would come when one or both of us would need a helping hand."

Brenna halted, this time turning to look him full in the face. "You *anticipated* all this?"

"I had to cover the bases if we didn't get out by air. We're here." They had arrived at the cross street that marked the end of the first block. "All right, you go on. Stay vigilant. If you are followed, no way is one of Marcus's thugs going to try to accost you out here on the open street. The local men would be all over him."

The expression on her face plainly said she didn't want to leave him.

"Brenna, this is just a precaution, that's all it is."

She didn't look any more convinced of that than his other reassurances that had preceded this one. But she offered no verbal misgivings. Her only question was, "You'll meet me at Tonya's, won't you?"

"Before you know it. Go."

Casey waited to see her turn and walk up the sidewalk. She would be all right, he told himself. She was a strong, capable woman. And it wasn't as if she were on her own. Tonya wasn't far, and she would look out for her.

Brenna had to be all right. He'd never forgive himself otherwise.

He watched her until she was out of sight around one of Crooked Lane's sudden, sharp bends. Then, reminding himself he was the one now completely on his own, Casey left Crooked Lane to travel several blocks along the cross street.

He had absolutely no destination in mind. His only objective was to lead any potential danger away from the vicinity of Brenna. So far, however, he'd perceived no one in pursuit.

That changed when he turned on another street that paralleled Crooked Lane and the three streets between. It would have been a mistake at any time for him to check over his shoulder. He wanted any enemy to think he was unconcerned.

Nor did he need to look behind him. If you were an FBI special agent, with enough assignments under your belt, you developed a sense of someone on your tail. And even with all these other people out here, Casey *did* sense he was being followed. The question was: *By how many? One man or both of them?*

There was a trick for finding out without giving himself away, and he used it.

Midway along the block, when the street was busy with motor traffic, he stopped at the curb with the intention of crossing to the other side. He kept leaning out and looking in both directions, waiting for the traffic to clear.

It was on one of these phony checks that Casey spotted him out of the corner of his eye. Although he permitted himself only the briefest of glances, there was no mistaking his tail several yards behind him. Other than himself, he was the only white guy in sight.

Damn. Only one man, and Casey had been hoping for both of them. That meant the blond was probably shadowing Brenna. He had to get to her, but first he had to deal with the goon behind him.

The traffic had momentarily cleared. Casey dashed across the street. There was an alley just ahead of him. He moved into it with a deliberateness that said this had been his destination all along.

After the blinding brilliance of the sunshine out on the street, the shadows in here were deep and dark. All to his advantage. Casey flattened himself against the blank brick wall, his body taut, his grip on the handle of the stout athletic bag tightening.

He didn't have long to wait. Probably fearing he would lose his objective if he hesitated, the goon came barreling into the alley with no reason to suspect he'd been made. And paid the penalty. The instant he appeared, Casey swung the bag hard into his stomach. The guy doubled over with pain, clutching his gut. Before he could recover, Casey dropped his bag to employ the tactics he'd been taught at Quantico.

With the edge of his right hand, using it like a blade, he chopped the side of his adversary's neck in one of its most vulnerable spots. Following that action almost instantly, he repeated it on the other side with his left hand slicing down with an equally effective result. Casey's target collapsed sideways with a groan on the brick pavement and was still.

Unconscious? To make certain of that, Casey nudged him with his toe. He didn't stir. Now that Casey had a better look at him, he realized there was something familiar about the guy.

Burly, a long ponytail and tattoos covering his arms. Where had he seen him? Right. That afternoon at the harbor front where he had paused to watch this same man direct the unloading of steel drums from a freighter.

It had been shortly after that, and a little farther along the waterfront, that he'd had a gun shoved into his back and a growled warning in an Eastern European accent to stay away from Brenna. Were the two men somehow connected?

He didn't have time for this. He didn't even have time to frisk that lump of flesh at his feet for a weapon.

Brenna! It was imperative he reach Brenna before Blondie could put his hands on her! He had promised her she would be all right.

Scooping up his athletic bag, Casey charged out of the alley and, legs pumping like pistons, headed for Tonya's.

Stay vigilant.

That was what Casey had told her to do before they'd parted. But how could she be vigilant without checking behind her every few minutes, an action sure to be a giveaway to her tail that she was worried she was being followed?

Anyway, she wasn't really worried about herself. Nervous maybe, but not worried. *That* Brenna reserved for

Casey. He'd provided assistance for her only a short distance off, but none for himself.

Except this block to Tonya's seemed much farther than a short distance away. She was so anxious to reach it she paid no attention to the heat of the advancing morning, the mingled noises on the crowded street, the spicy odors of cooking drifting from the open windows and doorways of the tenement buildings.

There it was on the corner! Just as Casey had described it! Tonya's!

Brenna resisted a last urge to glance behind her just once before she ducked into the restaurant. What she did do instead was send a silent, fervent message: *Casey, wherever you are at this minute, stay safe.*

There were two serving girls in the drab, faded dining room, setting tables for the coming midday meal. They ignored her as, obeying Casey's instruction, she headed straight for the swing door at the back. As expected, it opened directly into the kitchen.

A long, low table boasted a position of prominence in the center of the room. The black woman seated behind it was dicing tomatoes.

The owner of the restaurant, Brenna presumed. She could understand now what Casey meant when he'd said Tonya seldom left her work station. With her enormous girth, it must present a challenge for her to get around.

The smile that Tonya flashed Brenna across the table when she looked up to find her there could have competed with her body in width. Did Tonya always immediately welcome strangers like this who walked into her kitchen uninvited?

Brenna started to introduce herself. "I'm Casey McBride's friend, Bren—"

She got lopped off there with a sharp, "Hey, gal, you

tink I don't know who I'm talkin' to? No female on dis island got hair dat color. Yeah, I know who you—"

It was Tonya's turn to be cut off in midsentence, this time with the shrill ring of a bell.

"Up front tellin' us we got us a situation out there," she wheezed.

Brenna wouldn't have thought that a woman so heavy could move so fast. But with a shove of her feet beneath her wheeled chair, Tonya scooted clear across the room in a single flight, ending up in front of a thick door with a small, fogged window in the top.

"What you just standin' der for, gal?" Depressing a stout latch, she pulled the door back. "Git yourself in here!"

Ten seconds later, a startled Brenna found herself on the other side of the door, which had been snugly closed behind her.

There was no light in here, except for what managed to find its way through the fogged pane. And the little window was fogged, because it was cold in here. The kind of cold that had you hugging yourself.

She had been shut inside either a cooler or a walk-in freezer. Brenna couldn't decide which, but if given a choice, she'd opt for the cooler. If it was a freezer, Chicago-bred or not, she was afraid she wouldn't last long.

That bell must have been the dining room's warning to Tonya that someone, whose looks they maybe didn't like, had stormed into the restaurant, possibly looked around for a moment and then headed for the swing door. Which explained why Brenna had been hidden in the cooler.

This was as good a time as any to rid herself of her purse and two totes. Once she lowered them to the floor, her arms were free to wrap tightly around herself. Did it help? Not much. She was shivering now and fighting the temptation to dance vigorously in place.

There was the chance that any thumping on the floor could be heard, or even felt, in the kitchen, although the walls had to be thick enough to deaden the sound of voices. She could hear no conversation on the other side.

Nor did she dare to peer through the glass into the kitchen, and risk the satisfied-with-himself face of a pursuer staring back at her in triumph. She remained in the shadows in a corner, trying not to mind the icy currents drifting around her legs.

Who was out there? The blond? She hoped not. She carried the memory of a particularly mean-looking face from that morning when they had sighted him outside the general store. It could be his partner instead. It was silly, of course, to prefer one over the other. They were both the enemy.

On the other hand, it could be someone else entirely.

All Brenna knew for certain was she was cold, and growing colder by the second. If she had to remain in here much longer—

The swoosh of the cooler door being yanked open had her issuing a startled gasp.

"Brenna."

It was a familiar baritone voice carrying all the warmth she needed. Casey! Casey was here! She would be all right now.

She would have sworn her legs were so numb by now they wouldn't carry her. She managed just fine to rush forward, burst out of the cooler into a light that seemed blinding after the dimness she left and straight into his waiting arms.

And, oh, the blessed heat of those arms folding her tightly against his solid body. She felt his strong hands stroking her back, one of them lifting just long enough to tuck her head under his chin before it resumed its slow caresses.

Now, with her nose pressed against the exposed skin in the open top of his shirt, she could detect the slightly musky male scent of him mingled with a clean soap smell. Could feel his mouth brushing against her ear as he crooned huskily, "Casey has got you, baby. I'm sorry I wasn't here sooner. But I did come as fast as I could, sweetheart, so you're safe now."

Baby? Sweetheart? They had been endearments he had freely used when they were engaged, familiar to her then on a daily basis, and she had relished them. But he shouldn't be using them now. She should object.

Except…well, they signified the security both physical and verbal he was providing in this moment. And she hated to surrender that.

Maybe, though, Casey himself realized it was time to bring an end to the intimacy. He released her, permitting her to remove herself from his embrace.

"You okay?" he asked.

"Yes. Sorry to be so delicate. I guess it was the cold. You know how I always hated the cold."

Tonya spoke up from her chair at the table, where she had been watching them. "Sorry I put you on ice, gal, but I had to store you somewhere quick."

"It's all right, Tonya. You did what you had to, and I'm nothing but grateful for that. Anyway, I'm all thawed out now, and he's—" She broke off, gazing wildly around the kitchen, as if the threat that had come so near might still be here. "He is gone, isn't he?"

Tonya jerked a thumb over her shoulder in the direction of what apparently was the restaurant's rear door. "Out to de alley wid de rest of de garbage."

"Tonya told him you ran in here and out the back without stopping," Casey explained. "By now, if luck is still with us, he should be halfway to the other side of Georgetown."

"It was Blondie, wasn't it?"

"Yeah, it was Blondie."

"I *knew* it. I could feel him out here. And the other one? He came after *you,* didn't he, Casey?"

"Afraid so. I hoped to lead both of them far away and lose them, but—" He shook his head. "Instead, I ended up getting delayed in getting back to you having to deal with my own thug."

"What I can't understand," Brenna said, "is how they were able to locate us so fast."

"I got an answer for dat. My people down here, dey don't trust folks dey don't like de looks of. And what dey don't trust, dey don't talk to." A sadness crept into her voice. "But der's some of my people so poor dey don't have money to eat. Sometimes, if dey hungry enough, dey take de money and talk."

What could Brenna say to something like that except a lame "I understand."

Casey suddenly looked restless, as if worried one or both of the goons after them might come back. "We have to go."

"Go?" Brenna asked. "Go where? Where can we possibly go from here?"

"To a safe place where we can hide out until tonight?"

"And what happens then?"

"We get off St. Sebastian in the only way left to us."

Chapter 10

Maddening. Instead of troubling to explain what he had just dropped on her, Casey had turned to Tonya.

"Tonya, my friend, what are the chances of having you send over two of your daily specials to us at suppertime?"

"I'll fix you up somethin' you gonna like for sure."

"You're wonderful!"

Well, great. Just great, Brenna thought. The two of them obviously understood what they were talking about, and here she was left puzzling over another one of his mysteries. No, make that *two* mysteries.

Casey removed a roll of bills from his pocket, peeled off several of them and placed them on the table in front of Tonya.

"This is to pay for our suppers."

Tonya fingered the money. "Too much. What am I gonna do wit dis much?"

"If you won't keep it for yourself, then take any you

think is extra and buy a few meals for those people you were telling us about."

"You're a good mon, Casey McBride."

Brenna didn't have any argument with that. "And you," she said, bending down to hug Tonya, "are a good woman. Thank you for helping us."

Casey was already waiting by the back door for her, sunglasses in place, impatient for them to leave. Preceding her into the alley, he checked in both directions to make sure it was empty.

"You might want to tuck your hair under that baseball cap you brought along in your tote," he suggested. "It will lessen the chance of your hair being noticed and remembered."

Brenna complied. She wished she'd thought of piling her hair like this under the cap when the cabby had dropped them at the mouth of Crooked Lane. It might have diminished the possibility of Blondie learning where she went.

"It will do," Casey approved when, donning her own sunglasses, she turned to face him. "We go this way." He turned to the left along the cobblestones. She fell in step beside him.

"I assume you know exactly where we're headed."

He was too busy making sure they weren't being followed, that this time they had definitely lost their shadows, to answer her at first. When he did respond, it was with a vague "Uh, yes, I do."

"And that you made a prior arrangement for us to hide out there. Just in case."

"Well, yeah."

Of course.

They had come to the end of the alley and another

street. "Are we going to need a taxi to take us there, because I haven't seen any in this neighborhood."

"Nope, not many fares to pick up in this quarter. Not that we need a cab. It's not far to walk. Just up the block here."

"What is?"

"Where we're going."

Brenna decided she'd better change the subject. "Before we get there, wherever *there* is, suppose you tell me how you plan for us to leave St. Sebastian tonight, now that we've been prevented from getting on a plane."

"By water."

"Well, I know from my guidebook that none of the cruise ships currently dock here and that none of the freighters serving the island take passengers. I guess that leaves something much smaller and that you've already inquired about hiring it."

"Too risky. In that part of town, something like that could get back to Bradley in no time."

"Then what's the answer?"

"We steal a boat, which is why we have to wait until after midnight."

Brenna stopped on the pavement and turned to stare at him. "You can't be serious. You *are* serious."

"I am unless you have a better plan."

"Not at the moment."

"If one occurs to you, let me know."

And that was that. He went on, and she went on with him, both of them observant as they advanced up the busy street.

It wouldn't be crowded out here in the afternoon, Brenna realized. By the time the sun was overhead, the population of Georgetown would retreat indoors, away from the heat.

"Where do you suppose Blondie and his partner are right now?" she wondered.

"Not resting, you can bet."

"So, somewhere out there searching for us again."

"Right. And if I have a choice, make it far away from here." Casey halted, suddenly announcing, "We're there."

"Do I get to know now what *there* is?"

"Across the street. The hotel where we'll be spending the day."

Brenna looked across the street in the direction he nodded. The building he indicated was narrow-fronted, four stories tall and looked as though, if it hadn't been supported by the shorter buildings on either side of it, it would fall down. It was definitely a relic from another era.

Someone in the city had a sense of humor. The sign over the entrance boasted: *You want the best hotel in this town, traveler, you find it here at Jo-Jo's.*

"Let me guess," Brenna said. "No air-conditioning and no elevators."

"Ceiling fans and stairs are good for the cardiovascular system."

"So, tell me, there *are* rooms, aren't there?"

"Nothing fancy. Pretty plain, in fact. But they're clean and bug-free," he promised her. "I checked that out."

"Plumbing?"

"Most of the rooms have some form of plumbing."

She didn't permit herself to imagine what that form might be. "Just one more question. How did you happen to find this charmer?"

"Tonya recommended it. Turns out Jo-Jo is her son."

This deserved another dry observation, but Brenna felt she had been sarcastic enough. After all, they would only be spending the rest of the day here and part of the night. And who was she to get picky about whatever safe refuge was being offered to them by warm, helpful souls like Tonya, people who could be inviting trouble for themselves with their generosity?

"It looks like it will be just fine, Casey," she assured him, linking her arm with his. "And after spending time in that cooler, I don't need air-conditioning."

Across the street they went, through the front door and into a small reception area that was dim even after she removed her sunglasses.

"Brenna, this is Jo-Jo." He introduced her to the young man behind the counter.

It took only a brief glance for her to determine that mother and son had to have metabolisms that were polar opposites. Jo-Jo was sapling-thin, Tonya so heavy she needed her office-style chair with wheels to get around. But their smiles were the same.

Brenna offered her hand across the counter. Jo-Jo clasped it with an enthusiastic "It is my good fortune to welcome you to my hotel."

"Thank you, Jo-Jo."

"Good buddy," Casey addressed him, "is the room I looked at still available?"

"It is waiting for you with much joy."

"Great." Casey turned to her. "Brenna, I'm going to need a minute here with Jo-Jo."

Meaning, she supposed, he wanted it in private. "I'll wait for you over there on the stairs."

Crossing the reception area to the staircase, she seated herself on one of the lower steps. She could watch the two men from here conversing in earnest, though she couldn't hear them.

Casey's minute stretched into several before he joined her with an old-fashioned room key in hand. Brenna rose to her feet, dusting off the seat of her pants.

"Do I dare ask what secrets got exchanged, or would you prefer I didn't?"

"Hey, you're always accusing me of playing the mystery guy and keeping secrets from you. *I* share."

"Okay, share away then."

"It wasn't anything you couldn't have stayed to hear. After paying for the room, I had to find out if anyone had been around asking about us. There wasn't."

That was one relief, Brenna told herself.

"Then I had to let Jo-Jo know his mother was sending over two meals for us at dinnertime. He'll give us one long ring on our room phone when they arrive. But if someone he doesn't know tries at any time to get past him and up the stairs to our room, we've arranged that he'll alert us with two quick rings on our phone. Which we don't answer."

And *that* was not a second relief.

"Easy, babe."

"I know. Just a necessary precaution. So, we're all set with our room?"

"All set." He held up the key.

"Which floor?"

"Top." She must have groaned, because he defended his choice with a rapid "Common sense, Brenna. If anyone does come hunting for us, they've got to climb three flights to reach us. And that gives us three flights of time after Jo-Jo rings for us to get out."

"Just promise me one thing, Special Agent."

"What?"

"I'll only have to climb to the fourth floor one time."

"Wimp."

"I'd slug you now, McBride, but I'm saving my strength for the climb."

He laughed.

* * *

As Casey had indicated, the room wasn't much. But, though cramped and shabby, it was clean. Its furnishings consisted of a double bed, a chest of drawers, a couple of chairs and a small table. And that was it.

After locking the door behind them, Casey explained to her, "I chose this room because it's at the front with its window overlooking the street. We can see who's coming and going from up here. But be careful to stand at the side. We don't want to chance being spotted by anyone who might be watching out there."

"Just answer me this. If, God forbid, we should have to get out of here in a hurry, how do we do that without meeting who we don't want to meet coming up while we're heading down? An outside fire escape somewhere maybe?"

"There is one at the far back side of the hotel, but we've got a better emergency exit than that. Come see."

He led the way to a door that Brenna had presumed meant a closet on the other side. It was not a closet. When opened by Casey, it revealed a tiny bathroom that contained a sink, a stool and an open alcove with a rod for hanging clothes.

They would not be taking baths or showers. There was no tub or shower stall, but what fixtures there were were clean ones.

"I don't see an exit."

"Over here." Three easy steps brought Casey to a frosted window, which he unlocked and raised. "Look down." He made room for her. She looked.

A few feet below the window was the flat roof of the building that adjoined the side of the hotel. She supposed he considered it an easy drop offering an escape across that roof to...well, she didn't know and wasn't going to ask. She was simply going to count on never having to make use of it.

"Cool, huh? Another reason why I chose this room."

Damn, he actually sounded proud of his discovery. All these complicated advance arrangements of his were beginning to make her wonder whether they were more than just the thorough preparations of an FBI agent anticipating the possible necessity of an alternate plan.

As if what? As if maybe he thought that, instead of simply flying away, it might be more fun to actually—

She stopped herself. He'd never suppose anything like that.

This was merely a challenge to him, a realization that Marcus Bradley was an intelligent opponent who would not easily let his objectives slip away from him.

They returned to the bedroom where Casey opened the single front window and turned on the ceiling fan to circulate the air that was beginning to grow stuffy and warm. He checked his watch.

"Dinner is still hours away," he grumbled.

"When did you last eat?"

"Can't remember. Probably not since sometime early last night. Too bad we couldn't have risked stopping for something quick along the street or even begging a crust off Tonya before we left."

It was Brenna's turn to disclose a secret of her own she'd been withholding for just such a moment. Picking up one of her totes she'd placed on the floor, she sat down in a chair with it on her lap. He watched with interest as she searched through its contents.

"You got food in there maybe?"

"You're not the only one to prepare in advance," she said, producing four granola bars and two plastic bottles of water.

"Give," he said, eagerly snatching the bar and bottle she held out to him.

He perched on the edge of the bed, stripping off the wrapper on the granola bar and unscrewing the cap on the water bottle. Between bites and sips of her own share of the supply, she watched him as he alternately munched and gulped.

"Good," he managed to say.

"More?"

"Why not."

She passed him another bar. He polished that one off as well, finished the rest of his water and continued to sit there, looking as pleased as if he'd been treated to a banquet.

Brenna thought how on occasions like these he could be like a little boy. That was before she became aware of the smile he directed at her, altering her opinion to a quick *Or maybe not.*

It certainly wasn't the smile of a child but of an adult male, slow and lazy and communicating the kind of frank sensuality that made her stomach flutter.

The smile was spoiled seconds later when it morphed into an enormous yawn.

"Sorry," he apologized. Both of his eyes were looking a bit hooded.

"Just exactly how much sleep *did* you get last night before Zena King's brother came knocking on your door?"

"Not much," he admitted.

"And then you spent the rest of the night running around town rousing people out of their beds and getting them to promise you and your female friend sanctuary in their restaurant and hotel if they should need it."

"Not the whole night."

"No, what was left you used to visit ATM machines,

break into my quarters and convince me we had to get off the island. Since then you've been very busy taking me on the run and getting us into hiding. Casey?"

"What?"

"You're exhausted."

"No way."

"Come on, you don't get to play the big macho agent here guarding me around the clock. I don't need guarding. We're safely holed up here, aren't we?" She didn't give him the chance to answer. "Sure, we are. And, listen, I had a lot more sleep than you did. I'm fully awake and capable of being vigilant without you."

"Yeah? And what am I supposed to do?"

"I'll tell you what you're going to do. You're going to take advantage of this downtime to stretch back on that bed and sleep until I call you that our dinners are here."

"Forget it."

"Casey, listen to me. If you don't get some sleep, how useful do you think you'll be tonight when we really need you to be alert?"

She was glad she thought of this argument, because nothing else would have persuaded him. But after a moment of consideration, he was convinced.

"You win."

She watched him bend down, untie the laces of his tennis shoes and kick them off. Not satisfied with that, he peeled off his socks and stuffed them into the shoes.

"Ah, that's much better." He sat back, a happy smile on his face.

Brenna laughed.

"Listen, if you'd been pounding the pavement for hours, you'd be relieved, too, to shed your shoes."

Casey always did come up with excuses, usually weak ones, for removing his shoes and socks whenever he could get away with it. And that was why she'd laughed. Because the truth was, if the man had any addiction at all, it was going barefoot. Constantly.

That achieved, he swung his legs up on the bed, stretched out fully and closed his eyes. Almost the instant they shut, they snapped open again.

Casey popped up with a concerned "I want you to call me if there's the slightest sign that something may not be what it should be either in the hotel or out on the street. The *slightest* sign. No hesitations. You understand me?"

"I promise. Now go to sleep."

That must have been sufficient for him, because within half a minute she could hear his rhythmic breathing that told her he was asleep.

Brenna went on looking at him from her chair. Or, to be more accurate about it, she looked at his bare feet.

It was crazy to think that the bare feet of an adult male were in any way sexy, but his were. She didn't know whether it had to do with their size, their shape or even their strength.

Whatever the explanation, in the old days the sight of them could actually stir a slow heat inside her.

She used to wonder then if his feet, among all his other qualities, could actually be one of the reasons she fell in love with Casey McBride. She'd certainly had plenty of occasions to get familiar with them.

He'd never hesitated to wander barefoot around both his apartment and hers. She had asked him once how and when he'd acquired the habit. He had been reluctant at first to tell her, and then he'd explained.

"Going barefoot when I was growing up wasn't by choice. Not then. It was a necessity. My sister and I had only one pair of decent shoes apiece, and those had to be saved for school. The rest of the time, when the weather permitted it, we went barefoot. I not only got used to it, but in the end I preferred it."

Casey hadn't talked much about his background during their courtship, but Brenna had deduced from little things that his family was poor. But this poor? She'd had no idea. She couldn't bear to ask him about it, but after that she was unable to shake the image of a shack in the Kentucky hills.

It was shortly after she and Casey became engaged that her phone rang one afternoon. To Brenna's surprise, it was Casey's mother. She knew that her son was on assignment out of town, but since she and her husband had to be in Chicago on business, they would love to meet the woman Casey had chosen to be his wife.

Brenna met them for dinner at an expensive restaurant they not only selected but paid for. The McBrides, it turned out, had visited Chicago to deliver one of the Thoroughbred horses they raised. Not in the Kentucky hills but in the lush bluegrass country on one of those farms with a sprawling house, stables and acres and acres enclosed by gleaming white fences.

Casey had not grown up poor. He had grown up rich. When his parents finally understood Brenna's confusion, his father shook his head in an action of hopelessness and his mother laughed. She thought it was funny.

"Has he been telling those wild lies again about having to go barefoot? The truth is we couldn't keep shoes on his feet."

When Casey came home, Brenna tore into him, telling him he ought to be ashamed of himself going around letting people think he and his sister, Meg, were deprived kids.

"Your poor mother and father must be humiliated by those stories of yours."

"Mom and Dad? Naw, they think it's a hoot. Not Meg, though. I never could get her to go barefoot. She didn't know what she was missing, especially down at the creek. Nothing beats squishing mud between your toes."

In the end, Brenna came to realize that Casey's pretense wasn't all in fun. The reality was he was embarrassed that he came from money.

She never raised the subject again. However, she did go on being susceptible to his bare feet. To her relief, however, her fetish never applied to any other man.

And why should those feet be of any interest to her now when any and all attractions associated with Casey McBride were supposed to be long behind her? And remain there.

The afternoon wore on, Brenna's only companions the whirring of the overhead fan and the muted sounds of the traffic in the hot street below. She made an effort to keep her gaze averted from the rugged figure on the bed.

She was, after all, supposed to be alert for any sign of trouble. Which was why, at frequent intervals, she rose from her chair and went to the window, careful to keep out of sight as she checked the scene in the street. The only figures she saw were dark-skinned natives going about their business. Nothing and no one to be concerned about. They remained safe.

Safe enough at the present, anyway, from Marcus Bradley's relentless goons. But just how safe was she from the forceful warrior on the bed?

Chapter 11

"Casey, time to get up," she called to him.

When he didn't respond, Brenna leaned over the bed, gripped him by his hard muscled upper arm and shook him insistently.

The reaction she got this time was startling. His eyes flew open only an instant before he shot to a sitting position, his hands reaching for the gun in his belt. Only there was no gun.

He shook his head, as if trying to clear it of a lingering grogginess, frowning when he discovered her standing over him.

"Damn, don't ever wake an FBI man like that without some warning. You could get shot."

"I didn't think there was much risk of that. Considering."

"Oh, right," he remembered, "I had to surrender my weapon to the bureau." This realization was accompanied almost immediately by a look of alarm in those fascinating green eyes of his. "Hey, why *did* you wake me? Is there something wrong?"

"Our dinners are here."

"Can't be." His gaze went to the window where the last of the daylight was fading from the sky. "Jeez, Rembrandt, you shouldn't have let me sleep this long."

"You needed it." She watched him swing his legs to the floor. "Where are you headed?"

"Downstairs to get our meals."

"They're already over there on the table. Relax, McBride. It was all safely handled. Jo-Jo rang up as arranged to let me know one of Tonya's waitresses was here with the dinners from the restaurant. He assured me the girl was someone he knew and trusted. From the tone of his voice, I think she might be his sweetheart."

"Good for him."

"Well, anyway, I agreed to let her bring up the tray, cautiously met her at the door after she assured me there was no one else in the hall, received the tray, generously tipped her, then she left and I relocked the door. That's it. Oh," she added, "she did say Jo-Jo would collect everything in the morning and bring it down to the desk."

"Still," Casey grumbled, "you should have let me fetch the tray."

"Stop being such a grouch. I'm going into the bathroom to wash my hands. You might try getting something on your feet. Socks at least. I think there could be splinters in this old floor."

By the time Casey took his own turn at using the facilities, Brenna had the tray uncovered, the tableware in place and the two straight-backed chairs drawn up at either end of the table.

Tonya had packed the covered casserole so carefully it

was still steaming when, seated across from each other, they helped themselves to generous servings. Whatever it was, it not only tasted great, it smelled great.

"I can identify chicken, rice, tomatoes, both green and red peppers and seasonings I can't begin to name. How about you?" Brenna wondered.

"Who cares? It's food fit for the gods. Pass me some of that bread, would you? Thanks."

Tonya had accompanied the casserole with a loaf of crusty, grainy bread still warm from the oven. There was no question of it. The woman was a marvelous cook.

Brenna was not sure at what moment the mood of the meal changed. It was hard to identify since it was so gradual. But if she had to explain it, she would say it began soon after their initial hunger was eased.

That was when she became conscious of Casey concentrating less on his food and more on her. He began sneaking looks at her. Not ordinary looks but intimate, smoldering. Then those looks changed, becoming direct, boldly seductive.

What was going on here? But she knew what was happening, didn't she? It was a robust man who, having satisfied one appetite, was eager now to satisfy another. And why not?

Be honest with yourself, she demanded. *Even though you severed your relationship with him two years ago, convinced yourself in time you were no longer in love with him, you were never able to forget how dynamic he was in bed.*

Thrilling memories of the sex they had engaged in so freely and so frequently. Casey had taught her to be as aggressive as he was. But only with him. No other man after him, and there had only been a few, had aroused that kind of eroticism.

Brenna suddenly found herself wanting Casey now as much as he plainly wanted her. It didn't have to be emotional, did it? Just an unattached man and an unattached woman temporarily bonding in a healthy session of lovemaking. No complications.

But that was the trouble. There were always complications. How could there not be with a couple who shared a stormy history? All right, they had moved on. But nothing had changed. Not essentially. He was still committed to a work that, at any time, could place him in jeopardy. And, ironically, wasn't this one of those times?

It could begin all over again if she let it, couldn't it? Her starting to care too deeply, the fear of his never coming back to her except in a coffin. No, she couldn't risk it. *Wouldn't* risk it.

"I'm finished here," Brenna announced, abruptly pushing back from the table. "Can't eat another bite. Excuse me."

She got to her feet and went into the bathroom, shutting the door behind her. Her toothpaste and brush were here in one of the totes.

She'd always made a practice, whenever possible, of brushing her teeth after every meal. She hoped Casey remembered this and, recognizing the sounds behind the bathroom door as he would, didn't misunderstand why she was brushing her teeth.

When she came out of the bathroom, he had turned on a small, single lamp. She could see by its low glow that he had cleared the table and stacked their dishes and utensils on the tray. Everything was ready to be picked up in the morning.

"Guess I'll take my own turn in there," Casey said, brushing by her to enter the bathroom.

Having nothing else to do, Brenna strolled to the window, taking care to approach it from the side where she could steal glimpses of the street without being seen. Not that there was anything of either interest or concern to discover below her. The crowds of this morning had thinned by afternoon when the heat had driven them indoors out of the sun. It was much cooler now, but, except for a few people, the street remained quiet, almost empty of traffic.

Just in the time it had taken her to brush her teeth, the sky had darkened overhead. It was evening now. Full night really, but there were many hours to go until midnight when Casey had judged it would be safe enough to slip away from the hotel and make their way to the harbor front.

Brenna never heard the bathroom door open, didn't catch the sound of his steps crossing the room. Not surprising. She'd learned long ago that Casey had the ability to move in silence, surely an asset if you were working undercover.

She couldn't exactly say how she knew he was suddenly there behind her. *Close* behind her. Maybe because she felt the heat of that muscular body. Or simply sensed his presence.

Or could it be because she caught the distinctive masculine scent of him mingling with something minty on his breath? Yes, his toothpaste. Casey had brushed his teeth, as if preparing to kiss her…

Brenna swung around so fast she almost collided with him. What she intended to say, that he could forget what he was thinking, that it wasn't going to happen, didn't get said. The words stuck in her throat, lodged there by a pair of green eyes staring with such blazing longing into hers she was hypnotized by them.

When she found her voice again, she was able to do no more than croak out a hoarse, feeble "No, Casey, we can't."

His own voice was husky, strong with confidence. "Yes, Brenna, we can. We *have* to."

Casey was not the kind of man who forced himself on an unwilling woman. If she was certain of one thing about him, it was that. She had only to be insistent, and he would back away from her.

But Brenna did not resist, either verbally or physically, when his arms went around her. Her treacherous body betrayed her, melting against his strength as his embrace tightened. Her mouth, too, was ready for his when it angled across hers, opening willingly to admit his tongue.

She could taste the clean, fresh, minty flavor of him as that skillful tongue moved slowly, tenderly with hers. Then his kiss deepened, becoming something fierce, hungry. He held her so close she could feel the rigid hardness of his arousal straining against her.

Brenna had hoped after the passage of two years they were enough recovered from their broken engagement that Casey's physical allure for her, and hers for him, would have dimmed. But if anything, it had expanded, becoming so raw and savage it frightened her.

When she stiffened in his arms, his mouth lifted from hers. He held her a few inches away, his sultry, hooded gaze searching her face, seeking an explanation.

"Casey, what are we doing?"

"What we've both been wanting and waiting for since my first day here when I walked down that beach to you."

His answer was so solemn, so earnest that it carried a kind of promise to it. Brenna had no more objections. Whatever the outcome of what was to follow, for this night she was his.

Casey must have felt that. Without hesitation, he scooped her up in his arms and carried her to the bed, managing somehow to go on cradling her while he lifted the cover aside and deposited her full length on the sheets.

Placing himself beside her, he framed her face with his big hands and began to—

But, no, it wasn't her mouth he kissed as she'd expected. It was every other area. Her eyes, her nose, her cheeks, her ears, her throat. It was as if, having won her consent, he now had all the time in the world to do this properly.

When his mouth finally did settle on hers, it wasn't a kiss he delivered. Not at first. At first he gently caught her lower lip in his teeth and tugged on it. Played with it, using both teeth and tongue to nip and lick.

All this should have been familiar to Brenna, recalled from the past. It wasn't. She'd forgotten what an inventive lover Casey was, how even when they'd been together he had forever surprised her, managed something new.

She was moaning when he finally kissed her in the traditional way, the moans a wordless plea. The kiss was not a prolonged one this time.

Mouth abandoning hers, he raised his head just high enough to rasp, "What? What do you need? Something else?"

He was teasing her, damn him. She could hear his laughter underneath.

"Maybe this, huh? I know I do."

Before she knew what was happening, and without her assistance, he stripped her top off over her head, cast it aside, unclasped her lacy bra, rid himself of that garment as well and was devouring her breasts with a pair of eager eyes.

"Oh, yeah. This is better. *Much* better. But not good enough."

He cupped a breast with each hand, weighing their fullness, his thumbs caressing in slow circles. "I forgot how soft and silky they were," he murmured. "How sweet they tasted, too. Let's see if I remember right."

He lowered his head, his mouth fastening on one of her nipples, suckling strongly before moving on to her other breast.

Every one of his attentions was calculated to give her satisfaction. Even the stubble scratching the sensitive skin of her breasts—because it was probably yesterday since he'd last shaved—contributed to her pleasure.

But Brenna didn't want it all to be one-sided. She wanted to give as well as receive. Except that might be a problem. What he was doing to her felt so wonderful she hated to end it. But she had to.

By then fighting for air, she barely managed a quick "Wait!"

He lifted his head. "Problem?"

She nodded at his shirt. "That has to go."

He grinned. "And whose job is that?"

She sat up. "I guess I'm making it mine."

He sat up as well, twisting around to face her. "I'm all yours."

"A little help, please."

She motioned for him to lift his arms. He accommodated her. Reaching out, she grasped the hem of his tee with both hands, drew it over his head with one swift motion and rid herself of it.

The sight of his naked chest, its rippled muscles gleaming in the lamplight, had her almost dizzy with desire. She began to touch him, running her hands over his broad shoulders, down his pecs to his waist and back again. She felt him shudder, then was rewarded with a moan from him when, with thumbs and forefingers, she boldly pinched his own nipples.

She was startled seconds later as he barked out a sudden "Pants! What are we doing with our pants still on? Jeez, Rembrandt, you're still wearing your shoes. Come on, all of it off for both of us."

It was hard for Brenna to say just who was doing what to whom in the next few minutes. It seemed to be a tangle of hands getting in the way of each other as they either tried to do their own tugging and dragging or made an effort to help the other one.

Whatever the confusion, in the end they both managed to emerge completely naked.

The riveting evidence of his erection had Brenna convinced Casey was aching to join himself with her. His hands stroked her breasts, moving slowly down over her stomach.

She was on fire by the time he reached his destination, fighting for self-control when his fingers stirred through the nest of copper curls on her mound, searching for the core of her womanhood. Finally, as he parted her lips there and inserted his middle finger, she feared she'd lost the battle for control.

And knowing for certain she had when, after that finger had prepared her sufficiently, his mouth took over, fastening on her now swollen nub, sucking so powerfully she bucked like a wild thing. It didn't matter. His strong hands grasped her so tightly by her buttocks that he was able to keep her in place.

There was only one way to free herself, and he gave that to her with that relentless mouth building her to a pinnacle. She cried out when she crashed down on the other side, the spasms continuing to rock her even after he released her.

"You're all right now, sweetheart," he whispered, laying his cheek against her belly.

"If you call sweet torture being all right."

Brenna could feel her belly tremble under his chuckle over her description of her climax.

They rested like that for a long moment before he rose back on his knees and positioned himself between her legs. During that journey down her body, Casey had given her no opportunity to reciprocate. She could see now by the engorged length of his arousal how much in need of his own release he must be. She wanted to give that to him.

Lifting herself to a sitting position, she reached out for him, gripping his shaft. Its heat and hardness excited her. She could actually feel it throbbing in her hand as she squeezed her fingers around it, ready to pump it repeatedly from tip to base.

"What are you trying to do to me?" he groaned. "If you go that route, I'm not going to be able to hold back. And when I go off, I want—"

He interrupted himself there to pull away from her. His pants had been left hanging over the side of the bed. He must have shoved a condom into one of its pockets from a supply in his bag when he was in the bathroom. She watched him now as, reaching for the pants, he retrieved the condom, opened it and hurriedly sheathed himself.

"—to be inside you," he finished softly.

He was in no state to delay when, again between her legs, he positioned himself above her. Nor was Brenna. She was ready for him when he guided himself inside her, penetrating her up to his full length.

He paused only briefly, allowing her to adjust to him. Then he began to move. His strokes were long and rapid, his hips driving them. She answered him, body writhing under his, legs wrapped around him.

"That's fantastic," he rasped when the muscles at the mouth of her vessel contracted, squeezing his organ. "*You're* fantastic. I don't know how much longer—"

He broke off there, sucking in air, tensing in an effort to hold back. But both of them were so consumed with passion by then they were unable to stop the tide that engulfed them.

Brenna was the first to shatter in another blinding orgasm that tore his name from her lips. Casey almost immediately followed with his own release, accompanied by an unidentifiable sound rumbling from his chest, rising through his throat and emerging as a long, deep shout of victory.

Afterwards, he slowly sank down onto her in exhausted satisfaction. They stayed that way, holding each other, their bodies slick with the heat they had generated.

It finally occurred to him that his body was too heavy for her. "I'm crushing you," he said.

Before she could tell him she liked his weight and wanted him to stay where he was, he'd already levered himself off of her. It was all right, though. Rolling both of them onto their sides, he spooned himself against her, his arms going around her in a protective embrace.

They stayed snuggled that way, and eventually Brenna could hear from the sound of his breathing that he had dozed off.

She, herself, didn't sleep. She lay there, listening to the noise of the whirring fan above them and thinking about the sex they had shared. She had enjoyed it certainly, found it special even, but it had been nothing beyond the physical.

There had been no emotion really. Their feelings hadn't been involved. No mention of commitment beyond the present, as if they had wordlessly agreed not to mention the future.

Because there could not be another future for them. Casey was still attached to the FBI, still ready to go out on any risky mission that might be assigned to him. And she was still unable to bear the dangers of that.

So nothing had changed. And wasn't that a good thing really? And as long as they didn't talk about any of it, she could deny to herself that she might, *just* might be falling in love with him all over again.

Keep the emotions at a distance, she reminded herself.

Right. It was better that way. Better, but at the same time somehow terribly sad.

Chapter 12

Casey's nap, cuddled against Brenna, had been a brief but enormously pleasant one. After sleeping most of the day earlier, he shouldn't have needed a nap at all. But, hell, she had worn him out with that amazing sex.

A short nap, though, was all he'd needed to refresh him. The rest of the time between then and now he had spent watching over her as she had watched over him, as well as periodically checking the street.

Now was a few minutes after midnight. Dressed and ready, his bag at his feet, he stood over the bed gazing down at Brenna. She looked so peaceful he hated to wake her, but they needed to be on their way.

Hunkering down on his heels beside the bed, Casey reached out a hand. With the tip of his forefinger, he lightly traced the path of faint freckles sprinkled on her left cheek, following their route as they traveled across the bridge of her nose to her other cheek. Brenna frowned, swatting at what she must consider to be a pesky insect. Her eyes remained closed.

Stretching forward, he brushed a kiss on her mouth. This brought a more effective result. Smiling, she stirred and opened her eyes.

"It's time," he informed her softly.

For a half moment she looked confused, and then she understood. "It's midnight?"

"A little past actually. You need to get dressed, so we can clear out of here."

"Why did you let me sleep so long?"

"Same reason you let me sleep after we got here," he said, coming erect. "You might have had more sleep than I did last night, but it wasn't enough rest. And we're both going to need to be fully alert now."

"Give me a few minutes, and I'll be ready."

Rescuing her clothes from where they had been scattered in haste, she scooted toward the bathroom. The last sight Casey had of her before the door shut was of her tantalizing bare bottom.

And, oh, man, that was some view, bringing an instant thickening to his groin.

But he realized that all he could have at this point were the memories of a few hours ago.

As memories went, however, they were damn good ones. Some of them were innocent, like the fragrance of her silky hair. Others were downright wanton, such as the memory of her wet heat tightening around his pulsing shaft. Yeah, he'd settle for those.

He would have preferred staying on that course, but his thoughts shifted to something more serious as he continued to watch the bathroom door, waiting for it to open. Brenna and him. Did their lovemaking mean anything, or had it just been sex ignited by their situation? Something that, just as it had two years ago, been marked for failure?

Casey's feelings on the subject remained both uncertain and confused when Brenna emerged from the bathroom. He determined they would have to stay that way while he concentrated on getting them out of this mess.

He'd turned off the lamp while he was keeping his vigil. The light from the street was all they needed. It was sufficient enough to let him see she was dressed, bearing a tote in either hand and with her purse hanging by its long strap from her shoulder.

Unlocking the room door, he laid the key on the table.

"You're not going to drop the key at the reception desk?" she asked.

"No, Jo-Jo will know to find it here in the morning. We won't be leaving by the front door."

She didn't pursue it. He had her wait while he opened the door and checked the hall. Satisfied that it was clear, he signaled her to follow him.

When they passed the stairway that descended to the first floor, she understood without being told by what means they were exiting the hotel.

"We're headed for the fire escape, right?"

She had remembered. "Right."

The outside fire escape was located at the far end of the hall on the back side of the hotel. Access to it was not by a door but through a window. Brenna was not happy with the situation when Casey raised the sash, and she poked her head through the opening.

"It's one of those ancient iron jobbies pinned to the side of the building. The kind where you can see through the bars clear to the street."

"So?"

"Maybe it's not safe."

"Gee, I never thought of that. Okay, you go first," he directed her, "and if you fall through, I'll know not to follow."

He laughed when she glared at him.

"McBride, if you ever decide to be one of those spies who come in from the cold, you know, quit the bureau, I bet with that Irish mug of yours and the right routine, you could find work as a stand-up comic. Like at one of those dives under the 'L' tracks on Chicago's South Side."

He loved the way she nailed him with her own brand of humor whenever he tried to get funny with her. He'd missed that.

"Come on, I'll lead the way."

Swinging one leg over the sill, he ducked through the opening onto the fourth-floor platform. Brenna passed him his bag and her two totes, waved away the hand he extended to help her and joined him on the grating.

Shutting the window behind them, Casey preceded her down the zigzagging flights. The last one, more iron ladder than stairway, was one of those affairs kept raised for the sake of security. It took his weight on it to lower it to street level.

Brenna scrambled after him. If she'd been at all nervous during the descent, she'd been silent about it. He waited until she was clear before he lifted the rusty ladder back into its original position.

Turning around, he surveyed their situation. The light here was weak but just adequate enough to show him they were in an alley with trash bins ranged along the wall outside the back door of the hotel.

Like a wary animal, he raised his head, sniffing the sultry air, listening carefully. There was no sound. The night was quiet. The windows of the hotel rooms above them were dark. If there were other guests in the place, they had neither seen nor heard any signs of them.

Deciding they could advance, he took them to the end of the alley where it joined a street. "From here on," he warned Brenna, "we're going to have to be extra cautious."

"Thought that's what we were being ever since you showed up at the guesthouse," she pointed out.

Casey saw no need to respond to that. In fact, unless necessary, it was better for them not to speak at all. She seemed to understand this, maintaining a silence as he guided them through the maze of deserted, late-night streets in the direction of the waterfront. He could only trust his instinct was reliable about that.

Only once did Brenna break the silence, issuing a little yelp of alarm when something streaked in front of them.

"Relax," he whispered. "It was just a startled cat."

The cat and her reaction to it brought an end to the quiet after that. When they reached the corner, Casey heard the throbbing sound of reggae music. He judged it came from a couple of streets over, probably from an all-night bar.

Something less innocent than a cat and reggae music came out of the night another block on. Proceeding slowly down the street, the flashing blue dome on its roof identifying it, was a police cruiser.

Casey didn't hesitate. "In here," he directed, backing both Brenna and himself into the black shadows of a deep doorway.

He could feel her tension as they huddled there together, the cruiser advancing at a crawl. Casey was fairly certain that, unless one of them moved, they wouldn't be spotted. The doorway was too dark for that.

There was no mistaking Brenna's relief when the cruiser turned a corner and passed out of sight. The rush of her expelled breath told him that.

"Do you think they were looking for us?" she asked.

"Specifically? I doubt it. Probably just on routine patrol."

"But if Marcus does have considerable influence with the island police, they would have been instructed to at least keep an eye out for us."

That Casey didn't doubt.

"You know," she added, "it would have been a whole lot easier to get that water sample to Miami if we could have simply mailed it or sent it to the lab by a package service."

"And how reliable do you think either of those would have been with Bradley in control here?"

"Not very." She sighed, then added a quick "You do have the bottle safe, don't you?"

"It's right here in my bag, well hidden and cushioned against any impact. Let's move. We've still got a lot of ground to cover."

Casey understood that Georgetown was not a large city. But neither was it a small one.

There was something else he understood. Marcus Bradley wouldn't be a billionaire without relying on his considerable intelligence. Okay, he had sent his goons to hunt them down. But, knowing how big Georgetown was, he would have eventually realized there was little chance of finding them, that Brenna and Casey could be hidden anywhere.

Casey had surmised that Bradley would have called off his two men hours ago, at least by the time he and Brenna were locked inside the hotel room. Oh, the risk had still existed, but the element of danger had been slight. Otherwise, Casey would never have allowed Brenna to stand watch while he slept. He had no intention of letting her know that, though. He didn't want her thinking he didn't trust her, because he did.

This was the explanation for why, after that single pursuit this morning, they had not again seen anyone suspicious on the streets, either from the lookout of their room or on their journey on foot tonight. That didn't mean they hadn't still needed to be careful. Their enemy was unpredictable.

There was one thing Casey was certain of. Bradley hadn't given up. He would know that what Casey and Brenna needed was to leave St. Sebastian. He had blocked their escape by air. That left only the water.

Yeah, the cunning bastard was saving his thugs for the harbor. That was where the real threat waited. He and Brenna had a challenge ahead of them. Starting now.

They were nearing the harbor. The humidity in the night air had thickened. Casey could feel it, could smell the salt and the seaweed from the ocean.

He drew Brenna close against him, took care to make sure they hugged the shadows as much as possible.

She must have also sensed they were about to arrive at the waterfront, because when they reached a fork and he started to bear off to the left, she stopped him.

"Not that way. The docks for the sailing vessels and powerboats are along to the right."

"Yeah, I know. All the high-end stuff, which is why we're going in the opposite direction."

"Uh-huh. I'm guessing you're going to tell me just why that is."

"Because the docks to the right are certain to be flooded with security lamps and probably a guard or two patrolling them all night. Whereas the few docks off to the far left…"

"I get it. Where the cheaper stuff is parked and where no self-respecting yacht would ever consider being moored."

And also, Casey hoped, where none of Bradley's thugs

would be waiting for them. Chances were they would think the other area, with its dozens of choices, a more likely target. At least initially, which is why he and Brenna had to act fast.

Casey was right in his choice. What security lights existed here were few and scattered. And two of them, she noticed, were burned out and the bulbs had yet to be replaced. Nor were the docks themselves in the best repair.

No sign of any guards. No sign of anyone at all. He had her watching closely for that as she followed him in his swift tour from powerboat to powerboat.

He had a small flashlight he'd taken out of his bag, its beam narrow but strong. At each craft where he briefly stopped, he shone the beam through the windows at the gauges on the control panels, shielding the glow with his hand, before turning off the light and moving on rapidly to the next dock and the next boat.

"What are you looking for?" Brenna asked him.

"Fuel levels on the gauges."

She understood him without further explanation. "You're searching for a boat that's full."

"I don't want to take a chance of our going empty out there."

"And with no gas pump available here at the docks at this hour…" She trailed off as a thought occurred to her. "You haven't said just what our destination is. Assuming, that is, when you find the boat of your choice, you can get it started."

"The nearest island north of here with an airport and scheduled flights. They're out there, strung like pearls on a necklace. Shouldn't be hard to reach the closest one."

Brenna thought he was overly sure of their success, but

she offered no resistance, simply following him onto the next dock and the next powerboat.

"Ah, this is the one," he announced triumphantly, selecting the first boat they stopped at after checking its fuel gauge.

Brenna knew nothing about boats, but this one looked awfully old to her. It was a wooden craft on a single level, custom-built, she guessed. There was only one cabin, enclosed on all sides.

"Quaint," she remarked.

"Hey, she's a classic. Can you make out her name? *My Last Dollar.* Someone has a sense of humor."

The tide was in, which meant he had to lower himself less than a foot to the open, rear deck. Turning, he helped her aboard.

"But is it seaworthy?" she questioned.

"She's too well kept not to be. Locked, of course," he said, trying the rear door.

She watched him open his bag and take out a small case.

"Do I need to ask what that is?"

"My set of lock picks."

Which was how he'd gotten into the guesthouse.

"Keep a lookout while I go to work here."

A lookout, the man said. That's all she'd been nervously doing since their arrival at the docks. Where were they? she wondered. Marcus's hired thugs? Even though she and Casey had kept out of the light as much as possible, moved stealthily from boat to boat, their voices low, she expected the enemy to find them at any moment.

Brenna was anxious, wanting to get away before that could happen.

"I'm in," Casey said, opening the door. "I'll want you to hold the light here, please."

She hated to leave her watch on the deck. But, realizing he needed her, she joined him in the cabin. The light from outside, even with the windows all around, was so weak she could tell little. The wheel was at the front and what seemed to be lockers were at the sides under the windows.

He passed her the flashlight. "Keep the beam down as much as possible, less chance of its being spotted that way."

"Where do you want me to aim it first?"

"Run it along the floor. There! Stop!"

She had the beam pinned on a metal ring in the floor. "What is it?"

"Hatch for the inboard engine compartment."

Grasping the recessed ring, he lifted the hatch, motioning for her to shine it directly into the compartment.

"Yep, we've got us a four-stroke, powerful enough for our purpose. And here's the tool box over here."

He removed the metal box from the compartment, lifted the lid and examined its contents while she continued to hold the light.

"Plenty of tools but no sign of the spare key I was hoping for."

"That means you'll have to hot-wire it, doesn't it?"

"Afraid so."

"Can you? I mean, do you know how?"

"I've done my share of hot-wiring cars on behalf of the FBI when necessary. I've even hot-wired a couple of powerboats, and providing the system on this one isn't too sophisticated…"

He began to choose the tools he would need: clippers, a sharp knife, a roll of electrical tape.

"Bring the light up to the helm station," he directed her. "Can you get down on your knees and hold it underneath?"

Casey was already flat on his back on the cabin floor and wriggling beneath the control panel.

"Have I got the light low enough?"

"Fine. Just hold it steady."

She could hear him fiddling with the wires, muttering instructions to himself as he worked, cutting and peeling. To Brenna, it all seemed to be taking forever. She wanted to urge Casey to hurry, hurry before they were caught here. She didn't. She knew he was moving as fast as possible.

A moment later he reached for the roll of tape, slicing off a generous piece of it. "Just have to bind these two bare ends together, and then we'll see whether we get a spark from the battery to the ignition. Almost there."

Brenna held her breath. And was rewarded seconds later with the engine rumbling to life.

"That does it," Casey said, sliding out from underneath. "We're in business."

She got to her feet in relief, the flashlight shaking now in her hand as she checked through the windows. Had the sound of the engine alerted anyone? Were their pursuers already racing this way? If so, she could make out no figures.

Behind her Casey was piling the tools back into their box, storing it again in the engine compartment, closing the hatch.

"You can turn off the flashlight now. We have lights on the control panel. Come out on deck and help me cast off."

"Where do you want me?" she asked him when they were in the open.

"I'll go up to the bow and handle the line there. You take the one here in the stern."

When Brenna leaned over the gunnel to free the line from the piling, she discovered a long pole attached to the side of the boat. "Casey, there's a pole here," she called to him.

"It's a boat hook. There's a matching one on the other side. They're used sometimes to hook into a dock or push off from one. We won't need them here."

He must have detached his own line because, with the boat no longer moored, it rocked when she stood up. They were free! Now if only... She didn't finish the thought, saving it for what she hoped would be a prayer of thanks once they reached the open waters.

Back into the cabin they hurried, where Casey mounted himself on the pilot's stool while she resumed her watch at the window.

*Lucky. We are so incredibly lucky. Please, God, let it last, s*he silently pleaded.

She learned why the boat hooks weren't necessary. Narrow though their dock berth was, Casey was so capable easing the throttle into a stern position that they backed out smoothly.

From here, using both wheel and a forward position on the throttle, he turned the bow gently.

"I hate to steal this baby from what has to be her proud owner," he said as they crept away from the docks and across the harbor, all without a challenge. "But if we ever get where we need to go, I'm going to make it my business to see she gets returned to that owner."

Brenna nodded, her attention still fixed not on where they were headed but where they were leaving. No sign whatever of a pursuit. Yes, incredibly lucky.

Minutes later, they cleared the breakwater. Casey opened the throttle to a full position. With a roar, the boat leaped forward, cutting through the open sea. They were in the clear. It was time for that prayer of thanks.

Chapter 13

Casey consulted the gyrocompass to make sure he was bearing north. There was no opportunity to depend on the position of the stars, even had he or Brenna been able to adequately read them. The sky had clouded over, obliterating both stars and any moon that might have risen.

He'd had Brenna check the lockers for maps or charts. She didn't find any. They either hadn't existed on the boat, which was unlikely, or had been removed. He'd have to use the gyro and his sense of direction to get them to another island.

Not the most reliable means. The Caribbean Sea was a large body of water. It would be easy to miss any island at night like this. An inhabited island, of course, would mean lights. They would help.

There was an alternative. He could cut the engine while there was still plenty of fuel, drop anchor and wait for daylight.

He might do that but not yet. He wanted to make certain St. Sebastian was well behind them. They were already in good shape, though. They'd lost the telltale glow of Georgetown some time ago. Just the darkness now on all sides.

His confidence was premature.

Just seconds later, Brenna, who had stationed herself by the windows at the rear of the cabin, called out to him.

"Casey, there's a light behind us!"

"Something up in St. Sebastian's highlands maybe that we missed until now?"

"No, down at our level. Not steady either, like it's moving with the water. I think it's another boat."

"How far back? Can you tell?"

"Not possible. Light's too small. Although…"

"Although what?"

"I think it's growing brighter since I first spotted it. Casey," she reported, her voice lifting in urgency, "I think it's coming after us!"

"All right, don't get alarmed. Could be anybody just happening to be traveling in the same direction. Come on up here and take the wheel while I have a look for myself."

She came, but she wasn't happy about it. "Casey, I've never handled boats."

"Just keep the wheel steady. That's all you have to do. I'll be back before you can miss me."

A couple of minutes out on the open deck were all he needed to convince him that Brenna was right. There was something too deliberate about this boat, not just its being there but coming straight toward them, to be a coincidence.

Casey expressed his frustration in a string of soft but strong curses.

He wasn't going to kid himself about who was chasing after them. Bradley's bastards had finally managed to find them. How wasn't important. What did matter was the escalating brightness of the lights on that other boat, a sure sign it was closing on them.

That meant it was a powerful cruiser, something probably considerably faster than theirs.

He'd left Brenna too long at the helm. He went back inside, closing the cabin door behind him. She turned her head to look at him when he took control of the wheel.

"It's not good, is it?" she said. "I can always tell by how rigid you become."

He wasn't going to lie to her. "We're not going to be able to outrun them, but I'm damned if I'm going to kill the engine and just sit waiting for them. It isn't over until it's over."

Which might, he angrily realized a moment later, be sooner than later.

The glass in one of the rear windows exploded as a bullet tore through it, mercifully missing them, burying itself instead in the wood of the frame that surrounded the control panel.

"Brenna! Flat on the floor! *Now,* and stay there!"

She was down and hugging the floor when a second bullet whistled through the air. Where this one struck Casey didn't know.

"Were you hit?" she cried out. "Tell me you weren't hit!"

"I'm all right. I've got my head and shoulders low." All but his hands, which he kept on the wheel, were out of range.

Hell, the SOBs not only had a high-powered boat, they also had a high-powered rifle. And all he had was a knife. His fear now was there would be a hail of bullets, and one or more of them would strike something vital on their craft and put it out of commission.

Casey waited for that, but it didn't happen. Were those two bullets merely warning shots?

Brenna had the explanation for the failure of more gunfire. He was crouched over so far his vision was no longer on a level with any of the windows. But she must have lifted her head just high enough to get a glimpse of the windshield.

"Casey, it's raining! Raining hard!"

Sonofagun, fortune was smiling on them again. Although the sound of the engine had been too loud for Brenna and him to hear the rain on the roof, it must be thick enough to make it impossible for their enemy to sight them now. That overcast had ended up producing a blessing.

Best to be careful, he told himself when he eased back up on the stool and cautiously reached for the switch that activated the windshield wipers. Brenna was right. It was a heavy downpour. The wipers slashing rapidly across the glass were having a job of it clearing any kind of a view. Not that there was anything to see out there but the blackness.

"Hey, can I get up now?"

"Give it a few more minutes. I want to be sure it's safe."

Managing to lock the wheel into its present position, Casey left the helm and edged around the prone Brenna to the rear of the cabin where he peered through the side of the back window that remained intact.

He was unable to get so much as a weak glimpse of the running lights of the powerboat behind them. The rain was that solid. That being the case, the occupants of the other cruiser wouldn't be able to see them.

Doesn't prevent them from catching up with us, though, if we both maintain this course. In which case...

Casey hurried back to the helm station. He was unlocking the wheel when he heard from Brenna again.

"This floor is getting awfully hard."

"Sorry. You can get up, but hang on. I'm going to change course."

They were running in a northerly direction. He turned their craft east and into an absolute wall of rain. "That should confuse them."

Brenna, standing at his shoulder, observed, "Let's pray we lose them altogether. The question is, are we going to end up losing ourselves out here?"

"Better that than their finding us."

There was little likelihood of this as long as the rain continued, and so far it was falling without letup. No thunder or lightning, however, and scarcely any wind. Not enough, he thought, to make the sea more than a bit choppy, with only an occasional swell their craft cut through with a slight bounce.

Casey lost track of time and distance. He and Brenna didn't speak as they traveled on, maintaining their course with his eye periodically on the gyrocompass. All that changed was the rain. It was finally beginning to lighten.

When it was no longer a tropic drencher but merely a drip, luck failed them again.

"What's that?" Brenna asked sharply, referring to a sudden clunking sound coming from the engine compartment.

Before Casey could answer her—not that he had any clue—the engine sputtered, made a kind of gasping sound and died.

"I guess I don't have to ask what this is," she said. "It's the sound of silence."

She couldn't have put it better, he thought. Or, in this case, worse. Except for the faint slap of the sea against their hull, there was nothing. Not the reassuring rumble of the engine, not the patter of the rain. Nor, thankfully, so much as a distant whisper from the other cruiser anywhere in the area. The enemy had lost them.

And if anybody up there cares at all, it can stay that way.

The cabin was quiet until Brenna finally spoke up again. "Could we be out of gas?"

"The gauge was the first thing I checked, sweetheart. We've still got plenty of fuel."

"Oh." She waited a few seconds before her next question. "Shouldn't you maybe have a look at the engine?"

"I suppose I could do that." Not that it would do much good. Although he had a bit of knowledge on the subject, he was no mechanic. But if it made her feel any better…

Flashlight in hand, Casey left the helm, squatted down beside the engine compartment and raised the hatch. He was silent as he slowly circled the interior of the compartment with the beam of the flashlight, studying what amounted to the guts of the powerboat.

"Spot the problem?"

He looked up to find she had joined him. She knelt on the other side of the open well, a solemn expression on her face. Like a scientist gravely consulting with her colleague on their joint project.

"As a matter of fact, I do." Which surprised the hell out of him. "See this belt over here flopping uselessly?"

"Uh-huh."

"It shredded with wear and finally broke."

"And that's bad?"

"Yeah, it's bad. The belt is part of the water pump that cools the engine. Without the belt, the engine overheats and seizes up."

"And that's what happened?"

"Yes."

"Can you fix it?"

"If I had a replacement belt, I might give it a try. But there are no spares down here, just those cans of oil."

Turning off the flashlight, he lowered the hatch into place, rose to his feet and dusted off his hands. Brenna stood, as well.

"I guess," she said, "it would be stating the obvious to say we're stranded out here."

"Yep." Even the sea wasn't taking them anywhere. He didn't have to view it to know it had to be perfectly flat now. He could feel the absolute calm. There was no movement whatsoever beneath the boat.

"Do you suppose there's a chance of finding flares in any of the lockers?" she wondered. "Wait, though. That's no good. Setting off rocket flares that are seen for miles could—"

He finished the rest for her. "Send the bad guys straight to us."

"Casey, what are we going to do?"

"Wait."

"Until?"

"Daylight. There's bound to be a friendly boat sooner or later, and when they can see us and we can see them, we'll let them know somehow we're in distress and ask for a tow to a safe port." Without a radio on board or the cell phones they had ended up ditching in Georgetown, he realized they had no other choice.

Neither of them mentioned the possibility that the sooner-or-later boat could turn out to be the enemy.

"Guess I'd better put down the anchor," Casey said.

He went to the helm station, but either the motor that lowered the anchor wasn't functioning or the chain was jammed.

Going out on deck, he tried to hand-crank the anchor out. It was stuck fast, and in the dark he wasn't about to attempt any repair.

"No luck?" Brenna asked when he returned to the cabin.

He shook his head. "It doesn't matter, I suppose. In this flat sea, we're not going to drift any distance."

Back to the helm station he went where, except for one low light, he switched off all the power to conserve the battery. She had unfolded a couple of deck chairs in his absence. They settled down on them for what promised to be a long watch

Elbow propped on the arm of his chair, chin resting in the palm of his hand, Casey gazed at Brenna in the gloom. He'd always admired her spirit, but he had never before considered her capacity for courage. He guessed it was about time he did just that.

Yeah, he decided, she qualified for that. She might be worried about their situation. Who wouldn't be? But she wasn't fretting about it. She was doing exactly what a brave person would do—preserving her self-control.

He supposed he should be telling Brenna this, but that kind of thing could lead to a declaration of feelings. *Deep* feelings. And Casey wasn't prepared to go there. Not after she'd given his ring back to him two years ago. He maintained he'd long since overcome her rejection. The truth of it was, however, there were moments when he still felt the sting of that broken engagement.

She might not be a coward, but in that respect he was.

It seemed to Brenna they had been on the run forever. Two days actually, but they had been a very *long* two days. There had been no time for the expression of any personal emotions. Not even when they'd made love. Not really.

This, though, was a quiet interlude made for emotions. At least for her. But Brenna suspected Casey wouldn't welcome any introduction of the subject.

There was, however, one thing she'd been wanting to know almost from the moment he'd arrived on St. Sebastian. This seemed as good a time as any to approach it. Casey might not appreciate discussing it. If he refused… well, she would simply tell him she understood and let it go at that.

"Casey?"

"Mmm?"

"You've never explained your suspension to me. When I heard about it, I asked Will, but he didn't know."

"Yeah, the bureau has managed to keep a tight lid on it. They're good about achieving that kind of thing. When they've finished the investigation to their satisfaction and made decisions, they'll release a statement to the media, but until then…"

"I'm not the media."

"Meaning you're asking me to tell you."

"Even though we're no longer engaged, I still care about you, Casey. Naturally, I'd like to know."

He hesitated so long she thought he wasn't going to tell her.

"It isn't a pretty tale, Brenna," he warned her.

"I'd still like to hear it."

"All right, you insisted, so here it is."

Leaning forward in his chair, he told her the story in a deep monotone. A deliberate tactic she suspected in order to spare both himself and her unbearable emotions.

"Two other agents and I were sent from Chicago to another Midwestern city. The teenage daughter of a federal judge had been kidnapped by brothers demanding their terrorist father be released from prison. Negotiations to free the girl had broken down. That's when the judge demanded the assistance of the FBI. They knew by the time the three of us arrived where the daughter was being held."

Brenna noticed he was careful to avoid mentioning location and names, as well as any particular details. She respected that, permitting him to continue his concise account without asking questions.

"It was decided by people who should have known better that the only way to rescue the girl was for the three of us to break in there, weapons drawn while the two brothers were kept distracted. The result was a shootout, leaving both brothers dead and one of us agents wounded."

This time Brenna couldn't resist a brief "The judge's daughter?"

"Safe in a locked bedroom. When the other agent and I managed to get in there, we found her bound, gagged and blindfolded on a chair. What we didn't expect, what no one knew was that she wasn't alone. There was a kid in there with her sitting on the bed, a boy who couldn't have been more than ten."

Casey paused there, clearly reluctant to go on. *Something terrible is coming,* Brenna thought. *I should stop him from telling the rest.* But before she could do that, he finished in a rush. There was no monotone this time.

"Would you believe this kid, this child, had a gun hidden down at his side? We didn't see it. Didn't know a boy that young we assumed was another kidnapped victim could act so fast, be so accurate. Whipped out the gun and shot the girl in the chest. Turns out he was the son of one of the kidnappers. Now you know why I'm on suspension. Mental distress, the whole thing."

Brenna could manage nothing more than a stunned "Dear God." That and the fierce wish she'd never asked Casey to explain his suspension.

Even in this weak light she could see the anguish in his eyes. The blame he must be suffering at times like this for the death of the judge's teenage daughter. But how could he and the agent who'd been with him in that room have possibly anticipated such a swift, shocking outcome?

Brenna longed to go to him, put her arms around him, hold him in comfort for as long as he needed. But she knew him too well to try that.

This wasn't the first time she'd listened to him tell her, and always in a vague way, about assignments that hadn't gone well. Nothing as horrific as this one, but a few of them bad enough.

He'd always been ready for her to lend a sympathetic ear, but beyond that he was never willing for her to go. A masculine pride? She never knew, and she never trusted herself to ask. Those were the days when she began to fear for his safety in the field, not long after her father died and she started to question the wisdom of marrying Casey.

The two of them sat on in a long silence, neither of them stirring from their deck chairs. Brenna still wanted to do something for him that would demonstrate she cared. Something ordinary but thoughtful. That's when she remembered what she had noticed in one of the lockers when she had been checking through them earlier.

Getting to her feet, she crossed the cabin, crouched down and opened one of the locker doors. When she returned to where Casey was still seated, she bore a plastic bottle in either hand.

"What have you got there?" he questioned her. "Is that water?"

"Are you thirsty? I'm afraid it isn't cold."

She held one of the bottles out to him. He didn't hesitate to take it from her.

"Who cares, as long as it's wet. I'm dry as dust."

He had the bottle open, tipped back and was gulping from it while Brenna was still in the act of twisting the cap off her own bottle. She didn't get there. Not then. Not when she was suddenly distracted.

"Do you feel that?"

He lowered the bottle from his mouth. "What?"

"We're moving."

Brenna supposed she had sensed it first because she'd remained standing. But it took Casey only a few seconds to feel it, as well. "Damn if we aren't."

"We're picking up speed, too. What's happening?"

Casey was on his feet now and headed for the stern deck. She followed him out of the cabin and to the rail. Together they peered over the side.

"I don't see a friendly dolphin down there pulling us along," Brenna said, "but whatever it is we're getting a smooth ride out of it."

"You wouldn't see it, not even in daylight, unless you were very observant and knew the signs to look for."

"All right, since you're so smart, explain it."

"It can only be one thing," he said. "A current has picked us up. A very strong current."

"Carrying us in what direction? Can you tell?"

"Let's have the gyro answer that."

They went back inside, moving up to the helm station to consult the compass.

"Looks like we're headed northeast this time," Casey said.

And that, Brenna knew, could be very bad if this powerful current drove them out into the open Atlantic. Without an engine they would be helpless in ocean waters a boat like this wasn't constructed for.

They were both too restless to return to their chairs. Carrying their bottles of water with them, they went back onto the deck. They could better monitor the current out here.

This they had to judge by feeling the rate of the boat's velocity since measuring it by sight was out of the question. Or was it? Brenna wondered.

It began to seem to her after a bit that the night wasn't quite so black anymore. Imagination or reality? Stretching her head back, she scanned the sky overhead, searching it from horizon to horizon. There! A single star winked at her off to one side.

"Casey, look! I think the cloud cover is breaking up! No, not that direction. Over this way," she corrected him, pointing with her bottle.

That lone star had been joined now by another. As they continued to watch, sipping occasionally from their water bottles, rarely talking, more and more stars emerged until eventually the sky was clear of any overcast.

The stars were so brilliant, so numerous they provided a surprising illumination. Or was it the result of having had virtually no light before this except the little in the cabin, and so by contrast…

Casey must have been reading her mind, because he weighed in on it. "The night skies in the tropics away from the glow of towns and cities are like this, especially out at sea."

He would know, having had so many assignments in different climate zones.

They continued to stand at the deck rail, able now to distinguish the waters if not the current itself but continuing to feel its effect on the boat.

It was Brenna again sometime later who first sighted what lay directly ahead of them, and didn't know whether to welcome it or be alarmed by it. Either way, it was excitement that impelled her to clutch Casey's arm.

"Do you see what I see?" she said, referring to the sizable black mass that had suddenly loomed in front of them, seemingly out of nowhere.

"Both see it and hear it. Those are swells breaking on a shore, and if they're rocks and not sand we're going to be driven onto them."

Chapter 14

It was the current that saved them from disaster. As mercurial in its moods as a living being, in one moment it held them tightly in its control and in the next moment, as though bored playing with them, it threw them away.

Although cast now into friendlier waters off to the right, they continued to drift slowly but inexorably toward the land.

"Rocks or sand?" Brenna asked, trying to make out this section of the shore they would land on.

This time Casey's vision triumphed over hers. "Neither. Unless my eyes are playing tricks on me, that's some kind of channel ahead of us. A *narrow* channel."

Brenna could see it now, too. An inlet leading to... well, who knew what. "Is this going to be good or bad?"

"I'm making myself think good. It looks like we're definitely going to be sucked into the mouth, but if we should get hung up... Brenna, the poles! You grab the one on this side and I'll take the other! If it's necessary, we can use them to lever our way through."

For a few seconds she didn't know what he was talking about. And then she remembered. He was referring to the poles attached to the gunwales that were sometimes used to hook onto docks.

Leaning over the rail, Brenna took hold of the pole assigned to her. By the time she'd worked it free of whatever had it locked in place, the bow of the boat was already nosing its way into the opening.

"If you have to use it," Casey called to her from his side of the boat, "make sure you shove with the blunt end. You try with the hook end it'll just break off."

"Aye, aye, Captain Bossy." She didn't know whether what she heard in response was a laugh or a snort. Best not to ask.

It was a snug fit but not so tight that, if they'd had the engine, a good pilot like Casey couldn't have squeezed through the passage without contact. As it was, the boat, with no control, kept bumping and scraping, first on one rocky side and then the other.

The two of them were kept busy chasing from starboard to port with their poles and back again, helping each other to keep their craft free and moving. It was only in one place where the inlet turned, threatening to wedge them behind an outcropping, that it was necessary for both of them to exert considerable force digging and pushing to swing the bow back on course.

Once past that obstacle, they floated without further resistance into what they could tell by the starlight seemed to be a small, natural lagoon. There the boat came to rest. And so did Brenna, dropping her pole with exhaustion onto the deck.

Casey rid himself of his own pole, but he wasn't ready

to rest. There was a strong-looking tree that extended it-self from the bank over the tip of the bow. Going forward, he picked up the end of the bow's curled up mooring rope.

Brenna was just able to make out his form as he used the rope to lash them to the tree. A wise action to prevent them from getting caught by some other undertow that might tug them out to sea again.

When he returned, she had a question for him. "Are you laying any bets on just where we are?"

"You're funny."

"Meaning you have no more of a clue than I do. I don't suppose we can ask the natives."

"Could if there were any, but I don't see any signs of habitation. Like lights. Lights would be nice. How about you?"

She shook her head.

"Guess we'll just have to wait until daylight to know anything for certain."

"Casey," she said, getting serious, "when I knew back in Chicago that I was coming to the West Indies, I tried to educate myself. I read a lot and looked at maps, and one thing I learned was there are a gazillion islands in the Caribbean."

"Where are you going with this?"

"Just that a lot of them are populated, but even more of them are too small to have ever been inhabited. Not just small either but sometimes so remote they hardly ever get visited. What if we've landed on one of those islands? What if we're stranded here for weeks, even months, and without any supplies…"

He groaned. "You *would* mention food."

"I didn't. Not specifically. But I imagine there would be fish in the waters here and maybe edible plants. Why? Are you hungry?"

"Hollow after our workout with the boat hooks. It feels like forever since dinner was delivered to us at the hotel. I don't suppose you spotted something to eat in one of the cabin lockers."

"Just the bottles of water. If you're starving, though, I can oblige you."

"You telling me you've got food?"

"Follow me."

She led the way back inside, where the light was sufficient enough for her to find her way to her pair of totes. She crouched down beside them, digging through the contents of the nearest tote.

"What have you got in there?" he demanded with that boyish enthusiasm she never failed to appreciate. "What is it?"

"Now don't get excited. It's just bread left over from our dinner. I didn't want to throw it away, so I wrapped it up and stuck it down in the tote."

"Just bread, she says. Woman, right now that's a meal."

Brenna got to her feet with what was probably half of the loaf Tonya had sent to them. She expected Casey to grab it from her. He grabbed her instead. Or her face, anyway, framing it between both hands and leaning in to kiss her briefly but gratefully.

"Rembrandt," he said, "you keep getting better and better."

"Are you referring to my art or my food service?"

"Actually, I was thinking more along the lines of your mouth. But the food service is good, too."

He took the bread from her, tearing the piece in half and handing the rest back to her. They settled in their deck chairs, alternately eating and drinking from their bottles.

Halfway through her share of the bread, Brenna found herself yawning. How many hours had it been since she'd last slept? Or, for that matter, since she'd been relaxed enough to acknowledge to herself she was tired?

Finishing the last of his bread, Casey got up from his chair without a word and began to forage through the lockers.

"What on earth are you looking for?"

"This," he said, holding up a folded blanket. "Thought I came across one earlier. Actually, there are a couple more in here."

He hauled out the others. She watched him as he squatted down, spread one of the blankets out on the floor and folded it over lengthwise to make a double thickness.

"Best I can do in the absence of a mattress. It should soften the hardness of the floor. Come on, stretch out here and let me cover you with one of the other blankets."

"Casey, I don't—"

"No arguing. That yawn either meant my company is beginning to bore you, which I'd like to think isn't the problem, or you need a nap. We could both use one. After I tuck you in, I'll tangle myself up in this last blanket and get comfy next to you. How does that sound?"

"Like heaven," she said, although she wasn't sure she should have admitted as much despite whatever wild sex they had engaged in back at the hotel.

She was too sleepy, however, to let herself think about it. Restoring the wrapping on what was left of the bread to keep it from getting stale, she left it on her chair and placed herself on his makeshift bed.

Making good on his promise, he covered her with the second blanket, tucking it in on all sides. Brenna found it a touching action. Wrapping himself in the last blanket like a cocoon, he settled down close beside her.

Was that a kiss he planted on her neck? She wasn't sure. By then, she was already drifting off.

* * *

Brenna awakened to—well, she didn't know. It sounded like water splashing. Were they sinking?

Propping herself up on her elbows, she looked toward the stern deck. The door had been left open. The sound was coming from outside in the lagoon. Casey was no longer at her side. And something else. He had turned off the dim wall lamp in the cabin. It was no longer needed.

She could see through the windows a faint, gray light in the sky. The first sign of daybreak.

Combing the fingers of one hand through her hair, which had to be a mess, she threw the blanket aside, scrambled to her feet and went in search of Casey. He was nowhere on deck, but his clothes were, discarded in a heap.

"Where are you?" she called.

No answer. Her gaze went out over the lagoon, where the light was strengthening. Unable to see him, she hoped she had no cause for concern. She didn't.

The breath left her lungs in relief when a head suddenly bobbed to the surface out in the center.

"You scared the crap out of me!"

He laughed, arms and legs paddling slowly to keep himself afloat and facing her. The splash she'd heard must have occurred when he'd leaped into the water.

"Come on in and join me," he invited her. "It's as good as a warm bath, and frankly I was overdue for one."

She leaned out over the rail. "Since every article of your clothing is accounted for up here on deck," she said dryly, "I'm assuming you're wearing a bathing suit. One you happened to notice in the locker where you found the blankets."

"Wanna find out?"

"Please."

He swung around and struck out for the rocky edge of

the lagoon with powerful strokes. Reaching an enormous black boulder, he pulled himself up out of the water, upper arm muscles bulging.

That was a sight that was instantly trumped when, emerging from the sea like a primeval water god, he stood erect on the boulder's flat surface, his magnificently sculpted body streaming water.

Brenna decided she needed back every bit of the breath she had expelled.

"Satisfied?" he asked.

"Impressive."

He was not, of course, wearing a bathing suit.

"You ready to get nude and join me?"

"Think I'll just watch."

"There was a time when you weren't so modest and didn't mind parading around with me outdoors in the buff."

"We were engaged then."

"Ah, no. Even before that when we were first dating."

Oh, what the hell, she thought. She could use a bath herself, and if it meant stripping while he watched…well, it wouldn't be the first time.

"Stop smiling like the cat who swallowed the canary," she cautioned him as she added her shoes and clothing to the pile on the deck.

"And here I thought it was a lecherous leer. Ready?"

He didn't wait for an answer. Not that one was necessary since she was as naked as she could get. Launching himself from the boulder, Casey executed a neat dive back into the lagoon. Brenna didn't attempt anything that fancy, instead climbing over the rail and lowering herself by safe degrees into the water. He was right. It was beautifully tepid. She sighed with pleasure as she swam out into the center where he'd surfaced and was waiting for her.

"Everything but a bar of soap and a bottle of shampoo," she said, using her arms like slow wings to keep herself suspended.

"Sorry the management can't provide them."

He began paddling in circles around her.

"What are you doing?"

"Trying to admire you from all angles. Hold still."

He was in another mode now, a frisky seal playing with her. Then he was no longer there. He'd disappeared beneath the surface again. Where was he? She wasn't sure. Something brushed the back of her leg and was gone. A fish or Casey? She turned as rapidly as the water let her, but he was too fast for her. He was already behind her again, this time lightly pinching her buttocks.

Unmistakably, not a fish.

He startled her when he popped up directly in front of her.

So close in fact their noses almost touched. "Those contacts do anything for you?" he wondered.

"Like what?"

"I don't know. Get you all hot and bothered maybe?"

"Oh, was that you down there? And here I thought it was a shark."

He put his wet mouth against her ear. "They can be dangerous," he informed her gravely. "Savage."

"That's what I hear. Anything else I should know?"

"One thing."

"What?"

He lowered his voice to a whisper. "You don't have to wear yourself out staying afloat. You can put your legs down anytime and stand. Try it and see."

He was right. She found her feet touching a sandy bottom while her head and shoulders remained above water. The lagoon wasn't that deep.

"Gotta caution you, though. There's a bit of an undertow here. You should brace yourself with your legs apart to keep yourself from getting knocked off your feet."

She didn't trust his advice, but she was willing to obey it to learn what he was up to. "Like this?"

"Perfect." With that pronouncement, he jackknifed under the water, his legs flying up behind him like a dolphin flipping its tail.

The next thing Brenna knew he was gliding between her legs, out and around and back in again. This time, though, something fastened on her mound at the juncture of her thighs. His fingers? Or was it actually his mouth?

Whichever it was, he managed a sensation so enticing she felt as if that phantom undertow he had warned her of was about to knock her off her feet. That would have happened, too, if he'd been able to hold his breath a little longer.

When he came up for air, again in front of her, she challenged him with a weak "What are you doing to me?"

"Not enough, that's for sure. Not nearly enough."

She knew from experience that Casey had a talent for making a woman believe she was the most desirable female he'd ever encountered. Not by telling her but by showing her with his gifted mouth and hands. He did that now by claiming her mouth with his own. Owning it with a kiss so molten she would have sunk if his arms hadn't gathered her up tight against him. The man was incredible, destroying all feminine resistance. Hers, anyway.

When his marauding tongue finally withdrew from her mouth, he rasped a concerned "I think I'd better get you on land before we drown out here."

Turning over on his back, his arms cradled her to his chest. His strong legs pumping, becoming a pair of scissors, he towed her through the water to another boulder.

Its surface was also flat, but the water was so shallow here he was able to easily lift her out of it.

Brenna found herself seated on the edge of the boulder, feet dangling in the water, Casey facing her from where he stood up to his thighs. He was close. *Conveniently* close, she decided.

"You're safe now."

She hadn't been in danger out in the middle of the lagoon, and he knew that. But she could be in danger here, she thought, eyeing the growing erection aimed in her direction like a heat-seeking missile.

"Sun's coming up," she observed.

"So am I."

"Yes, I can see that."

He leaned into her, supporting himself with his fists planted on the rock on either side of her. His green eyes glittered in the rising sun.

"Know what?" he said.

"I'm not even going to guess."

"Your breasts want to be touched."

"You're sure of that, are you?"

He nodded slowly. "But since my hands are busy holding me up, I'll have to send in a substitute. How's this?"

She had no complaints when, with lowered head, his mouth kissed her nipples in turn, sucking on them so strongly she squirmed in unbearable pleasure.

"Oh, the things you do to me, sweetheart," he muttered roughly between licking and lapping.

The things *she* did to *him?* Somebody was reversing something here. She was the one getting all the attention.

"Am I going to survive this?" she moaned.

"Let's see."

His mouth transferred to her mouth for another lingering kiss. She could feel down below the tip of his arousal thrusting at her, demanding her attention. She gave it to him, her hand slipping between them to close around that hot length, squeezing it, pumping it.

He pulled back with a groan from both her mouth and her hand. "Too soon, too soon. I want both of us ready for this."

Having straightened up, he no longer needed his fists to support himself. That left one of his hands free to travel to the portal between her thighs where he located the bud inside. He began to stroke and rub it, slowly at first and then with increasing speed.

Brenna could feel the pressure building. Apparently, Casey sensed it, too. He went at it in a lusty urgency until she cried out his name as he tipped her over the edge. The release came in a series of wild, blinding spasms.

"Now," he murmured. "Now we're ready."

Then, no longer able to restrain himself, he offered her his erection. She accepted it, feeling its heat, as she guided it to her willing, waiting opening.

It was as far as she went. As far as she had to go. Casey was in control from here, proving his capability as he eased into her yearning wetness. He didn't rest until his length was fully inside her.

Seated as she was on the boulder, Brenna found it necessary to steady herself by gripping his shoulders, her fingers digging into his hard muscles. He voiced his approval when her legs clamped around his tight buttocks.

"That's right, baby. That's real good. Just relax now and let me do the work."

Oh, yes, it was good. Good then and even better, *much* better, as he drove into her with slow, measured strokes. But relax? That was impossible when, through her haze of passion, she strained to hear his whispered endearments, attempted to return them with her own.

They were on this raging ride together, laboring for the climax that came too soon. His own orgasm swiftly followed her own. Spent, he rested his head against her breasts while she caressed the stubble on his cheek. It was an aftermath she treasured, but it was all too brief.

She understood his action when he straightened away from her. They couldn't linger in this state, not with a threat that might still be out there.

"You ready to swim back to the boat?" he asked her.

Before telling him she was, she took one last look at him standing there in the water. The sun was above the horizon now, its slanting rays bronzing that superb body that had given her so much joy.

It was a sight that brought a lump to her throat.

"No breakfast," Casey lamented after they dried themselves and dressed.

"I saved the last of the bread," Brenna informed him, "but it's probably stale by now."

"Stale or not, it's food."

"How's our water holding out? Did you happen to check?"

"Still some bottles left."

After that cherished interlude they'd shared in the lagoon, she hated to think about the hard reality of survival. But if they didn't find sources of food and water in this place, they would soon be in trouble. For the moment, however, they had the bread and the bottled water.

The sun was so pleasant they dragged the chairs out on the stern deck. They were silent as they sat there eating and drinking. Brenna still had that lump in her throat, but the reason for it had changed from happy to sad.

Sad because she was no longer uncertain of her feelings

for Casey. Back at the hotel she had worried she might be falling in love with him again. Now she knew she *was* in love with him. It didn't matter whether, broken engagement or not, she had never stopped loving him, only deceived herself she had, or whether this was a new love.

Either way, it had *hurt* written all over it. How could it not when, struggled though she had, she still hadn't managed to overcome the lesson of her mother. Because the terrible memory of how her mother had suffered when Brenna's father died in that blaze remained fresh. As did the recollection of how in the months that followed the life slowly went out of her.

Brenna had experienced that same desperation when Casey had been captured and held in the Mideast. New love or old, she refused to repeat those fears for his safety.

This was foolish. She had no indication her love was anything but one-sided, something she had to deal with on her own. Intimate though they had been back at the hotel and here in the lagoon, Casey had said nothing about his feelings for her.

The closest he'd come to anything like that was telling her in their hotel room, "I've missed us like this."

Meaning what? The sex they'd shared? And if that was all...

"What are you thinking?" he asked her now.

She started, realizing he was smiling at her. It was not a happy smile but one that she thought carried a kind of somber regret. She wanted to ask him about it but decided it was better to just let it go.

Instead, she lied. "Still wondering where we are. Daylight doesn't help any, does it?"

"Well, it tells us what the land looks like anyway."

Brenna had already observed it was not flat. The terrain rose abruptly from the shore, climbing toward the summit of what could be defined as either a high hill or a low mountain. It was hard to tell since it was entirely covered in vegetation. There was no sign of anything resembling a building, no sound but the calls of the sea birds. It seemed they were alone here.

A breeze blew across the deck. Brenna shivered. The moving air wasn't responsible. The breeze was mild. It was the sudden absence of the warm, cheerful sun. She looked up at the sky to see clouds gathering. It would soon be entirely overcast again.

"I think it's time," Casey said, "that we go exploring. We need to learn more about this place, try to find food and water."

"I agree, but those approaching clouds look like rain. We could end up trekking through mud with the only clothes we have soaked."

He eyed the sky. "I don't think they indicate anything serious. Nothing like a downpour, probably just a drizzle. As for staying dry…"

He got to his feet, motioning for her to follow him inside. *What now?* she wondered, watching him squat on his heels and open one of the locker doors.

"I noticed this stuffed in here when I found the blankets."

"What is it?"

She couldn't tell, not then when he withdrew it or when he stood, shaking it out for her inspection. Whatever it was, it looked like it was plastic-coated. It also looked a bit dingy.

"It's a rain poncho, hood and all. Okay, maybe a bit worse for wear, but it should keep you dry."

"What are you wearing? Is there another poncho hiding in there?"

"Just the one. But I've got my own rain gear with me."

Opening his bag, which he'd dumped into a corner when they'd first boarded *My Last Dollar,* he produced a lightweight, thin nylon jacket with an attached hood. Brenna assumed the garment had been waterproofed.

She looked from the jacket to the poncho. Although she said nothing, he had to know what she was thinking.

"Look, I'd trade, but the poncho is too small for me, and you'd be swimming in the jacket."

"Please, it's all right," she assured him in her best martyr's tone, the one that had never failed to elicit a grin from him when they were together back in Chicago. She earned one now.

Outfitted in protective poncho and jacket, with the precious water sample Casey wouldn't risk leaving behind tucked in a zippered pocket and the toolbox knife strapped to his leg, they left the boat for the shore.

The drizzle that Casey had predicted was falling when they picked up a narrow trail that ascended the hillside.

"This beats struggling through the jungle," he said.

"What do you think?" she said. "An animal trail, or something cut by human hands?"

Casey had no opinion on the subject. His only interest was in fresh water, and that was answered by a clear brook tumbling toward the sea. As for food, banana plants were plentiful, and coconut palms rimmed the shore. These could be supplemented by catching fish.

Although Brenna was grateful for the presence of these needs, her enthusiasm lay in another direction.

This forest is a botanist's dream, she thought.

She could recognize only a fraction of the plants whose sprawling growth was so luxuriant on either side of the trail. Philodendron vines clinging to the trunks of trees, moss and waist-high ferns and, of course, flowers everywhere. Many she knew; others were nameless.

All of it made an impression on the senses, but the rain pattering on the forest created a special mood. It polished the broad leaves, emphasizing their glossiness. Deepened the perfume of blossoms like frangipani. Heightened the colors of hibiscus and anthurium. Even the wet earth itself had its own pleasing scent.

It was, in Brenna's estimation, an unspoiled paradise.

They clambered on up the trail, trading few comments, saving their breath for the climb. Halfway up the mountain, they emerged onto a level, natural terrace.

The terrace was clear of all growth, but it was not empty.

To their surprise, the center of it was occupied by the remains of a crude, open-sided shelter constructed of a framework of bamboo poles and a roof of palm leaf thatch that had fallen in on one side. If there had once been walls woven from the same material, they were long gone.

Brenna gazed in wonder at the skeleton.

"Casey," she said slowly, her voice as soft as the rain, "I *know* this place."

Chapter 15

Casey turned to stare at her. "Are you saying you've been here before?"

"Not in person, no, but in memory."

"That doesn't make sense either."

"It does, if you know I read about it in my St. Sebastian guidebook."

"You telling me we're back on St. Sebastian?"

"Of course not. But the island—and that's what this is—was recommended as a place to visit, if you had the time and access to a boat. The article was written by a naturalist. I think his name was David Yates. He built the shelter here for himself and spent weeks on the island— Maroa, I think it's called—observing the unique fauna and flora."

"What else do you remember?"

"That the island is a couple of hundred acres in area and that the article described a place of anchorage for a small craft only. I think that's got to be our lagoon." She swung away from him to look at the heights still above them. "I would love to come back here one day and paint this wild place."

"You might want to rethink that."

"That's a funny thing to say. Why would I want to do that?"

"Because before the day is over, it's very possible you won't have such pleasant feelings about the island."

There was such a severe tone in his words that she turned back to face him. "What are you trying to tell me, Casey?"

"Just that apparently you weren't the only one who read that article and learned about the lagoon."

His face wore the same severity as he looked back the way they had come. Not just back and down but out as well. "You see it?" he asked her.

Brenna followed the direction of his extended arm pointing seaward, discovering then what he indicated. The sight had her heart sliding in the direction of her stomach.

Cutting through the water was a powerful cruiser rapidly approaching the island. Not just randomly either. The craft was headed directly toward the mouth of the lagoon. There were at least three people on board. Two of them, males, stood on the bow deck. That meant a third had to be inside at the controls.

Even at this distance, Brenna could identify the blond of their burly nemesis. The second, darker one had a pair of binoculars trained on the lagoon, which meant he hadn't missed the presence of their boat.

"They've found us," she said flatly.

"Probably been checking out other islands in the area before tackling this one."

They had been deluding themselves, thinking they were

safe here. Or at least Brenna had allowed herself to believe it. Even in their carefree moments, Agent Casey McBride wouldn't have abandoned his realistic conviction that the enemy wouldn't give up.

"Maybe they won't be able to anchor," she said, clinging to hope. "We had a heck of a time squeezing through the channel, and our boat is smaller than theirs."

"The tide was out then, the water a lot lower than it is now. They'll make it through into the lagoon all right."

"Casey, what are we going to do?"

"Get the hell out of this clearing before they point those binocs up this way and spot us."

"Do we go down or up?"

"Up, I think. If we go down, we could run into them on the trail. All I know for sure is we have to stay ahead of them. If we can evade them long enough, we stand a chance of locating a good place to hide ourselves. It's all we can do."

She knew what he was thinking. She was thinking it, too.

Their pursuers were armed. There was no forgetting this after last night. And she and Casey had no weapon, except his knife.

Not much use against three men and their guns.

"So we run."

"Yeah, we run, but first…"

She watched him unzip the pocket in his jacket and remove the small, sealed bottle of water.

"I don't want to risk having this on me any longer. It's better if it's hidden."

Brenna understood how vital it was to Casey to safeguard what had been entrusted to him. And how determined Marcus Bradley must be to get his hands on that water sample and destroy it before it could be tested. One of the spies he had everywhere on St. Sebastian would have learned what Zena King had planned and how she had managed to arrange for the sample to be passed to Casey.

Marcus was too clever after hearing this information not to have had the well immediately shut down or, more likely, had its supply altered to an innocent state. The sample Casey had in his possession, the only one in existence, was dangerous to the billionaire. Because even if the well was now neutralized, its content had damaged Freedom's women, and the sample could prove that. Marcus had to prevent it from reaching the Miami lab. His hired thugs were the solution. She had no doubt who they were. She had glimpsed the two dark-haired ones around the villa, so it was only logical to assume they worked for Marcus.

Not the blond one, but because he was one of the trio it made sense to believe he was one of Marcus's thugs.

Brenna watched Casey as he searched for a place to conceal the bottle. He finally settled on a break in the shelter's framework.

One of the upper bamboo crosspieces had tugged out of the socket in the upright that supported it. Casey squeezed the small bottle into the hollow end of the crosspiece, jamming it back into the socket, then tightening the connection with his fist, pounding the upright on its opposite side.

"That ought to do it."

Brenna was suddenly aware the rain had stopped. Looking around, she saw mist rising from the jungle, heard the repeated calls of birds answering one another as they flashed from tree to tree, their plumage brilliant.

She hated that this incredibly beautiful island was about to be violated by Marcus Bradley's goons.

"Come on, Brenna," Casey urged, "we need to be gone before they pick up the trail."

"And our footprints. There was no way we could avoid leaving them in all that mud."

"We'll have to try to do better this time. I don't see any signs of a path leading from here to the top of the island, do you?"

Brenna shook her head. "It looks like one was never worn or cut through."

"Then we do without."

She found the expression, "Easier said than done," never more true in the struggle that followed. Casey led the way, weaving through thickets of bamboo, wading through palmettos, thrashing through curtains of vines while she kept close behind him, feeling guilty because he was doing the major work of forging a route for them.

The only advantage of all this dense vegetation was the dead, fallen leaves and fronds that so thickly littered the forest floor, making it less likely they were leaving noticeable footprints in the damp earth.

What progress they made was hampered at times by walls of impenetrable growth that forced them to detour left or right, searching for a way around or through the barriers. It was a slow advance but always up, steadily up. And all the while Brenna wondered where they were. How far, how close?

She and Casey didn't discuss this concern. There was nothing to be gained from that. All they could do was climb and keep on climbing.

Her leg muscles ached, her breath grew shallower.

Would they never reach the summit?

Light years seemed to pass before Casey announced, "We're there!"

She didn't need him telling her this. Nor, although the growth had thinned considerably, did she need to see it.

The terrain had leveled off, which meant she could *feel* underfoot they had crested the mountain top.

Brenna started to say something, but he put a hand on her arm, silencing her. "You hear anything behind us?"

They both listened. She shook her head. "Nothing. I don't even hear the birds now."

"Me either. That means they're not close yet. We still have time. Have you caught your breath yet?"

She nodded, keeping to herself how tired she was after their tough climb. She knew, however, from the way he looked at her that he sensed it. She also realized they had yet to find any safe place to hide, and he was still hoping for this.

"Let's go," she insisted.

They moved forward. Within yards, they left the last of the growth behind them. They had reached a flat, clear zone, but that didn't last. A matter of less than a hundred yards more brought them to the sloping edge of a wide, deep basin.

Brenna found herself looking down into a circular bowl whose bottom was entirely covered by a mass of lush vegetation.

Casey close beside her was puzzled by the abrupt changes in the terrain. "What's this all about?"

"I think I have the explanation. We're standing on the rim of the volcano that long ago created this island. And that down there—"

"—is the ancient crater," he finished for her, understanding the differences now.

"Casey, the crater could offer us the perfect hiding place. Look how thick the growth is down there. The crater sides aren't steep. We could scramble down there in seconds and lose ourselves in all that stuff."

He didn't hesitate to veto her plan. "It's a trap. If all

three of them come after us with rifles, and figure out we're down there, which eventually they would, all they'd have to do is spread out along the rim, come after us from different sides and close in on us."

She appreciated his objection. "Yes, but if we stay up here on the open rim…"

"Yeah, we're not going to do that. We're going to follow the rim around to the other side and head down the opposite side of the mountain. And we're going to try to do that before we end up being targets."

She fell into step beside him, asking herself whether she had enough energy left to go on the run again so soon, even if this time it was down instead of up. She didn't worry Casey with this, however, as they followed the rim with as much speed as he must have thought her capable of at this point.

When they reached the other side, it offered them a clear view across the crater to the place where they had started. They had left the spot empty behind them. It was no longer empty. The well-armed hunters had arrived. One of the three men shouted something, gesturing excitedly in the direction of Brenna and Casey.

"We've been found, Rembrandt. Time to disappear."

Side by side, with Casey holding her hand, they fled from the rim, hurrying down the slope that descended the mountain. There was no time to search for any rabbit hole to a lava tube.

Unlike the heavily forested route they had traveled on their ascent, this side of the mountain, except for sparse growth, was practically barren. The windward and leeward sides of the island, Brenna thought. One wet, the other dry. That meant there was no place for them to take cover. All they could do was try to keep ahead of their pursuers.

Both she and Casey kept checking behind them. As of yet, the trio was not in sight. It was perhaps this vigilant action that made them unaware of what lay ahead of them.

Without warning, the land suddenly dipped into a hollow. No time to detour around it. They plunged down into the depression, raced across its narrow floor and up the other side.

Casey stopped when they reached the ridge. "Go on," he urged her.

She knew what he was doing. They were vulnerable here after losing vital moments in the hollow. He was placing himself between her and the enemy. Risking himself to protect her, damn him.

She opened her mouth to oppose his intention, but he would have none of it. "We don't have time for this. I'll catch up with you. Just go!"

She went, tearing down the long slope in front of her. There was grass here. Some of the rain must have reached this side of the island, because the grass was wet with it. It was then she made the mistake of looking over her shoulder for Casey.

Losing her footing on the slick grass, she went down on her stomach. Before she could pick herself up, she was sliding down the incline like a sled on snow.

When she managed to finally stop herself, Brenna found her head hanging over the sharp edge of a precipice and looking down into the sea far, far below her. The situation had her in a state of shock.

Brenna hadn't permitted herself to feel any intense fear during their long flight. There had been neither time nor energy for it. But now she knew a genuine terror.

Her natural response was to push herself away from the dangerous edge. Only that didn't work. Her hands had ended up trapped under her own weight. Trying to free them resulted in both hands and arms getting caught up in the folds of the poncho.

She was near panic when a voice above her commanded, "Stop fighting it. You're making it worse."

Casey! Thank God he had arrived on the scene.

"Here, let me help you."

She felt his strong hands on her ankles, dragging her away from the edge just far enough to safely turn her over on her back.

"You really did it this time, Rembrandt. Got yourself so tangled up in that damn poncho it's going to take my knife to cut you out of it."

He'd been crouched down beside her. In order to reach the knife that, in its sheath, had worked around almost to the back of his thigh, he got to his feet.

The sun had managed some minutes ago to finally break through the cloud cover. Its light flashed on the sharp, steel blade of the knife Casey removed from the sheath. A knife intended in that moment to rescue the woman with him, not as a weapon of attack. But that was how it was apparently perceived by one of the three figures that had topped the ridge of the hollow behind them.

A rifle raised to a shoulder fired, its *bang* reverberating around the mountain. Brenna heard Casey curse in pain, watched him clutch his arm where blood was already seeping through the sleeve of his jacket.

The impact of his being hit was powerful enough to send him staggering in a daze toward the edge of the precipice. He teetered there for a few seconds that seemed like forever to a horrified Brenna. Then, shaking his head as if struggling to clear it, unable to correct his footing, he leaned slowly forward, out into space.

Poncho or not, she must have somehow managed at one

point to flip back over on her stomach, raise herself on her knees and crawl forward. She was conscious of nothing but her howl of anguish, the long, loud "Nooooo!" she sent after Casey as he plunged down out of sight.

Working her way in desperation through the flattened grass, she reached the spot where he had gone down, peered into the sea that had received him so hideously far below. She prayed for him to surface, to still be alive, but there was no sign of him. He had vanished, and she was in a despair as deep as those waters.

A pair of large hands closed roughly over her shoulders, yanking her to her feet and swinging her around to face a burly figure with a long ponytail and tattoos covering both of his bare arms.

Brenna choked out an angry "Take your hands off me!" as he began to pat her down.

He ignored her command, finished his exam and reported to his two comrades, who had joined him, "She's clean."

She fought her hands and arms free of the poncho, ready to lash out at all three of them. Her captor with the tattoos seemed amused by her attitude of defiance.

"You try anything," he warned her, nodding in the direction of the bearded man whose rifle was now resting loosely in the crook of his arm, "and Ion here won't like it. Ion has a mean temper."

She didn't care. Her safety no longer mattered. "Your Ion is a rotten coward. He cruelly shot a man who never had a chance to protect himself."

Presumably their leader, the first man spoke to the tall blond who had dogged Casey and her from the beginning. "Karl."

That and a jerk of his head at the spot where Casey fell was all Karl needed to understand. He came forward and knelt at the edge of the cliff. Catching her breath, Brenna watched him gaze down over the side. She hoped for something encouraging, but she didn't get it.

Blondie got to his feet, shaking his head. "Either Ion's bullet killed him, or he drowned down there. Water looks deep, but with plenty of jagged rocks poking up. Maybe he struck one of those. Either way, there's no sign of a body. What say we get out of here, Lew, and back to the boat?"

"Not so fast. There's still the matter of the well sample." He confronted Brenna again. "It wasn't on you. Where is it?"

"Where do you think? It was in Casey's pocket. Thanks to your buddy's bullet, you'll never have it now."

"Doesn't matter. If it's at the bottom, it's no longer a threat. What counts now is that we still have you. And guess what? You're going back to St. Sebastian with us. Got somebody there real anxious to see you again."

Marcus, she realized. She would face his Bradley wrath, of course. Not that she cared. Nor did she take any satisfaction from knowing that the water sample was safe where Casey had hidden it. Maybe one day it would matter, and if it wasn't too late she would try to see it recovered and the promise to Zena King realized, but at the moment…

She had dared to love him again, and now he was gone. This time for good, and all she had left was a terrible grief. How was she supposed to live with that?

He had survived for two reasons: the first being the luck that had dropped him into deep water instead of smashing his body against one of the sharp rocks that lifted their heads above the surface, like an army of scattered sentinels.

The other reason he owed to his nylon jacket. Air had

collected beneath it on his long plunge downward, expanding it sufficiently enough to cushion his contact with the water. Without it, he might have been submerged to such a depth that he could have drowned before fighting his way to the surface.

But now that balloon was deflated, and he was out of advantages.

Casey was in trouble, and he knew it. *Felt* it. His arm throbbed where the bullet had penetrated. Blood continued to slowly leak from the wound there. If he lost too much, there was the risk of passing out, sinking to the bottom in a state of unconsciousness.

As it was, with only one good arm, he was having trouble staying afloat. The surf didn't help. It was far from heavy, but strong enough to have immediately pinned him against the wall of the cliff. No beach here, no shallows either. Just the black cliff with its overhang blocking the head of the rock far above him.

Casey searched its face, looking for— What? Some way to rescue himself when there was none? He refused to accept that. There had to be—

That's when he spotted it. Down there to his right, about twenty feet away. A ledge above the water. If he could manage to pull himself up onto it, he would be safe from drowning.

The ledge was already occupied by a dead, gnarled tree that had grown out of the fractured rock decades ago, its trunk and limbs curling down over the edge.

Hand over hand, he scraped his slow way along the cliff face, his legs moving just enough to maintain a state of vertical buoyancy. He felt stupid having lost the strength he'd always been so capable of demonstrating.

But what strength did remain finally brought him directly below the ledge. He rested a moment. Then, raising his arms as far as he was able to reach, he managed to lock his fingers over the edge.

It was no good. He would need more than his fingers to lift himself onto the ledge. Even if he could extend his arms high enough to have the full use of both hands, there was the problem of his wounded arm. It burned like hell. He doubted it would withstand any lasting exertion.

His gaze cut away to the tree on his right. One of its thicker limbs descended a fair distance below the edge of the ledge. It looked stout enough to bear his weight. If he could climb aboard that limb, drag himself along its length, he might be able to swing onto the ledge.

There was no way to know without trying.

Positioning himself beneath the limb, he made a grab for it. His arms were able to wrap around it, but the injured one hurt like hell with the effort.

He hated this weakness that came from the pain and loss of blood. The same weakness that had cost him his balance on top of the cliff.

He willed himself to ignore the pain.

His body, from years of training, took the strain of his clinging with every muscle to the limb. The dead tree did not. With a sudden tearing sound, the whole tree, roots and all, ripped away from the ledge. It came tumbling down, pitching Casey back into the sea.

When he surfaced, the tree was floating beside him. He no longer had the option of the ledge, but he did have the tree. With his last remaining strength, he draped himself facedown over the mass. His final thought before he lost consciousness was of Brenna.

When the tide turned, it took the tree and Casey with it out to sea. But he had no awareness of that. Nor did he realize, when he briefly regained consciousness again, that the island was no longer in sight. His fuzzy mind was only able to dwell on Brenna.

Where was she now? With the enemy, of course. Enduring what? But he didn't want to consider her being hurt in any way. The idea of it infuriated him. He damned himself for not being there to protect her. He had failed her by falling over that cliff. A woman so important to him that...

That was as far as his mind took him before it shut down again.

It must have been hours later, with the tree still bobbing on gentle swells, that Casey became vaguely conscious of a pair of dark hands as gnarled as the tree lifting him from his driftwood raft, passing him to another pair of younger, waiting hands.

Chapter 16

White Rose Plantation. That was where they were taking her, not Marcus's villa in Georgetown. Brenna didn't have to ask them to realize that. She recognized the road they were traveling that passed through the dim tunnel of arching trees.

She remembered being on this road before with Casey, and the uneasy feeling it had generated. Brenna hadn't understood that feeling then, and she didn't now. How could she have anticipated the road led to the old sugar plantation, and that her first sight of the place convinced her there was something bad connected with it?

People claimed without evidence to sense things like that all the time. She hadn't believed any of those claims. Not until she'd experienced the phenomenon herself.

Brenna had never had a reason to imagine she would be a passenger in the green sedan, the vehicle she and Casey had referred to as the green demon. But this was where they had installed her, in the backseat with the burly Lew squeezed close on one side of her, the mean-tempered Ion on her other side and Karl at the wheel up front.

None of them had spoken since leaving the harbor, where she'd been held on the power cruiser until this morning when the summons came. If they'd decided a long dose of silence would intimidate her, they could forget it. Brenna refused to be unnerved by any of these thugs.

Emerging from the tunnel into bright light, they reached the gates of the plantation. Karl turned into the mouth of the drive and stopped. They waited while he got out of the car, unlocked the gates and swung them open.

Brenna could see the great house in the distance at the end of the long, straight avenue leading to it. It still struck her as having a sinister look about it, but she wasn't afraid of what might be waiting for her inside. She had lost her fear when she lost Casey. Without him, she simply no longer cared.

That feeling remained with her when moments later Karl parked the sedan in front of the galleried mansion. The three men conducted Brenna up the wide steps and into the house.

"Wait," Karl told her.

He went off into the shadowy gloom toward the rear of the house, presumably to announce her arrival. The other two stayed with her in the enormous entrance hall that lacked nothing in elegance.

Originally, this room must have impressed visitors with its sweeping grand staircase and finely detailed woodwork. Now it had a tarnished look and a smell of slow decay. Did Marcus want the mansion like this, both inside and out, in order to maintain a look of desertion that would help to hide what was going on here?

Karl returned to report, "He'll see us now."

They escorted Brenna down a long, wide corridor to a closed door. Karl opened it without knocking, ushering her into a spacious, high-ceilinged room. The collection of moldering books on its shelves indicated it was the library.

A massive, antique desk dominated the room. She wasn't surprised by the presence of the silver-haired, handsome man seated behind it. Hadn't Casey informed her he'd learned Marcus Bradley was the current owner of the plantation? And that it was the site of suspicious activities?

Marcus was reading what looked like a report. Or pretending to, at least. Brenna knew he was aware of her standing there, but he took his time about looking up. When he did, he ignored her, directing his attention to Karl with a brusque "McBride?"

"Dead. Ion wounded him with one of the rifles. McBride sailed over the side of a cliff into the sea and never surfaced."

"And the water sample?"

"Went to the bottom with McBride."

"You're certain of that?"

"We thoroughly searched both her and their boat. Not a trace of it. It was with McBride all right."

Brenna knew there was no need for Marcus to ask these questions in front of her. He could have done that before she was brought into the room, or even late yesterday when his three goons had returned with her to Georgetown. Probably *had* done it then. He wouldn't have wanted to wait to learn the outcome of their pursuit.

All this now was a performance calculated to give him the satisfaction of seeing her angry over her capture or, better still, grieving for Casey. She didn't give him that pleasure. She stood there without any overt emotion.

Finished with his questions, Marcus addressed Lew. "Take the truck and go back to port. There's another ship-

ment coming in. I'll expect you to deliver it here tonight.
Karl, Ion, you can leave me now with my guest. Stick
close. I'll call you when I need you."

When they were alone, with the door shut, Marcus finally looked at her directly with those ice-blue eyes. He
didn't stand or invite her to be seated. He just kept looking at her as a grandfather clock in the corner ticked off
the seconds.

There was a time not long ago when, in the end, Brenna
would have looked away from that steady, disturbing gaze.
Now she just continued to silently meet it.

When he spoke at last, it was in that low, suave voice
familiar to her, except this time there was a note of mocking sorrow in it.

"Do I need to tell you, Brenna, how deeply disappointed I am? I had plans for you and your future. Plans
for *us.*"

"Us?" She shook her head in disbelief. "I'm not sure
what that means, but I never could have been serious about
you. Not even before I learned what you are."

His gaze narrowed. "And just what is it you think I
am?"

"Not think. *Know.* You're the lowest form of human
being, Marcus Bradley. Playing benefactor by providing
that village up the road with a reliable supply of clean
drinking water. But it wasn't so pure, was it? You had
something introduced into the well. Something that robbed
those people of their God-given right to reproduce. Or are
you going to deny that?"

"Deny it? I'm proud of what I've achieved. The world's
population is out of control, especially in poverty-stricken
regions whose people can least afford to bring more babies into their villages where health is a serious issue.
Those places need to have their populations reduced. My

method is a humane one, which is why, along with others I've banded with, we propose to offer more wells here in the West Indies, Africa, South America."

The man is a raving maniac, Brenna thought. He actually believes he has the right to play God. "Reduce? Don't you mean *eliminate?* Because that's what it sounds like to me."

"It's a matter of survival," he insisted.

"No, it isn't. I'll tell you what it is, Marcus. It's you and your racist friends wanting to wipe out people you think have the wrong color of skin. There's nothing humane about introducing that evil formula of yours into their drinking water."

Enraged, he came to his feet, slapping his hands on the desk as he leaned toward her. "It was my every intention to make you one of the world's most famous painters. I could have done it, too, Brenna."

She believed him. Why not, when it was a billionaire's influence responsible for her refusals to listen to either Will or Casey when they had tried to warn her about Marcus Bradley? She'd wanted the success Marcus could offer her. That had been then, but now...

"I can make my own fame, Marcus. I don't need you to do it for me. As a matter of fact, I'm thoroughly ashamed of myself for ever producing any paintings for you."

He was actually shaking with anger. She had never seen him like this before, never known him to be capable of losing his composure. "You'll regret those words," he promised her. "I'll make you regret them before I'm through with you."

She had no answer for him. He didn't deserve one.

The last of his self-control deserted him when, lifting his head, he shouted, "Karl, Ion, get in here!"

They must have been waiting just outside. Flinging

the door back, they practically tumbled into the room at the same time.

"Take her upstairs," Marcus ordered them. "Lock her in the secure bedroom. You know the one. What are you staring at me for? Do it!"

Even before he opened his eyes, Casey was aware of the strong odor of fish. It seemed to permeate everything around him.

Well, at least his nostrils were working. Yeah, and his sense of touch, too. He could feel himself lying on something that seemed like a narrow bunk. How about his sight?

He tested that by cautiously letting his eyes drift open. What he saw was clear enough but confusing. Two men stood at the side of the bunk, gazing down at him solemnly. One was young, the other older. Both were black.

That much he could tell, but nothing else. The light in here was very poor. Wherever *here* was. Maybe a cabin on some kind of boat. This seemed right since he could feel himself being slowly rocked on what must be easy swells.

Were they talking to him? In this gloom, he couldn't make out whether either of their mouths was moving. If they were speaking, all that was registering was silence.

He tried to speak. "You two picked me up off that floating tree, didn't you?" Curiously, he could hear himself just fine.

Neither of his rescuers answered him. Maybe they didn't understand English. He tried again. "You saved my life. There aren't thanks enough for something like that." Still no reaction.

Casey lifted his arm, prepared to shake their hands in a demonstration of gratitude. Whoa, big mistake. He'd forgotten the wound. His movement had been too sharp and sudden.

His face must have registered his soreness. The elder
of the two men put out his own hand, not with the intention of shaking Casey's hand but to gently press his arm
back down on the bunk.

"What you tryin' to do, mon, make dat ting go bleed-
ing again after we cleaned an' wrapped it up?"

"You do speak English."

"Sure, we speak English. What you tink?"

"That I owe you all around," Casey said humbly, conscious then of the dressing on his arm. "So, just who am
I thanking here?"

His savior poked himself in his chest. "Dey call me
Big Jimmy back in Georgetown. And dis here is my boy,
Little Jimmy."

The two of them didn't exactly fit their names since
the son was bigger than the father.

"I'm Casey McBride. This is your boat?"

"Sure. Fishing trawler," he said proudly. "You lucky to
be on such a fine boat."

Georgetown, Casey thought. That meant they were
from St. Sebastian. Brenna would have been taken there
to be confronted by Marcus Bradley. Bradley wouldn't be
pleased by her escape with a man who had sworn to get
a sample of water from the well he had funded to a safe
lab in the U.S.

The billionaire hadn't hesitated to have Zena King
killed. Would he order the same for Brenna? He had to
get to her. He had to prevent Bradley and his thugs from
harming her in any way.

"How long have I been here?" he asked Big Jimmy,
making an effort to stay calm.

"We collected you from the sea around dis time yesterday afternoon."

A whole day! He had lost a whole day on this boat! Arm or no arm, he couldn't waste another minute!

It was when he eased himself to a sitting position in the bunk that Casey realized he was naked except for his boxers.

"My clothes. Where are my clothes?"

"We hung 'em up ta dry."

"Can I have them now, please?"

It was Little Jimmy who fetched them from out on deck. The garments stank from fish when they were brought to Casey, but he ignored that. As he dressed, taking care of the injured arm, he realized the trawler's engine was silent.

"How soon are you going back to port?" he questioned Big Jimmy.

"Us? We don' leave until after we lift dis next net we got to lay down. If dis catch is good, den we go."

Casey tried to convince him how urgent it was that he return immediately to St. Sebastian, but Big Jimmy obstinately refused to listen. Casey couldn't blame them. Their livelihoods, and that of their families, depended on the fish they caught. And until the trawler's ice chests were full…

They had removed Casey's wallet from his pants and safely placed it on a shelf above the bunk. It contained all of the money he hadn't spent in Georgetown, and what remained was considerable. It should have remained dry in the zippered wallet. Casey offered to pay them whatever they asked to get him back to St. Sebastian without further delay.

The proud Big Jimmy turned him down. He and his son earned what money they needed by catching fish. And that was that.

Casey went up on deck with them when they returned to work. The engine was fired back to life, the current net laid down, the trawler on its slow way again.

Neither of the Jimmies asked him to explain how he'd ended up in an unconscious state with a gunshot wound, clinging to an uprooted, dead tree. Apparently, in their world a man was entitled to his privacy, whatever it involved.

Casey wanted to help them in their operation, both as a way to thank them and to hasten the work. But they wouldn't have it, pleading a risk to his arm. He suspected it wasn't that as much as, without a knowledge of what was needed, they felt he would be more of a hindrance than a help.

He was left to himself, trying not to get in their way as he paced the deck, frantic now to reach St. Sebastian and find Brenna. He told himself it wasn't too late, that she was still alive and he would do whatever he had to to save her.

Casey wouldn't let himself believe anything else. How could he when Brenna was so vital to him? When he so desperately needed her in his life?

All right, so she had sent him away two years ago, strongly, firmly resisting the possibility of any permanent future for them together. The danger of his work terrified her, and as long as he was an active FBI agent…

But they were different people now, a little older, a litter wiser. Weren't they? Sure, they were. And given the chance, Casey was convinced this time around he could change her mind.

He just had to. It wasn't a matter either of having fallen in love with her all over again. The truth was, he'd never fallen *out* of love with her. Which was why he was going so crazy thinking about her.

Hold on, sweetheart, until I can get to you, he silently begged. *Hold on for me, please.*

* * *

Brenna sat on the edge of the four-poster bed, casting her gaze around the room. It was spacious, high-ceilinged and its detailed woodwork as finely crafted as the rest of the mansion.

There was even a connecting bathroom, possibly created out of a dressing room some decades ago, because a house of this age wouldn't have had indoor plumbing. Not originally.

From what she had glimpsed elsewhere in the place, this bedroom had suffered the same wear and neglect as the other rooms. Holes in the Persian rugs, cracks in the walls, flaking paint and peeling wallpaper.

Any visitors to the house, willing to overlook these flaws, however, couldn't help admiring the luxuries built into it. The same level of luxury the villa back in Georgetown boasted of. With a prominent difference. Brenna couldn't remember having noticed any bars on the windows of its rooms.

This bedroom had them, as well as the bathroom window, making it her prison. At least until Marcus decided what her punishment was going to be. Maybe this waiting was deliberate, part of what she was meant to suffer.

If he believed that's what he was achieving with her, he was wrong. She had more than enough to be despondent over. *Casey.*

Was this devastation what her mother had experienced when she'd lost the man *she* loved? If so, Brenna knew only too well what her mom must have endured. She had never fully understood that before now.

What was she doing? Casey wouldn't want her to sit here like this grieving over him. He'd want her to make some effort to escape.

Now that was a challenge. A second-story bedroom, bars at all its windows and the only way out a locked, very solid door.

The flight attendant strolled down the aisle, checking the passengers to make certain their seat belts were fastened for the aircraft's imminent landing.

Will Coleman was among those passengers. In his case, an anxious one. Not because he had any problem with flying. Being a sports writer traveling with the teams made him a seasoned flier. His anxiety was not for himself but for his sister.

Having heard nothing back in Chicago for several days from either Brenna or Casey McBride, Will had worked himself into a state of concern. He'd been unable to contact them on their cells. Nor could any authority he reached on St. Sebastian provide him with a satisfactory answer. It left him wondering if Marcus Bradley was responsible for those evasions.

Convinced by then something bad was happening down there on the island and that he needed to be there, Will told his editor at the paper he had a family emergency and caught a flight out of O'Hare that would connect him with St. Sebastian.

He managed to be one of the first off the plane when, after taxiing to the gate, it released its passengers. He didn't want to chance missing out on a rental car.

It was midafternoon when he drove into Georgetown. Before leaving home, Brenna had provided him with the address of Bradley's seaside villa, where she would be staying in the guesthouse. The rental's GPS directed him there.

It looks like the kind of place a billionaire would own,

Will thought, surveying the villa when he got out of the car. It also looked deserted.

He didn't bother going to the villa's front door. He went instead to a matching, much smaller structure that couldn't be anything but the guesthouse.

The tropic sun was hot on his back as he waited after knocking. When no one came to the door, he went around to the side and peered through a window. He could see Brenna's easel in the corner of what appeared to be a sitting room. Her other painting gear was nearby, including her camera.

She can't be out on location then, he told himself. So where is she?

Hopefully, there was someone at the villa who could tell him that. He turned his steps in that direction.

There was a bell at the front entrance. He rang it and waited. This time someone answered the door. From the way she was dressed, she was either a maid or the house-keeper. Hispanic, he guessed.

"I'm trying to find Brenna Coleman," Will told her. "Is she around?"

The woman hesitated, as if she might have been in-structed not to impart information without prior permis-sion.

"I'm her brother, Will Coleman."

That was enough for her to yield a reluctant "I have not seen the miss lately, sir. She spends the days away from us painting."

"She's not out painting today. Her gear is still in the guesthouse."

The servant looked startled, as if wondering how he could know that. Will didn't enlighten her, asking instead, "How about Mr. Bradley? Is he at home?"

She shook her head. "He is at the place of the construction every day. It's to be a fine resort, you understand." Her round face brightened. "Maybe the young miss is there with him."

"How do I find this construction site?"

She provided him with directions, seemingly relieved to be rid of him when he thanked her and turned away. His questions had apparently made the chubby lady nervous.

Why? Will wondered. Was she withholding something or simply uncomfortable with strangers at the door?

He was concerned by Brenna's absence when he climbed behind the wheel of the rental and drove away from the villa. But he had no reason yet to be seriously worried.

The planned resort was located on the shore, a few miles beyond the airport. Will found it easily enough—an ambitious, sprawling project with work crews crawling all over it. There was no sign of either Bradley or Brenna.

He spoke to the superintendent in charge of the construction. The man, a blunt American from Texas, had never met Brenna. He didn't know the current whereabouts of Marcus Bradley. The billionaire hadn't been near the site for several days.

It was late afternoon when Will drove back to Georgetown. He was more than just worried by now. He was alarmed. Something was not right. Something was very wrong.

Should he go to the cops? No, not yet. Casey. If he could find Casey…

He remembered his friend was staying in a rental cottage on the beach. What was the name of the place? Fair Winds. Yeah, that was it.

Pulling over to the side of the road, he activated the GPS and learned that Fair Winds was on the shore road on the other side of Georgetown. It was rush hour, making the city a bitch to navigate.

The sun was sinking beyond the highlands as he crawled through the traffic on the busy harbor front. He was stopped at a traffic light when he spotted him on one of the docks, coming off a battered fishing trawler. Tall, broad-shouldered and even at this distance the unmistakable good looks that had drawn the interest of more than one woman when he and his friend had visited the bars. Casey.

Brenna had dozed on the four-poster. When she woke up, darkness was closing in outside. She couldn't read her watch. How long had she been kept here? There was a lamp on the bedside table.

Fumbling for the switch, she turned it on. That was when she heard a key turning in the lock of the hall door. The scraping sound of it had her immediately alert. Sitting up, she swung her legs to the floor, her gaze cutting to the door.

It was pushed open, bumping against the wall on her side. Brenna waited for someone to appear in the doorway, but a moment elapsed before a thin, short young man, probably still in his teens, glided into the room bearing a tray with covered dishes on it.

Apparently, Brenna thought wryly, *I'm about to be fed. Maybe the proverbial last meal of the condemned.*

The young man barely glanced at her. He was more concerned about locating somewhere to rest the tray. Finding it on the flat surface of a scarred desk beneath one of the windows, he crossed the room, placed the tray there and began to uncover the dishes.

Brenna wasn't interested in the menu. Her attention was riveted on the open door and the sudden realization that the boy couldn't be very intelligent. Otherwise…

He went and left the key in the lock.

It was an opportunity not to be missed.

Her server was silently indicating her waiting food, inviting her to eat. Brenna replaced her shoes, got to her feet, and addressed him.

"I want to wash my hands. I need a fresh towel in the bathroom. The one there is very soiled. Can you please get me one?"

He looked at her blankly. It was obvious he didn't understand English. Maybe he'd been hired to work here for that reason, because what he didn't understand he couldn't gossip about. Brenna pointed to the bathroom, pantomiming the act of drying her hands on a towel. He was slow in reacting, but she finally got what she was trying for when he went into the bathroom to check out the situation for himself.

Brenna bolted to the door, slammed it behind her as she made a swift exit into the corridor outside and relocked it. She was removing the key and placing it on a chair when she caught the muffled sound of fists pounding on the other side of the thick door.

Poor little guy. She hated to leave him like this, imagining the trouble he was going to be in when they learned the prisoner had not only tricked him but he'd gone and let her escape. At least he had something to eat until then.

That was as much concern as she had to spare for the young man. She had to worry about herself now. Getting out of a single room was one thing. Getting out of a whole house and away from a fenced estate before she was discovered was entirely, maybe impossibly, something else.

She could hear Casey's deep, mellow voice telling her: *You're on your own now, Rembrandt. Show me what you're made of for both of us. Get going.*

Chapter 17

"Being dead," Casey said.

Will stared at him, his only reaction a mystified "Huh?"

"You asked me what I was doing on an old fishing trawler, and I'm telling you. I was being dead, and for now I'd like to keep it that way."

"Casey, what's going on? And where the hell is my sister?"

They were seated in Will's rental car parked at the side of the street across from the dock where the sports writer had discovered Casey coming off the trawler. For a quick moment he considered Will in the gathering darkness.

Time was vital, but he could use Will to help him find and rescue Brenna. For that, Will would need to know the essentials.

"All right," Casey said, "but I'm going to make this quick, so listen and don't ask questions."

There was just enough light from the lamps on the dock

when he was finished with his abbreviated version of the story that he was able to register the shocked expression on Will's narrow face.

No point in discussing it. Other priorities waited.

"Your turn," Casey urged him. "And don't waste seconds telling me."

Will made his account a short one, starting with what had impelled him to fly down to St. Sebastian.

"All right," Casey said when he was done, "what you've told me is useful. Unless the housekeeper or the construction superintendent was lying to you, always a possibility, we can eliminate those choices. They weren't likely places for Bradley to hold Brenna anyway."

"Don't you think it's time we went to the police?"

"Absolutely not. Bradley controls this island, and if the cops learned I was alive, they'd consider me a fugitive from justice and pop me into a cell."

"Then where do we look for my sister?"

"I think I know. I think I knew hours ago on the trawler. There's only one logical place. An old, remote plantation called White Rose. Let's move. I'll give you directions along the way."

Casey wouldn't let himself believe Brenna wasn't there and unhurt. Anything else was unthinkable.

Brenna knew that if she went to the right, it would take her to the grand staircase and the entrance hall below. That would be the most direct route to the front door. On the other hand, brightly lit as she remembered it was, it carried the risk of her being sighted and apprehended.

She chose the other direction, thinking there must be a back staircase in a house this size. She was right. It was located at the far end of the corridor, a plain, ordinary flight that would have been used by the house servants when the plantation was active.

Brenna descended cautiously, not just to keep herself from being caught but also because the stairway was so poorly lighted it was a safety issue.

She paused at the bottom of the flight, hanging back in the shadows to look and listen. She had glimpsed no one since escaping from the bedroom where she'd been held, heard nothing.

There was no sound down here either, no voices to be overheard. And no sign of any movement.

The closed stairway emerged on another corridor, a broad one. The same corridor off which the library Marcus was using as an office was situated? She couldn't be sure of that. In any case, it was deserted. Well, she'd made it this far.

But it wasn't anything to celebrate. Not until she was out of the house, and even then...

Half expecting a shout of discovery and the pounding steps of pursuit behind her, Brenna went to the left and crept along the wide hallway. Wherever she was, it felt like the far rear of the mansion.

There had to be a back exit. Probably more than one.

The corridor turned here, and she turned with it. At the end of this shorter passage was a closed, double door. What was a door of this distinction doing along here in what ought to be strictly the service region of the house?

Brenna's hand closed on one of the brass latches, resting there, hesitating to open the door. Why? Was she afraid an evil something would leap out at her?

Anything was possible in this creepy old place. Including her overactive imagination.

Impatient with herself, unwilling to be the coward Casey would have fought for her not to be, she depressed the latch and pressed the door back. What waited for her on the other side was totally unexpected.

For a few seconds there was total blackness inside. Then, with a startling suddenness, the area was blasted with bright light. After her initial surprise, she concluded that opening the door must have tripped an electronic signal that activated the lights.

Had it been a large kitchen bathed in light, or the backyard she'd have welcomed, she would have understood and accepted it. It was neither one. What she found herself slowly walking into was a vast hall.

On the side walls were tall windows, tightly shuttered on the outside to prevent anyone from looking in. Ornately framed pier glasses hung between the sealed windows, and from the scrolled ceiling high above her were suspended massive crystal chandeliers. It was an imposing hall, and it didn't take a whole lot of Brenna's imagination this time for her to understand it had been built as a ballroom.

There must have been some magnificent parties here long ago with the whirling dancers reflected in the long mirrors. Not anymore. The spacious hall served in another capacity now.

Although the chandeliers were dark, modern fixtures above gleaming counters provided the white light. Spread along those counters were all forms of apparatuses, most of it unknown to Brenna but some of it just familiar enough for her to realize this was a laboratory.

The same laboratory, she was ready to believe, where the formula introduced into Freedom's water supply had been engineered. This, then, was the secret of White Rose, the reason why Marcus Bradley had acquired a remote plantation and fenced it off from the world. All to protect a laboratory that must remain hidden.

Brenna knew she should be on her way out of here, but she was compelled to linger just long enough to investigate a series of enormous glass jars ranged along shelves against the far wall. It wasn't until she approached those jars that she began to understand what they contained floating in a clear liquid that was probably formalin.

Art had been her only interest in college, but majoring in it had required that she study anatomy. It had been just science back then, learning both the exterior and the interior of the human body in order to accurately replicate it in your chosen medium.

But this wasn't science. This was a collection of what Brenna regarded as profane souvenirs, a kind of chamber of horrors bottled by a twisted mind to be on display. What other purpose could they possibly serve?

It was the anatomy classes years ago that enabled her now, as she went along the row of jars, to identify various parts of the female human body. Portions of women who had once been alive.

Their bodies desecrated.

Brenna retreated, backing slowly away from what angered and sickened her. Not just the jars but her own greedy curiosity that had cost her to waste minutes. Precious minutes that should have been used in escaping this place in order for her to let the world outside know what was happening here.

She owed that to the women whose lives had been sacrificed for the sake of heinous experimentation. And she owed it to Casey who had died to save her.

It was when she turned to run that Brenna saw on one of the lab counters what she hadn't noticed until now. The hot, blue flame of a Bunsen burner.

The realization of its presence shocked her. Because, being left lit as it was, meant that someone had been working here. Surely only minutes ago. And when he returned, as he must any second now, he would discover her.

* * *

"Stop!" Casey barked. "Pull over to the other side of the street and park there under that banyan tree."

Although he had to be puzzled by the order, Will did as he was told, risking a collision by racing across the traffic and coming to rest beneath the banyan tree. Its crown was so broad and thick Casey figured the rental wasn't likely to be spotted here, particularly after dark like this.

It was a different matter on the other side of the street. Because that was the area of the waterfront where the freighters loaded and unloaded their cargoes, it was well lighted.

It was those lights that had made it possible for Casey to discover an activity in progress that had triggered his memory on two levels as they'd been crawling by in the rental.

"Why are we wasting time stopped here?" Will wanted to know. "What's got you so interested?"

"See that truck over there with its open bed in back being loaded with steel drums?"

"Yeah? So what?"

"I saw this same thing happening here once before. It didn't mean anything to me then. It does now. With all I've learned since then, I'm ready to swear those drums contain chemicals bound for White Rose Plantation."

"How can you be sure of that?"

"See that guy directing the loading? The one with the ponytail and all the tattoos? He works for Bradley. He's one of the three goons who chased Brenna and me down."

"All right, but why does this matter now?"

"Because you and I are going to be on board that truck when it pulls out of the loading yard."

"What!"

"No, I'm not crazy. I have a good reason for my intention. Driving out there to the plantation in the rental here seemed the only option at the time, only I knew it would present a problem when we got there."

"Like?"

Casey explained how the entire property was framed by a high-security fence. And how the gates to the drive were kept closed and locked. They would have to leave the car where it wouldn't be discovered, scale the fence and work their way up to the mansion without being seen. All actions that would require time they couldn't afford if Brenna's life was in imminent jeopardy.

"But if we're out of sight on that truck when it arrives, we sail right through the gates and up to the house."

"Sold," Will agreed. "One thing, though. How do we climb aboard that truck without being detected?"

"Yeah." Casey searched the street in both directions before settling on a plan. "See the van parked a little way down from the loading gate on the other side? We take cover behind it, and when Ponytail is busy turning out of the yard into the street, we move."

They took care after leaving the rental to cross the street at a spot directly opposite the van, where the light was so poor there was little chance of them being noticed from the loading yard.

Once safely concealed behind the van, Casey's only concern was that the owner of the vehicle would arrive and challenge them. Either that or drive off, exposing their presence. Thankfully, neither one occurred.

Nor did they experience any difficulty when Ponytail, finally behind the wheel of the truck, was nothing but oc-cupied looking both ways for a break in the traffic at the exit of the yard. Seizing the opportunity, Casey and Will rushed out from their cover behind the van. Hauling them-selves into the bed of the truck, with Casey making an effort to ease the stress on his wounded arm, they crouched down out of sight among the drums.

They were rolling along the shore highway when an observant Will wondered, "I noticed back where there was light that all of these drums are marked in big letters with the word *Brennbar.* You have any idea what that means?"

Casey's overseas assignments had required that he be familiar with some of the major foreign languages. "Yeah, *Brennbar* is German. It means *flammable.* And with the size of those letters, I'd say the indication is that what the drums contain is *highly* flammable."

There seemed to be no exit from the mansion by way of what had once been its ballroom. Brenna's only choice was to flee back along the route she had come. There had to be some way out of the house other than the front entrance. She just needed to find it before they learned she was on the loose.

Too late.

Brenna was stopped before she even began. The double door through which she had entered the ballroom was already ajar. Three figures came through the opening. Marcus led the trio, Karl with his white-blond hair and stoic, Nordic face followed, and a third man she didn't know brought up the rear.

Brenna stiffened, refusing to show any fear as they surrounded her on three sides, cutting off any possible escape. Marcus was smiling in that despicable way of his as he considered her.

"Our bird seems to have gotten out of her cage, gentlemen. Karl, you should have known better than to send that stupid boy up with her tray. She obviously took advantage of poor Joseph. Well, no serious loss now that we have her back. Let's keep it that way, Karl."

Marcus jerked his head in the direction of the double door.

The obedient Karl went to stand in the opening, blocking it off with his solid body.

Looking pleased with the situation, Marcus spoke to her, friend to friend. "Now that you found the laboratory, you deserve to have a tour of it. Oh, but then I imagine you couldn't wait for that, could you? Would I be wrong in thinking you already had a good look around, saw the state-of-the-art equipment, the computers and, of course, the fascinating specimens in the jars?"

Every word out of his mouth was a mocking one intended to humiliate her. But she'd be damned if she ever let him see it affect her that way.

He didn't wait for her response, probably realizing he wasn't going to get one. Instead, looking suddenly remorseful, he addressed the third man. "What's wrong with me? I'm being rude, forgetting my manners. Let me correct that. Doctor, let me present our guest, Brenna Coleman."

The little man in the white lab coat and thick glasses nodded to her by way of acknowledgment.

"Brenna, this is Dr. Milosz. You need to be impressed by him. He's a brilliant chemist. He created the marvelous formula we hired him to engineer for us here in this laboratory. Doctor, why don't you give her a brief description of how you achieved that?"

"It would be my pleasure."

Brenna detected a slight European accent. Considering his name, maybe Polish. There was something else she observed at the corner of his thin mouth. He had a nervous tic.

"If you will step this way…"

With Marcus crowding in behind her, she had no choice

but to follow the doctor to one of his work stations where he pointed out various chemicals on the shelves. His explanation of what components he'd blended and repeatedly tested before he achieved success was wasted on her.

The nerve at the corner of Dr. Milosz's mouth twitched all the while as he introduced her to the formula he had manufactured in this room. He seemed nothing but proud of his clever ability to halt the reproduction process in women without their being aware it had been artificially accomplished.

Brenna must have registered her disgust on her face. Milosz didn't observe it, but Marcus did.

"I don't think she's paying sufficient attention to your lesson, doctor. Perhaps this over here will be of more interest to her."

He went back to the other side of the room, expecting her to follow. She remained where she was.

"Perhaps we need Karl to encourage you. He's very capable when it comes to persuasion."

From the slow smile on the thug's mouth, Brenna knew he would love the opportunity to use force. She had a choice. She could either willingly submit to Marcus's will or be manhandled by Karl. That kind of brutal treatment could end up injuring her, making her incapable of an escape. And naive though that intention might be, she still hoped for it.

It was wiser to join Marcus where he stood by a covered something she hadn't noticed until now.

"That's much better, Brenna. You can't fail to be fascinated by this latest addition to my collections."

She couldn't prevent the gasp that resulted when he whipped off the cover, revealing what was underneath. It was a chair, but not an ordinary chair.

"I purchased it from an American prison that was no

longer in use and had it shipped down to me. Original, isn't it? But you're looking alarmed. You don't think— Oh, no, no, this isn't an electric chair. Nothing that uncivilized. But you can see by the leather straps on the arms and at the legs, this was a chair used for executions. In this case, the gas chamber. Try it, why don't you?"

"I don't think so."

His voice altered, going from pseudo pleasant to genuine harshness. "I insist. And if you refuse, there's always Karl." He thrust his face down into hers, his blue eyes cold with contempt. "Have you forgotten my promise to you that you'll regret turning on me? This chair is my means of making that happen. Karl, get over here."

The blond left the door and joined them.

"Strap her down in the chair. If she gives you any trouble, you have my permission to do what's necessary. Meanwhile…" Marcus turned away, calling across the laboratory to Dr. Milosz where he waited on the other side.

"Doctor, do me the favor of preparing a syringe containing a strong dose of your formula."

"Do I understand that you want me to inject Miss Coleman?"

"That's the intention."

"You realize, don't you, Marcus, that once it's in her system she'll never be able to conceive?"

"Of course. It's exactly what she deserves." He turned back to Brenna with a soft, taunting "For the rest of your life, Brenna. It will stay with you for the rest of your life."

Dear God, he's a lunatic. They're all lunatics. To rob a woman of her right to bear a child. It's unthinkable…

But if Marcus Bradley had his way, it was about to happen to her.

She'd wanted a baby. One day, that is, when she was established as an artist and had the time and means to get pregnant. She and Casey had discussed it during their engagement, planned for it. It wouldn't happen now. Casey would never father their baby.

Wait a minute. She wasn't thinking straight. Marcus was just tormenting her. Knowing what she did, he couldn't afford to let her live. Oh, he would let her suffer for a time with being infertile while he kept her captive. That was his way of punishing her, but sooner or later she would be killed.

That didn't mean she was going to willingly submit now to any form of injection.

She fought Karl with the fierceness of a mother bear protecting her cub, but he was too strong for her. In the end, spewing curses all the while, he secured the leather straps around her wrists and ankles.

Bound to that chair as she was now, Brenna felt like a helpless victim about to be sacrificed on a satanic altar.

Chapter 18

Casey could feel the truck swinging into the end of the driveway and stopping at what he presumed were the locked gates of the plantation. There was a pause and then an exchange of voices.

From what he could tell where he and Will were hidden on the bed of the truck, the driver had to be leaning from his open window, calling to another man behind the gates. "Ion, is that you?"

"Who else? Don't I always get the crappy jobs? Boss kept Karl up at the house and sent me down to wait for you. You took your sweet time getting here."

The voice, bearing traces of an Eastern European accent, was familiar to Casey. He had heard it before. When and where? It took a few seconds before his memory kicked in.

Yeah, that was it. The day along the waterfront when the gun had been shoved into his back and this bastard had snarled a warning into his ear to stay away from Brenna. A threat that had to have originated from Marcus Bradley.

Ion, huh? His presence at the waterfront back then made sense now. Casey knew the driver tonight had been collecting another chemical delivery that day, and this Ion must have been there helping him.

"Come on, open up. Boss is eager to get these chems."

"You know why, don't you, Lew?"

Casey could hear a jangle of keys, one of which he supposed was unlocking the gates.

"I guess you're going to tell me, aren't you?"

"He and Milosz are trying to stockpile the stuff so they get enough batches to send overseas to all the cabal members at the same time. Problem is, the chem brew in the vats needs to be mixed and refined until the solution—"

The driver cut him off there with an impatient "Since when did you get so freakin' interested in science? No, don't tell me. Just get the damn gates open."

Ion must have done that, because the truck pulled forward and stopped. Casey supposed the driver, Lew, was waiting now for Ion to close the gates, relock them and climb aboard the vehicle for a lift back to the house. When the passenger door opened and slammed shut, he knew he was right.

Casey waited for them to be rolling again before signaling Will to be ready to jump down. Lifting his head, he saw the lighted great house looming ahead of them. The truck slowed when it reached the turn in the drive that would take it around to the back of the mansion.

It was then Casey swung down from the open rear of the truck. Will followed. They took cover in the shrubbery at the side of the house. It was only when they were out of sight and hearing that Casey spoke softly to his friend.

"We need to find a way inside this mausoleum. Let's try the back. They'll probably be taking the drums in that way. With any luck, we might be able to slip through."

"I'm with you. Lead on."

The two men worked their way through the shrubbery. They stopped when they rounded the corner of the house. Ahead of them, beneath the glow of a yard light, sat the truck. Ion and Lew were there, securing three of the heavy chemical drums on a forklift.

Casey placed his mouth near Will's ear. "Can't see any entrance inside the house from this angle," he whispered.

"Looks like what used to be a horse stable across the yard from where they're working," Will whispered back. "How about we backtrack where it's dark enough to slip around to that stable without being spotted and take up position there?"

A few minutes later they were hugging the shadowed side of the derelict stable. Their situation gave them a clear view of the yard and the back wall of the mansion. There was still no sign of an entrance.

There had to be one, Casey thought. The burly Lew was already seated on the forklift, ready to trundle the drums to where they would be needed.

"I'm gonna take a quick smoke break while you're gone," Ion said.

"You'd better be here waiting when I'm back to help with the next load. And you'd better get out of sight before you light up. You know what a fit the boss will throw if he catches you anywhere near those chems with a lighted cigarette."

Lew had already swung the forklift around and was on the move when Casey realized Ion, cigarette in one hand, lighter in the other, was headed directly toward where he and Will were hiding. Presumably, the bearded bastard meant to share their shadowed wall.

Casey made a quick decision. If he and Will were going to find Brenna and get her out of that decaying mansion, they would have to start taking down these goons. This was as good an opportunity as any to begin.

Casey was ready for the guy when he rounded the corner of the stable and came to a halt, his eyes bugging in disbelief. Not a surprising reaction since the man lurking at the side of the stable was supposed to be dead.

Casey gave him no time to think about it.

"Hi," he greeted him cheerfully. "Remember me? I remember you."

Casey's fist was ready and eager. It shot out with the force of a piston, connecting with Ion's jaw. Casey didn't care what his wounded arm might suffer from that blow. It felt too good to mind. Almost as good as seeing his target drop to the ground and stay there.

"Guy must have a glass jaw," Will observed.

"Yeah, looks like he's going to be out for a while. Hey, you see where the other one disappeared to with that forklift?"

How much longer did she have, Brenna wondered, before her body was injected with that foul fluid that would make her forever barren?

Dr. Milosz was still preparing the syringe on the far side of the laboratory, and Marcus remained with him watching the procedure. Karl hovered close to the chair that held her, guarding her. Which was pointless since she was incapable of going anywhere.

She was startled when a bell rang toward the rear of the hall. Was it an alarm of some kind? None of the three men were surprised by it.

"That would be Lew with the first of the drums," Marcus remarked to no one in particular.

Brenna saw him pick up what looked like a remote control. His thumb must have punched a button. To her amazement, a wide section of the back wall of the hall slid open to admit a forklift. The man with all the tattoos—Lew, wasn't it?—was seated at the controls operating the machine, its extended carriage supporting three of the drums.

"Where's Ion?" Marcus wanted to know as the forklift rolled into the laboratory.

"Waiting out at the truck to help with the next load."

Satisfied that Ion had been accounted for, Marcus went back to watching the doctor. Brenna's own gaze was on the forklift and its current load proceeding slowly toward the front of the hall.

She could guess what those drums contained. Chemicals needed to manufacture more of the junk that would be pumped down wells all over the world. The very thought outraged her.

The forklift had come to a sudden halt. Something strange was happening. Its frozen driver was staring directly into one of the long mirrors mounted on the front wall.

From her position in the chair, Brenna was unable to see what had captured his attention in the pier glass. What she could detect from his profile, however, was the horror on his face. As if he were looking at a ghost from the past.

But the mirror wasn't reflecting the past. What it was reflecting, she realized, was the back wall of the laboratory.

Something or someone was there outside the opening, and it couldn't be Ion. Not to elicit such incredulity from the man on the forklift.

It was both a night and a setting for seeing ghosts. Brenna understood that when the tall figure of Casey McBride, hands down at his sides curled into fists, strode through the opening.

She choked on a sob of astonishment that rose from deep inside her. It couldn't be him. How could it be?

It took her a few seconds to know that it *was* him. He hadn't died. He was real. As real as her brother, Will, who entered behind him.

Brenna had no time to process any of it, to experience the joy it deserved. What happened next happened so swiftly, so violently there was a surreal quality to it.

Lew in his shock must have lost control of the forklift. As he yelled wildly, the machine spun rapidly in the direction of the lab counters. Brenna could only guess that, in his effort to correct his mistake, he somehow activated a wrong lever.

The carriage dropped, kicking off the three drums it had supported. The impact of them striking the hard floor was so strong that while the first drum remained sealed, the other two popped their lids. No longer contained, their chemical contents gushed out onto the floor.

One of those rolling drums smacked into the bottom corner of a lab counter. The same counter on which the forgotten Bunsen burner still sprouted its intensely hot, blue flame. The collision forced a geyser out of the open drum, the fluids raining down on the counter, leaking over the sides to join the widening lake on the floor.

It needed only the merest trickle of the inflammable chemical coming in contact with the Bunsen burner to ignite the fluid. The resulting fire licked a trail across the counter and down the side. When it reached the spreading liquid on the floor, and it did so with an unbelievable swiftness, it resulted in a situation so volatile it was like an explosion.

That's what it seemed like to Brenna who, helpless in the chair, could only watch with terror what followed.

The six men in the laboratory were galvanized into immediate action.

Lew left the forklift behind in his race to the far side of the laboratory to assist Marcus and Dr. Milosz, who were already taking down fire extinguishers from the wall there.

Casey and Will rushed toward Brenna, Casey shouting to her brother, "Will, get Brenna unstrapped from that chair and the hell out of here! Looks like I've got another job that's gonna occupy me!"

She knew he meant Karl, who, like a dumb, stubborn ox, refused to disobey his order to guard her. Even in this crisis, he was determined to oppose any effort to free her.

A frantic Brenna didn't know where to look. At Casey and Karl locked in combat, at Will striving to unfasten her bindings or at the inferno raging out of control. An inferno aided by the first barrel which, unable to resist the heat, erupted its contents. The chemical that had been Marcus Bradley's ally was now his enemy.

The extinguishers were of little use against a chemical blaze that trapped Marcus, Milosz and Lew behind a wall of encircling fire.

Will had her out of the chair and standing, his hand gripping hers. "Come on, Brenna, we need to go."

"Not without Casey."

"Trust him. He won't lose this fight. Not unless he has to worry about you."

She was torn in two directions, but in the end rightness prevailed. Dragging her hand out of Will's grasp, she headed in the direction of the double door through which she had entered the hall.

"Not that way!" her brother pleaded behind her. "The opening in the back wall!"

"There's a boy locked in a bedroom upstairs. I won't leave him there to burn."

It was with a desperate prayer for Casey, and a last glimpse of him still struggling with Karl, that Brenna left the laboratory. Will stayed protectively behind as she ran through the corridors that brought her to the back staircase. She took both the flight and the broad hall with as much speed as possible.

She was out of breath when she arrived at the locked door. Her hand shook as she endeavored to turn the key.

"Here, let me," Will insisted, unlocking the door for her and flinging it back.

The sight of a very frightened young man inside was all Brenna needed to realize her choice of whether to stay with Casey or come up here was the correct one.

"You have to go, Joseph. The house is on fire."

She didn't know whether he understood her words or not. There was no questioning his action, however. He fled past her and Will, headed for the main staircase.

"Don't even think about trying to go back to the laboratory," Will said. "I can already smell the smoke up here."

Recognizing the wisdom in that observation, Brenna led the way to the front staircase, descended them with her heart heavy and her mind on Casey and reluctantly walked through the main doorway that Joseph had left open in his flight.

The last glimpse she had of the young man was of his slight figure running down the drive in the direction of the gates. She had the feeling Joseph would no longer want anything to do with White Rose Plantation.

Brenna was hardly aware of Will propelling her away from the house. "I deserted him," she said when, putting a safe distance between themselves and the mansion, they sank down on what was left of a once-proud lawn.

"Stop punishing yourself. We both did what Casey wanted us to do."

She clutched her brother's arm. "What if he doesn't make it out of there? Will, I couldn't bear to be cheated of him a second time. First on Maroa, and now this. Life just can't be that cruel!"

"You weren't cheated of him on Maroa. He didn't die. And you won't be cheated of him here."

"Then where is he?"

"Give him time. He'll come."

Brenna wished she could be as calmly convinced of that as her brother. Silent now, they sat there in the grass and gazed up at the great house where tongues of leaping flames, using the ancient, dry timbers as their fuel, had already eaten through the roof.

Brenna covered her mouth with her hand to prevent herself from sobbing aloud as she watched smoke curling from the walls of the building. The windows that weren't shuttered glowed orange with the blaze that raged through the rooms inside. No one could survive that.

"Look," Will said, pointing to the side of the mansion. A tall figure had come around from the back and, like a phantom, was approaching them through the veils of drifting smoke.

But Brenna knew that gray form emerging from the mist was no phantom. Even before Casey, having sighted them, arrived where they were waiting, she was on her feet and flinging her arms around him so fiercely she almost knocked him off his feet.

He managed to stay upright, enduring her face pressed tightly against his chest and the tears that must be soaking his grimy tee.

"Hey, what's this?" he demanded, those wonderful hands of his stroking her back. "You're bawling like a baby."

"Can't help it," she choked. "You put me through hell."

"Yeah, I have a habit of that, don't I? But I'm here now. See?"

His hands shifted, holding her away from him so she could get a better look. That's when she heard him sharply sucking in his breath, as if he were in pain.

"You're hurt!"

"Naw," he reassured her. "It's just the bullet wound from Maroa. It's still a little tender, and after wrestling with Blondie—"

"What happened in there?" Will wanted to know.

"Flattened him in the end. He was unconscious when I dragged him out and dumped him in the backyard. Don't know about that SOB, Ion. I didn't bother checking on him. I was in too much of a hurry to find the both of you."

"And the others?" Brenna asked. "Marcus, Dr. Milosz, Lew?"

Casey shook his head. "Didn't make it. There was no saving them."

Brenna was too drained by then to care one way or another. And so, apparently, was Casey.

"The arm is okay," he said. "But I'm ready to get off my feet." He dropped down in the grass next to Will, drawing Brenna down beside him, holding her close with the arm that hadn't been shot.

The three of them huddled there, solemnly watching the mansion being consumed by a roaring firestorm so bright it lit the night sky above them.

"There's one thing for sure," Casey grimly remarked.

"No more of that damn formula is going to be produced in there."

Brenna added an earnest "And nowhere else when the world finds out what happened here."

Chapter 19

They sat three across on the flight to Miami, Will in the window seat, Casey on the aisle and Brenna sandwiched in the middle.

The two men were asleep. She on the other hand was very much awake. She supposed she should be resting as they were, but she feared her mind was too active to shut down long enough for a nap.

There was plenty to think about. The last two days had been hectic ones for the three of them. With Marcus Bradley dead and no longer in control of St. Sebastian, the island's authorities had been willing to take action. It was either that or be targeted by the media, whose worldwide coverage of the events had already broken the cabal, putting its members at risk of prosecution.

The Georgetown police, listening to Brenna and Casey's story, had caught Karl and Ion and jailed them. Never having believed Joseph was anything but innocent,

Brenna never mentioned the young man. As for Curtis Hoffman, they were told he flew back to the United States before any of the recent events at White Rose, and if he were to be investigated and charged it would have to be there.

The only matter of any real importance was the water sample Zena King had entrusted to Casey. Because Marcus Bradley had ordered Freedom's well neutralized after learning of the sample's existence, it was more imperative than ever to recover that sealed bottle.

Casey had hired Big and Little Jimmy and their trawler to take them back to Maroa, where the water sample remained undisturbed in the hollow bamboo. Towing the crippled *My Last Dollar* behind them, the trawler returned to Georgetown. As he'd promised himself, Casey had generously compensated the forgiving owner of the cruiser for both its use and repair.

That achieved and the water sample tucked safely away inside Casey's carry-on, they had boarded the flight for Miami.

Everything addressed and neatly settled, Brenna thought wryly. Everything but Casey and her. There had been no time to sort out things between them. Or was it because one, or possibly both of them, were reluctant, even afraid to resolve their present feelings for each other?

She looked over at Casey where he was slouched down in his seat, hair tousled, long legs stretched out as much as he could in front of him. The sight of him never failed to awaken an urge to touch him intimately.

In Miami, while we wait for the results on the lab's chemical analysis, Brenna promised herself, *we'll have plenty of time to discuss just where we're at with each other.*

* * *

But it didn't work out that way.

After landing at Miami-Dade Airport, they grabbed two cabs. Will had decided to remain in Miami with Brenna and Casey long enough to learn the lab's findings firsthand before flying back to Chicago. He went off in the first cab to obtain rooms for them at a beachfront hotel, leaving the second cab for his sister and Casey, who didn't want to lose any time delivering the water sample to the lab waiting for it.

Having replaced their cell phones Casey had recommended they discard while on the run, they were able before leaving St. Sebastian to inform the laboratory by phone the sample was in their possession and on its way.

The private facility Zena had so enthusiastically recommended was near the school where she'd been training. The building in which it was located was an ordinary one, but they were impressed by the able technician who met with them. A tall, gangling man approaching middle age introduced himself as Aaron Fowler.

"We were shocked here by Zena's death," he said. "She had such a promising future, but you folks probably know that."

"We do," Casey said. "And believe me she won't be forgotten. Certainly not on St. Sebastian where her people valued her so much."

"You can trust us with her sample," Fowler assured them. "Our chemists here are the best. I know the media is waiting to tell the rest of this outrageous story, and for that they need our findings. I should caution you both, though, that it takes time to do a thorough, reliable analysis."

"Are you telling us," Brenna asked, "that we won't know for a while?"

"You'll hear from us at the earliest possible moment," he promised them, taking charge of the small, sealed bottle Casey placed in front of him.

"Sounds like that moment could amount to days," Casey said in the cab that carried them toward Miami Beach where Will, who had reached his sister as they came away from the lab, reported the three of them were booked into White Sands Hotel.

Days. In one way, she knew that was a disappointment. In another, it would provide the unhurried opportunity she longed for to discuss their feelings for each other, to determine just where they stood.

But once again her expectation was blocked. Casey's cell phone rang. *Now who?* she asked herself. There were only a couple of possibilities. With their phones and numbers being so new, there had been little time to notify people of the changes.

Brenna didn't have to guess, however. Although for her the conversation was one-sided, she knew from its content that Casey was speaking to someone in authority from the Chicago division of the FBI.

His face was sober when he ended the call.

"What?" she asked.

"I'm being summoned back to Chicago for a final question-and-answer before there's a decision."

"When?"

"On the first flight I can get."

"And if you and the others get cleared?"

"Then we get reinstated to active service status."

"Meaning you won't be here to learn the lab's findings. You'll be out in the field again."

"Brenna, no. It doesn't work that fast. I'll have time to get back here before I'm assigned to another case. You'll see."

"I'll count on that." She made the effort to sound cheerful about it, not wanting him to see she was close to despair. That she feared the next time she heard from him his suspension would have been lifted and he would be involved in a fresh case somewhere far away.

They wouldn't talk, not now, not then.

Her brother was waiting for Brenna in the lobby when the cab delivered her to White Sands Hotel.

"Where's Casey?"

"He isn't coming. We had to have the cab take him back to the airport."

She and Will were close. He'd always known from just looking at her face when something was wrong. "All right, what's happened?" he wanted to know.

"He had to return to Chicago on the first available flight." She explained as briefly as possible why. She didn't tell him that, when their cab dropped him off at Miami-Dade, his departure and the kiss that accompanied it were fleeting.

There was a moment of silence before Will muttered a guilty "Uh-oh."

"Uh-oh *what?*"

"I called my editor at the *Trib* to let him know I was back in the States. He wanted to know why I wasn't somewhere more specific than that. Like back at my sports desk in Chicago."

"You're flying home, too, aren't you?" She would be alone in Miami waiting for those results. No brother to keep her company and her mind off Casey. It was a dreary prospect.

"Not until later tonight. We have until then. Let's go out to the swimming pool. They're serving lunch there. We can talk."

Yes, she needed to talk to someone who understood her. And that would be her brother.

The pool was located in a large courtyard with wide bands of alternating brick and stone framing it on all sides. Wrought-iron tables and chairs, shaded by colorful umbrellas, were scattered around. Pots and upraised beds, overflowing with flowers, added to the ambience, making it a pleasant place for casual dining.

After they'd ordered, Will leaned toward her with an earnest "All right, what's bothering you?"

"Why should you think anything is bothering me?"

"Oh, please, after all these years you think I don't know. It's Casey, isn't it? What's he done?"

"It's what he *hasn't* done that's made me unhappy."

Will tipped his head to one side, examining her critically. "You've gone and fallen in love with him again, haven't you?"

"I'm not sure I ever fell *out* of love with him."

"So what's the problem?"

"I love him, but I don't think he's capable of loving me back. Not anymore. I can't really say I blame him. I was pretty rough on him when I broke our engagement. Something tells me he never got over that."

"I find that hard to believe about Casey."

Brenna lifted her shoulders in a little shrug. "It could be, too, that he's been waiting for some safe indication of just how I feel about him."

Will shook his head. "After the way you greeted him when he turned up outside the burning plantation house? I don't think your emotions could have been any plainer than that."

"The thing is—"

Before she could go on, their server interrupted them with their orders, iced tea for Brenna, a cold beer for Will and BLTs for both of them.

When she'd departed, brother and sister began to eat their sandwiches. Brenna resumed the conversation between bites.

"The thing is, whatever our feelings for each other, Casey may not be interested in a reunion. He can't have forgotten how, when I gave his ring back to him, I could no longer bear his dangerous assignments."

"You must have gotten over all that after what the two of you shared down in St. Sebastian. Brenna, you thought he was shot and drowned and later that he perished in the fire. And he survived all of it, and you survived your desperation. What more do the two of you need?"

"But none of that was by choice. Marrying him would be giving him my permission this time around for him to go out on those deadly assignments. He must sense that, maybe thinks by not telling me he loves me he's providing me with a ticket to walk away. Who knows? Could be I'm not strong enough to withstand the dangers. That I'm no better in that department than Mom was."

Will lowered his glass, wiping beer foam off his upper lip with the back of his hand, looking exasperated by her defense.

"There's one thing you're forgetting, Brenna. Mom knew Pop was a fireman and always would be when she married him. She knew the danger and hated it, but she loved him too much not to risk it. How about you?"

Brenna gazed back at him, ashamed of herself. He was right. What her mother could be she could be.

"I don't know what we're discussing all this for," Will wondered. "Haven't you and Casey talked about it?"

She shook her head. "There's hasn't been any time."

"So you make it a priority when he comes back."

She hesitated before admitting to her brother what she'd been fearing ever since she'd dropped Casey off at the airport.

"I'm not sure he is coming back to Miami. I'm not sure when I hear from him again he won't already be on assignment."

After Will left, Brenna expected to have a dull time of it waiting to hear about the findings from the lab. Much to her surprise, however, neither the first day after his departure, nor the second, were solitary ones.

It started when she was having breakfast out at the poolside where she and Will lunched the previous day. A thin, middle-aged woman approached her table. Brenna looked up as the well-dressed woman spoke to her with a hesitant "Ms. Coleman?"

"Yes, I'm Brenna Coleman. How did you know—"

"Generous tips can do wonders. One of the bellhops in the lobby pointed you out. As for learning you're staying in this hotel…well, the reporter who interviewed you here told me. I'm afraid there isn't much that stays private anymore."

Very true, Brenna thought. She and Casey had been all over the news ever since the story broke in St. Sebastian. But what was this particular mystery about?

"I seem to have interrupted your breakfast. My apologies for that."

"It's all right. I was finished except for drinking the last of my cup of coffee, um—"

"Valerie. Valerie Hoffman."

The name wasn't familiar to Brenna. Or was it? "What can I do for you, Ms.—"

"Valerie. Just Valerie. I apologize for intruding on you like this," she went on quickly, "but when I read you were in Miami… My husband and I have a vacation home here, though our permanent home is in Chicago. Anyway, I had this sudden impulse to speak to you. I promise I don't want anything from you, other than to share a proposal of mine and, hopefully, to have your opinion."

This could be nothing but a scam, but there was something genuine about the woman. Brenna decided to take a chance. All she need do was listen. "You'd better sit down and tell me what this is about."

"Thank you." Removing her sunglasses and revealing a pair of gentle eyes, she settled on a chair across from Brenna. "I think you met my husband in St. Sebastian when you were both guests of Marcus Bradley. Curtis? Curtis Hoffman?"

Brenna stared at the woman. Valerie Hoffman. The wife of Curtis Hoffman. No wonder the woman's surname had seemed vaguely familiar. She was the author of the secretive, unfinished letter Brenna had discovered in the guesthouse.

She must have registered her shock. Valerie noticed that and misunderstood. "I don't blame you, Ms. Coleman, for—"

"Brenna, just Brenna."

"Well, I don't blame you for your reaction. Curtis isn't always a likeable man, and for you to have learned he was involved in that horror down there…"

Should she tell her she had found and read her private letter? Brenna quickly decided to just keep it to herself.

"But here's the thing where Curtis is concerned. I'm ashamed to say I let him control me. That is, I did until I read what courageous people you and your friend were in exposing Marcus and his associates. You were an example to me what a woman should be. What I should have been all along."

"That's very flattering, but I'm nothing special, Valerie."

"I don't agree, only that isn't why I'm here. Curtis and I are no longer together. I don't know what's going to happen to him concerning his part in this awful thing, and I don't care. What I need you to know is that the big money Curtis let people think he had was never his. It was always mine, family money I inherited."

"I don't understand why you need me to know this."

Brenna watched Valerie take a slow, deep breath. "This is what I'm proposing. I want to make amends with my money for being connected, even in the reluctant, minimal way I was, with Marcus Bradley and his madness. For not making an effort to bring my husband and the rest of them down."

Brenna was still puzzled. "How?"

"I understand his construction of a luxury resort and attached casino is at a standstill, without much chance of its ever being completed."

"That's what I hear."

"I'm going to buy that project and see it finished as a fully staffed, free clinic for St. Sebastian's native population. And I'm going to call it the Zena King Clinic in honor of the woman who gave her life fighting for the health of her people." Valerie sat back in her chair, gazing at Brenna. "Do you think what I want makes sense?"

"What I think, Valerie Hoffman," Brenna said slowly, her emotions threatening her self-control, "is that the people of St. Sebastian will regard you as their saint."

Will phoned her the evening of the next day, wanting to know how she was doing on her own.

"Fine," she said, knowing she was lying, knowing she was lonely and restless and aching for Casey.

"You hear from Case?" her brother wanted to know.

"No. I imagine they're keeping him busy at the bureau going over all the details again before they make a decision whether to reinstate the agents involved in what went down that day."

"Brenna?"

"What?"

"Why don't you call him?"

"He has my number if he wants to talk to me."

And that was the problem, wasn't it? There had been no contact from him since his departure. Was this his way of telling her it was over between them? This time for good? That he was an FBI agent with all the risks it involved, and he couldn't bring himself to change that for her?

To her surprise, Aaron Fowler from the lab called her the next morning. "We have the test results for you."

"This soon? I thought from what you indicated it would be much longer than this before we could expect to hear anything."

He chuckled. "So did I. Turns out, though, this was one job our chemists couldn't wait to get their hands on. Can you come out to the lab so I can go over the findings with you?"

"Yes, I can grab a cab right away and be there in minutes, if that works for you."

He assured her it would. Before she knew it, she was facing the technician across his desk. "I think you'll be pleased with what we learned," he began.

He went on to explain how, with some effort, they were able to break the formula down to its chemical components, how they were able to recognize those components, how they were blended and what effect that blending had on the women who drank it without knowing it was in their water.

He must have noticed how her eyes had glazed over, because he broke off at that point with a knowing grin. "I'm thinking chemistry was never a strong subject with you."

"Sorry, it wasn't," she apologized.

"Doesn't matter. I've got several printouts here with a written report of the chemical analysis. You can look at them later or just hand them out to the people who would like to have them. The only important thing for you to know is this—whatever its creator believed, the formula is not a permanent one. It lasts only as long as the women continue to drink the water laced with it. With no one now placing the formula in the water supply, the effects will begin to fade."

"Are you saying—"

"No permanent damage. With a bit of time, the women will begin to conceive again."

That news would have meant everything to Zena. Fanciful of her or not, Brenna wanted to think that wherever her friend was now she would be celebrating.

In the taxi on the way back to her hotel, Brenna realized she had some calls to make. It might take work, but she had to somehow reach Zena's Aunt Cleo in St. Sebastian and let her know the women of Freedom would soon be able to bear children again. She should also inform the reporter who had interviewed her of this positive development. Will would want to learn of it, too.

And Casey? That was less of a certainty. He'd promised to return to Miami in time for the lab results. That, of course, hadn't happened. In all fairness, both of them had been given to understand it would be some time before those results would be available. Neither of them had anticipated it could be this soon. Still…

She decided not to do anything yet about trying to contact Casey. Her mind right now was in too much of a turmoil where he was concerned.

When she arrived back at the hotel, Brenna went directly to her room, parked her purse and the analysis reports and prepared to make her calls. And didn't.

Not yet, she thought. It could wait for a little while. She wanted first to sort out some things in her head. *Needed* to do that.

Not here. Outside in the open where she had a better chance of clearing her mind.

Locking her door, she went down to the lobby, left her key at the front desk and exited the hotel, headed for the beach across the street.

A moment or so later found her seated in the sunshine on a bench, gazing out at the incredibly blue waters that were in such sharp contrast to the glaring white sands of the sloping shore. The beach was far from crowded. A few scattered groups of sunbathers. Parents wading in the shallows with their kids. Someone paddling on a float.

It made a colorful scene, but for once Brenna wasn't thinking about painting pictures.

Casey, of course, was on her mind instead. These days it was always the subject of Casey. There was no longer any question of just how vital he was to her. If she'd learned nothing else on St. Sebastian, she had learned that.

With her brother's help, she had even determined she was strong enough to overcome whatever fears might threaten her when Casey was on assignment. *If,* that is, she was given the chance.

And there was the big question. Did he still care about her? Care about *them?* Or was that gone? Is that what this long silence of his meant?

If that was true, she would have to deal with the loss

of him. It would be very hard, harder than it had been when she'd given him up two years ago. But what choice would she have?

The sky above her was clear. There were no clouds to obscure the sun, but the day suddenly seemed to dim.

Brenna didn't know how long she sat there on that bench, knowing she needed to return to her room and make those phone calls but somehow unable to summon the energy to move.

"Ha, this is where you got to! Guy at the front desk said he saw you headed this way. Rembrandt, when are you gonna learn to keep your cell phone with you? Ever since my plane touched down I've been trying to reach you to let you know I'm here."

Was she hearing that cheerful voice behind her just because she yearned to hear it? Brenna twisted around on the bench to make sure she wasn't imagining his presence. There was no question of it. The familiar, devil-may-care figure of Casey McBride was striding toward her across the sands.

She didn't wait for him to reach her. Springing to her feet, she rounded the bench and flew at him. Nor did she wait to see if he would take her in his arms and kiss her. She took the initiative herself the second she reached him.

There was a startled look on his face when Brenna reached up, pulled his head down to her level and kissed him so ferociously she almost toppled both of them in the sand.

"Wow!" he said when she finally released him. "If that's the kind of welcome I'm going to get, then I've got to go away more often."

"I wouldn't make a habit of it, mister," she said severely.

"Whoa, first she kisses me, then she accuses me. What did I do wrong?"

"Silence, that's what. I didn't hear a word from you the whole time you were gone. For all I knew, you were never going to return."

"Hey, didn't I promise I'd be back? And here I am. As for not contacting you…I hardly had a minute to sleep I was so busy the whole time I was in Chicago."

"Doing what exactly? Come on, tell me."

"Well," he began and then stopped, shaking his head. "Nope, I think I'd better make certain of what's important before I divulge."

Perplexed, she watched him fish around in his pocket, withdraw something around which his hand was tightly closed and drop down on one knee in front of her.

"Brenna Coleman, will you marry me?"

It wasn't until he reached for her hand that she got a good look at what was in his other hand. And recognized it.

"That's the ring I gave back to you two years ago. You kept it all this time?"

"I figured there was a chance I might need it again. I hoped as much, anyway. With the same woman, of course. Who else was I going to love like that?"

"Right."

"Uh, I'm still kinda waiting for an answer here."

"Oh, sorry. Yes, I'll marry you. Do I have any other choice when I'm so crazy in love with you?"

"Thank God."

He slid the ring on her finger where it felt so familiar. And so very right. "You don't get it back this time," she said.

"Let's make sure of that."

Getting to his feet, Casey folded her into his arms, demonstrating his own love with a kiss that was long, deep and a promise of a solid future together.

"So," she said when he finally released her, "tell me what kept you so busy in Chicago. Have they made a decision? Was your suspension lifted?"

"That was taken care of the first day. By noon, actually."

"Casey, listen. This time I won't try to stop you from going out into the field. I can't say I won't worry when you're on assignment, but I'll keep quiet about that."

"Not necessary. The FBI was ready to put me to work again, but I've had my fill of adventure. St. Sebastian was proof of that. I've quit the bureau. I'll be staying home in Chicago."

"You're serious? But doing what?"

"An FBI buddy of mine is also handing in his resignation. We're going to combine our savings and start a security company. It's something I've been thinking about for a while. So that's what I've been doing these past couple of days, getting the preliminaries going. What do you think?"

"That with your FBI experience you're sure to be a success." She had yet to tell him about the lab results, but that could wait.

"What are we standing here for? We're wasting all this beautiful white sand." Hopping first on one foot and then the other, he shed his shoes and socks. "Come on, what are you waiting for? Get those sandals off and join me."

"You're asking me to walk the beach barefoot with you?"

"Why not?"

Yes, she thought, *why not?* Casting off her sandals, she accepted the big, protective hand that closed around hers. He was already squishing sand between his toes, inviting her to join him in the activity.

"Feels nice, huh?"

"Tell me," she asked him as they set off down the beach, "do you expect us to go through life together barefoot?"

"Yeah, pretty much."

It sounded perfectly reasonable to her.

* * * * *

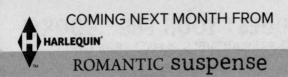
Available May 6, 2014

#1799 CAVANAUGH UNDERCOVER
by Marie Ferrarella

Agent Brennan Cavanaugh's covert job in the seamy world of human trafficking turns personal when he meets the mysterious Tiana. Suddenly he's risking his life—and his heart—to save the undercover madam who's out to find her sister.

#1800 EXECUTIVE PROTECTION
The Adair Legacy • by Jennifer Morey

When his politician mother is shot, jaded cop Thad Winston gets more than he bargained for during the investigation with the spirited Lucy Sinclair, his mother's nurse. But keeping his desire at bay proves difficult when Lucy becomes the next target...and his to protect.

#1801 TRAITOROUS ATTRACTION
by C.J. Miller

To rescue the brother he believed dead, recluse Connor West will trust computer analyst Kate Squire. But the deeper they trek into the jungle, the hotter their attraction burns. Until the former spy realizes Kate knows more than she's telling...

#1802 LATIMER'S LAW
by Mel Sterling

Desperate young widow Abigail McMurray steals a pickup to flee an abusive relationship, never realizing the truck's owner, K-9 deputy Cade Latimer, is in the back. But rather than arrest her, the lawman takes her under his protection and into his arms.

REQUEST YOUR FREE BOOKS!
2 FREE NOVELS PLUS 2 FREE GIFTS!

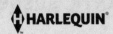

ROMANTIC suspense

Sparked by danger, fueled by passion

YES! Please send me 2 FREE Harlequin® Romantic Suspense novels and my 2 FREE gifts (gifts are worth about $10). After receiving them, if I don't wish to receive any more books, I can return the shipping statement marked "cancel." If I don't cancel, I will receive 4 brand-new novels every month and be billed just $4.74 per book in the U.S. or $5.24 per book in Canada. That's a savings of at least 14% off the cover price! It's quite a bargain! Shipping and handling is just 50¢ per book in the U.S. and 75¢ per book in Canada.* I understand that accepting the 2 free books and gifts places me under no obligation to buy anything. I can always return a shipment and cancel at any time. Even if I never buy another book, the two free books and gifts are mine to keep forever.

240/340 HDN F45N

Name	(PLEASE PRINT)	

Address		Apt. #

City	State/Prov.	Zip/Postal Code

Signature (if under 18, a parent or guardian must sign)

Mail to the **Harlequin® Reader Service:**
IN U.S.A.: P.O. Box 1867, Buffalo, NY 14240-1867
IN CANADA: P.O. Box 609, Fort Erie, Ontario L2A 5X3

Want to try two free books from another line?
Call 1-800-873-8635 or visit www.ReaderService.com.

* Terms and prices subject to change without notice. Prices do not include applicable taxes. Sales tax applicable in N.Y. Canadian residents will be charged applicable taxes. Offer not valid in Quebec. This offer is limited to one order per household. Not valid for current subscribers to Harlequin Romantic Suspense books. All orders subject to credit approval. Credit or debit balances in a customer's account(s) may be offset by any other outstanding balance owed by or to the customer. Please allow 4 to 6 weeks for delivery. Offer available while quantities last.

Your Privacy—The Harlequin® Reader Service is committed to protecting your privacy. Our Privacy Policy is available online at www.ReaderService.com or upon request from the Harlequin Reader Service.

We make a portion of our mailing list available to reputable third parties that offer products we believe may interest you. If you prefer that we not exchange your name with third parties, or if you wish to clarify or modify your communication preferences, please visit us at www.ReaderService.com/consumerschoice or write to us at Harlequin Reader Service Preference Service, P.O. Box 9062, Buffalo, NY 14269. Include your complete name and address.

HRS13R

Desperate young widow Abigail McMurray steals a pickup to flee an abusive relationship, never realizing the truck's owner, K-9 deputy Cade Latimer, is in the back.

Read on for a sneak peek of

LATIMER'S LAW

by Mel Sterling, coming May 2014 from Harlequin® Romantic Suspense.

"Let me see, Abigail. I won't hurt you, but I need to know bruises are the worst of it."

"That…that *crummy* button!" The words came out in the most embarrassed, horrified tone Cade had ever heard a woman use.

He couldn't tell whether the trembling that shook her entire body was laughter, tears, fear, pain or all of the above. She swayed on her feet like an exhausted toddler, and he realized she might fall if she remained standing. He sank back onto the picnic table bench and drew her down with him. She drooped like a flower with a crushed stem, and it was the most natural thing in the world to put an arm around her. In all his thug-tracking days he'd never comforted a criminal like this. How many of them had wept and gazed at him with pitiful, wet eyes? How easily had he withstood those bids for sympathy and lenience? How many of them ended up in the back of the patrol car on the way to jail, where they belonged?

But how quickly, in just moments, had Abigail McMurray and her gigantic problem become the thing he most needed to fix in the world. He felt her stiffness melting away like snow in the Florida sun, and shortly she was leaning against his chest, her hands creeping up to hang on to his shoulders as if he were the only solid thing left on the planet.

Now I have the truth.

He had what he thought he wanted, yes. But knowing what had pushed Abigail to take his truck wasn't enough. Now he wanted the man who had done the damage, wanted him fiercely, with a dark, chill fury that was more vendetta than justice. He shouldn't feel this way—his law enforcement training should have kept him from the brink. He hardly knew Abigail, and the fact she'd stolen his truck didn't make her domestic abuse issues his problem.

But somehow they were.

He felt her tears soaking his shirt, her sobs shaking her body, and stared over her head toward the tea-dark river, where something had taken the lure on his fishing line and was merrily dragging his pole down the sandy bank into the water.

Aw, hell. You know it's bad when I choose a sobbing woman over the best reel I own. Goodbye, pole. Hello, trouble.

**Don't miss
LATIMER'S LAW
by Mel Sterling, coming May 2014 from
Harlequin® Romantic Suspense.**

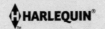

ROMANTIC suspense

CAVANAUGH UNDERCOVER
by **Marie Ferrarella**

A thrilling new *Cavanaugh Justice* title from *USA TODAY* bestselling author Marie Ferrarella!

Agent Brennan Cavanaugh's covert job in the seamy world of human trafficking turns personal when he meets the mysterious Tiana. Suddenly he's risking his life—and his heart—to save the undercover madam who's out to find her sister.

Look for *CAVANAUGH UNDERCOVER*
by Marie Ferrarella in May 2014.

Available wherever books and ebooks are sold.

Heart-racing romance, high-stakes suspense!

www.Harlequin.com

HRS27869

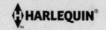

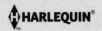

HARLEQUIN®

ROMANTIC suspense

TRAITOROUS ATTRACTION
by C.J. Miller

**From steamy jungles to opulent palaces...
it's nonstop action, danger...and passion!**

To find a "dead" agent, intelligence analyst Kate Squire
needs the man's brother—retired Sphere operative Connor
West. His skills as a trained assassin are essential for her
mission...but not so much her slamming, raw attraction for
the man himself....

For a loner like Connor, trekking into the jungle with a
secretive killer blonde at his side is not textbook. Caught
between armed insurgents and hungry predators, he fears
Kate may be his deadliest threat...until their very agency
turns on them. Stranded, outmanned and outgunned,
Connor has nowhere else to turn. Trusting Kate may be the
only way to get them out alive....

Look for the TRAITOROUS ATTRACTION
by C.J. Miller in May 2014.

Available wherever ebooks are sold.

Heart-racing romance, high-stakes suspense!

www.Harlequin.com

HRS27872

HARLEQUIN®

A *Romance* FOR EVERY MOOD™

Love the Harlequin book you just read?

Your opinion matters.

Review this book on your favorite
book site, review site, blog or your own
social media properties and share
your opinion with other readers!

Be sure to connect with us at:
Harlequin.com/Newsletters
Facebook.com/HarlequinBooks
Twitter.com/HarlequinBooks